rage against the machine

GIVEN PATH TRILOGY
BOOK ONE

endorsements

H. Meadow Hopewell has given us a tremendously vital novel for our times as we grapple with the benefits and potential perils of artificial intelligence. Along with the importance of the subject matter, I became immersed in her storytelling, as the characters and twists in the plot kept me mesmerized throughout. It's uplifting to read something so essential and enjoyable that also strengthens my relationship with God.

—**Scott Mohr**, author of the afterlife thriller *A Heaven to Die For*

Rage Against the Machine is captivating, highly entertaining, and thought-provoking. I was forced to consider the possible physical and spiritual dangers of advancements in artificial intelligence. I became emotionally attached to the characters and I was on the edge of my seat, cheering them on. Hopewell's superb pacing helped to bring the action scenes to life. As a Christian, it was uplifting to read about God protecting and directing his people to combat evil. I highly recommend *Rage Against the Machine* by H. Meadow Hopewell to all avid readers.

—**Juan Lynch** for Readers' Favorite

rage against the machine

Book One of the Given Path trilogy, *Rage Against the Machine*, presents the riveting—and frightening—possibilities of biotechnology. How many of them are already in play on our planet, only the powers that be could say. Herein lies a thrilling tale as Roare Murdock-Galloway races to expose sinister schemes that threaten the very existence of humanity. H. Meadow Hopewell has woven a gripping plot with danger, intrigue, and cyborgs. Join Roare on this fast-paced journey of faith and purpose.

—**Irene Chambers**, Onward Editing fiction editor and Gold Member of Christian Editor Connection

rage against the machine

GIVEN PATH TRILOGY

BOOK ONE

H. MEADOW HOPEWELL

PUBLISHING THE POSITIVE
Plymouth, Massachusetts
A Christian Company
ElkLakePublishingInc.com

copyright notice

rage against the machine

Library Cataloging Data

Names: Hopewell, H. Meadow (H. Meadow Hopewell)

Rage Against the Machine, Given Path Trilogy Book One / H. Meadow Hopewell

360 p. 23cm × 15cm (9in × 6 in.)

ISBN-13: 9798891342804 (paperback) | 9798891342811 (trade paperback) | 9798891342828 (e-book)

Key Words: Christian science fiction; Christian sci-fi suspense; speculative fiction; transhumanism and God; artificial intelligence sci-fi thriller; strong female lead; forgiveness

Library of Congress Control Number: 2024947291 Fiction

dedication

To my husband, Malcom, my family, and the true friends who had my back since the beginning of this ongoing odyssey.

acknowledgments

Well, M.C., it's been a long journey, but we finally made it, and both lived to tell the tale. Your limitless patience, encouragement when I wanted to call it a day, and relentless support should've earned you the Noble Peace Prize, but instead you got this book. I'm indebted to your inspiration and love. Much love to you.

The prayers of family members who spoke this project into existence. I'm humbled by your belief in me. Love you all.

To my comrades in arms and "true" friends who cheered me on and kept me focused throughout this project, I adore you all and I'm eternally grateful.

I am in deep gratitude for all the editors who steered me into a creative direction that formulated *Given Path*. They are truly a tour de force and the backbone of my book. They pushed my level of creativity I didn't realize I had. I could not have completed this novel without them.

But God ...

chapter one—spotlight

You can't manipulate people who know how to think for themselves. —Trish Mercer

Roare Murdock mused about conducting her interview as a holograph. She wouldn't have to be present on the set, wouldn't have to stare at an audience of strangers, and wouldn't have to pretend she was chill about live interviews. Only, today wasn't that day. Giving interviews—on a network TV show, no less—came with the territory of a film director, but that didn't mean she had to like it.

From the stylist's chair, Roare could hear the commotion outside her dressing room. *There's so much buzz, you'd think they were expecting POTUS.* Chaotic environments froze her blood. Clutching the arms of the chair, she fought the urge to bolt out of her seat.

Cameramen screamed obscenities at anything that looked or moved wrong. Production assistants, scriptwriters, bodyguards, and whoever else made up the heartbeat of *Spotlight* maneuvered like ants building a bridge to eternity.

She wished the stylist would stop fussing. Her hair was fine, makeup perfect, and clothes suitable. Her stomach was now churning like an overachieving cement mixer.

She didn't even do selfies and never took a liking to social media. She valued her privacy and preferred keeping a barrier between herself and the public—called it self-preservation. Betrayal from friends during the worst times of her life had birthed her suspicious nature, limiting the number of people she was willing to trust.

She'd blamed herself for allowing her agent to talk her into this. Arlo Sassoon had dropped the interview on her suddenly without time to dispute. Despite their bickering, she trusted Arlo—he worked hard to further her career and force her out of her comfort zone to build her confidence in handling the public. Usually, she resisted, then slowly warmed up to his ideas—sometimes. Arlo was the older brother she wished she had.

"Fabulous!" The overanimated stylist stepped back and ran a handkerchief over his bald head.

Maybe he *should do the interview.* Roare provided a fake grin to appease him, closed her eyes, tuned out the chaos outside the door, and focused on her breathing.

The associate producer bustled in sporting a wireless headset, armed with an iPad and a black box. The AP set up her mic and escorted her to the stage. Roare waited behind the blue velvet curtain and was told to stand on the big blue X. "You're on in three," said the AP.

Spotlight's host, Mason Yates, stood from his leather chair, straightened his tie, and smoothed his suit jacket, preparing to welcome his guest. His chest protruded like a deprived marigold craning its petals to soak in the sun. "Tonight, our special guest, in a rare interview, is the multitalented and stunning Roare Murdock." He clapped and turned toward her.

The audience applauded as the AP waved Roare onstage. She remembered her assistant's coaching to appear nonthreatening—toss her long, black hair over her shoulder and wave to the enthusiastic audience. Some shouted her name. A man whistled. Monitors to the sides of the stage signaled them to quiet down.

Roare nodded and said, "Thank you." *Pilar Elyas, you'd be proud.*

Mason motioned her to a cushy leather chair opposite his and sat, welcoming her with his carefully applied Hollywood grin. Of course, he said it was spectacular to have her, and of course, she thanked him for the invitation she detested. The host was known for manipulating guests to reveal personal aspects of their lives they'd rather not share. Roare couldn't understand why young people loved his show when she deemed him cringeworthy. *Great choice, Arlo.*

More compliments and demurs. Roare reminded herself to smile.

"*Substance* is a powerful film," Mason said. "Life-changing. How does it feel to win an Oscar for Best Documentary Feature?"

"The success of the film was completely unexpected. I'm deeply honored and grateful. The production process these past three years was overwhelming."

"You've rebounded well from a dark period in your life. Can you tell us how you pulled through?"

Roare's smile faltered. *Evidently, "private life is off limits" is too many syllables for him. This interview may end sooner than he thinks.* "Yes. By God's grace, I recovered from drug addiction. During my rehabilitation in the Berkshires, I developed a passion for gardening, growing purple coneflower and milkweed wildflowers."

Mason crossed his legs. "Why wildflowers?"

"They grow naturally in the wild. If a garden is overly manicured, it can choke the life out of the flowers. It was

3

cathartic for me. And it helped me decide I didn't want my creativity inhibited. Drugs blocked my imagination."

"A switch inside you turned on."

"Being amid wildflowers eased my anxiety, increased my focus, and brought me closer to our Creator."

"Freedom and peace within can't be bought," he said.

"The revelation destroyed my desire for drugs completely. Nowadays, before I start a new film, I take a walk through a field of flowers."

"So you can only start a film in warm weather?"

"I'm all grown up. I travel where I need to go." *I've already said too much. I'm sure he knew all that anyway.*

"So your *problem* inspired you to take on such a heavy subject?"

"After I won my battle over ketamine, a couple of close friends died of heroin overdoses. They thought they had control over addiction. They couldn't fathom the truth—until it was too late. Addiction is seductive, wickedly powerful, and a growing epidemic. I grew tired of wallowing in grief and had to fight back." She gazed at the audience. *These are real people. People who need to hear this. To join the fight. Okay.*

"Obviously, film was the best medium to make a powerful statement, to change lives," he said.

"At least the movie could disturb people enough to see the disaster. These drugs vaporize lives, ruin families—genetically, mentally, spiritually—sometimes irreversibly." *Thank God Mom threw me out when she did.*

"You dedicated the picture to your friends," Mason said. "Truly a gripping, tragic, yet heroic piece of work—a lot of profound messages filled with hope. What a substantial achievement."

"I couldn't have done it without God, the testimonies of those who've overcome addiction, those still in the fight, the

4

NYPD narcotics unit, and counselors—everyone's openness, exposing their struggles, sharing their stories. They're the heroes. It's their movie, not mine. We all won the Academy."

"We're all grateful you made it." Now Mason addressed the audience, "Ladies and gentlemen, those who haven't seen *Substance* still have a chance before it leaves theaters."

He paused while the audience applauded.

"You have two Oscars under your belt, Roare. Your debut, *iWonder*, a comedy about the risks of online dating, won too. Though your adoring fans are waiting anxiously for your next picture, your talent doesn't stop with directing. You're also a giant in the local jazz scene, I hear."

"I play a little," Roare's voice hardened. "Just a random thing." She scoffed internally. Clenched her fists. *I tried to smile, but we had agreed to stay out of my personal life. This rodent doesn't follow contractual agreements. Why am I not surprised.*

"Your passions don't end there, do they? NYU graduate, you're involved with genetic engineering—"

"Nope. You've got that wrong." Roare's face twisted. "Wherever you're getting your information, that part isn't true."

Mason cleared his throat. "I stand corrected, but you are an activist for children rescued from human trafficking—"

Roare stood. *Mason has probed too deep into my private life.*

The audience began to murmur.

"You don't want to discuss that. Okay. How does your husband handle being overshadowed by your stardom?"

"Why don't you ask him? Your questions are irrelevant to the film, and you've breached our agreement on respecting my privacy."

Roare overheard an audience member whisper, "Ooh, I bet he didn't like that."

Then, she heard the AP's shrill tone in Mason's headset. "What's going on? You're going to lose her if you keep this up."

Mason flinched, then continued. "But an interview with you is unprecedented. We want to get to know you." He shifted in his seat and smoothed the sleeve of his blazer.

Roare pursed her lips. *Mason doesn't care. He gets pleasure out of making his guests squirm. What a worm.* "Fair enough." She faced the audience. "This is who I am: God is my pulse, grace is my creativity, humility is my success, and compassion is my inspiration."

"Did your family influence the roads you've chosen?"

Without acknowledging Mason, Roare remained fixed on the audience. "Thank you so much for coming tonight. Please, please talk to your loved ones about drugs. See the film. Get it into the light. It could be a discussion starter. One person informed could be one life saved."

She walked off the set, through the studio, stripping off her mic, ignoring crewmembers trying to get her attention, and straight to her husband who was waiting for her at the rear exit. Wyatt wrapped his arms around her.

Despite her apparent success, depression was setting in. She felt emotionally violated, backed into a corner. Losing her cool wasn't exactly the impression she wanted to leave her audience with. So much for learning how to handle public confrontations. She had taken three steps back.

They walked around the building, flagged a Yellow Cab, and headed home.

The whole drive uptown, Wyatt held Roare's hand, but she was still disappointed she'd let Mason get her so upset. By the time they were sitting in their living room, flutes of champagne in hand, she'd calmed down a little.

She raised her drink, and the two glasses clinked. "To the interview being over."

They sipped. She closed her eyes and tucked her lower lip under her front teeth.

"You look serious," Wyatt said.

"Mmm." She gazed into his steel-gray eyes. She had loved his eyes since the moment they'd met at a nonprofit conference years ago. "I could've handled things better tonight."

"He's lucky you didn't clock him on national TV."

She gently banged her head against his chest. "You know better. I'm an artist not a fighter. But when my private life is exposed, I come apart. Why do I do that?"

He swiped a stray hair from her forehead. "How much are you trusting Jesus?"

Darn Wyatt! He took her out of her comfort zone unlike anyone she knew—in a good way and for valid reasons. She drank more champagne. "We're a perfect pair. Sure, I trust but I don't have your razor-sharp intuition and consistent faith. I'm still building enough confidence to find a little peace as a believer."

"Trust is a building block to—"

"Unwavering peace within, I know. What I would give to have the kind of hope that would move me to my core— sheer surrender and contentment. Trouble is, I'm not sure I want to go through the trials it takes to get there."

Wyatt put his arm around her shoulders and pulled her against him. "You've come a long way, Gobo." Her husband had given her the nickname as a cute reference to her concern over creating mood lighting for unfolding drama.

She poked him in the side. "You're incredible at times."

"I never said I was perfect, but neither are you." He stroked her right cheek.

She pulled away and turned to face him more. "Don't I know it? If Jesus has always watched over me, then why is there an invisible wall between us? I struggle to believe I deserve anything he gives me. At times, it would be easier to disconnect from him—but at the same moment, I want to grab on."

"You'll break past the barrier, and he knows it. You have no idea what you're worth to him."

"That's the problem, I don't know. I ask him why he let me fry my braincells with drugs for so long. How come my so-called friends betrayed me? Why did my father abandon me?"

Wyatt cradled her hand in his. "There will always be some trial, some wall of fire we have to pass through to reveal what we're made of."

Roare chuckled. "Sounds like iron sharpening iron." The tension of the interview finally dissipated, and she relaxed.

"Despite your doubts, you're already on a path with purpose—making documentaries to expose evil. It'll test what you're made of. For now, enjoy the benefits of the success he's given you." Wyatt sipped the last of his champagne.

Roare leaned closer and kissed his lips. "The testing is what worries me. I hope I'm ready. Listen, I'm drained. Can we call it a night?"

"It's a night."

Roare closed her eyes. *God, I know you've got my back too. Be patient with this twenty-six-year-old kid. I'll figure life out eventually. Please show me where to go.*

chapter two—process

The light shines in the darkness, and the darkness has not overcome it. —John 1:5

Still unsettled from the interview the night before, Roare regretted not calling her agent sooner. *Arlo will have some choice words for me. And I for him. Can't wait.*

Seated at the kitchen island, she ate oats while reading the Bible app on her phone. Closed her eyes. *Thank you, Lord, for this day and all you've given me. Clarify any words spoken to me today, and use me to glorify your name and encourage others. The world is a mess. Bring evil into the light. Turn hate into love, malice into kindness and peace. If you want me to be part of shaking up the world, guide me in the right direction. In Jesus's name. Amen.*

With a mug of green tea and her cell phone, she got comfortable on the sofa and auto-dialed Arlo.

"What have you to say for yourself?" he snapped.

"And a fine morning to you, Arlo. I've called to have it out."

"I'm justified in being aggravated with you."

"And right back at you. This promotional gig you set up was trifling and irresponsible, to say the least. I'm actually shocked he isn't off the air yet!"

Arlo moaned. "All right, pipe down. Poor judgment on my part. Look, I know you didn't want to do this interview, but I can count on less than three fingers when you have given an interview. You need exposure."

"Not in that way."

"Think of it as a requirement as a celebrity out of loyalty to your fans."

Roare huffed. "Arlo, this is nauseating. We fight over the same things repeatedly and get nowhere. We need to come to an agreement."

"I agree."

"What about podcasts or radio talk shows? People still do listen to them you know—how about *Tomorrow's News Today*? Work with me here."

Arlo sighed. "If you weren't so successful, clever, and a master negotiator, I'd drop you. Let me put some feelers out. But I insist you have your assistant crank out some nuggets about your next project or harmless nonpersonal clips on social media. Does that sound fair?"

"I suppose, but no more TV interviews, or I walk!"

"It's a fair compromise. Here's a news flash though—walking off the show last night earned you kudos as a rebellious celebrity. Stirs more intrigue. Fans adore that young-defiant image. You have the saints on your side."

"Good thing for both of us."

"Truce?" he said gently.

"Yes. Thanks for understanding me."

"I'm trying. You'll owe me one."

"I know. Let's talk soon. Enjoy your day."

"You too, kid."

As soon as she hung up, the phone rang. *Oh no, another intense chat.* "Good morning, Mom. You saw the show last night?"

"Uh-huh," Lane said.

"Go on, let me have it."

"You were fine, daughter dear. I'm proud of you. Your success is anointed, and you'll keep having interviews. Is your success so difficult to accept?"

"Getting prophetic again? I'd love a normal mother-daughter conversation just once. And for the record, there won't be any more interviews." Roare uncurled from her seat on the sofa and stretched.

"Why? I would've thought live interviews would serve you well."

"It's a magical place for me behind the cameras, but in front of them, I'm an alien. I don't want my personal life on display for the whole world to critique."

"Honey, your life is not your own. People will want to see more of you. You have prophecies to fulfill."

"Whose prophecies—yours or God's? Yeah, perhaps God owns my life, but the world doesn't. Don't put that claim on my life. And it doesn't sound like something God would say." Roare drifted toward three floor-to-ceiling windows off the living room and peered out. She placed a free hand on the window to feel the temperature outside. A childhood habit. The view overlooking Riverside Park always gave her a sense of peace during conflict.

Roare heard her mom say, "I'd admit I was embellishing things a bit. Maybe in time, you'll see what I see."

"Mom, I know you mean well, but I never know what's going to come out of your mouth. Every time we talk, you come up with revelations about my future. You told me about meeting Wyatt before I met him, when I would marry, winning the Academy award before I was even nominated. Mom, don't you understand it takes the thrill out of surprise? Spare me some of the details please. It's intrusive." She stormed away from the window and dropped herself on the sofa again.

"I suppose it is. Maybe I'm wrong in giving you inside information. You're not a normal person."

Roare's mouth dropped open. "What the devil do you mean by that?"

Lane sucked her teeth. "That came out wrong. I only meant to say that few are chosen to be on the frontlines for the kingdom of God. It's a huge mantle to carry, and he believes you can carry it."

"Whatever he's tasked me to do, I hope it comes to light soon. This mystery and waiting are exasperating, but there are *issues* I need to fix within my spirit—the Holy Spirit gave me a dream about how to improve my heart while I was filming *Substance*. Hating my absent father is probably the cause of my anxiety and anger, in part anyway, and I'm working through that." She sank onto a plush pillow.

"And you're doing well. He'll iron out those concerns for you. Help him by releasing your hate and hang-ups to the wind. You've got to accept how God is using you for something monumental, whether you presume you're a likely candidate or not. Your films will give birth to a future generation of fearless fighters."

Typical. Roare placed her feet on the marble coffee table. "Appreciate the pressure."

"It wasn't intentional. I wouldn't be a mom unless I shared what was prophesied to me by my pastor and confirmed by three other people. My dear daughter, I know it's a lot to absorb but God has his reasons for you being born and spared. He knows what's ahead for you. Forgive me for being overprotective."

"Oh, Mom, I forgive you, but maybe hold back a little information, please?"

"Yes, I suppose I can, but I can't help whom God chooses. You won't know your assignment until it's right before you. Naysayers will challenge you, and when you expose evil, opposition will come. There's no room for cowards, and you aren't one of them."

"I'm not ready to step into that role." Roare sighed. "I don't want to surrender my life and die to save the world." *I knew this would be a heavy conversation.*

"You're already doing what you were meant to do. Trust your instincts. Hire a bodyguard to fend off distractions. And pray. Nothing happens without a reason."

"C'mon. I can look after myself." Roare rolled her eyes. *I guess I don't fully understand or accept the gravity of being a celebrity and having someone look after me.*

"Your pride is talking. Yes, I'm being a protective mama bear. Don't wait until something terrible happens before you want protection. I know the perfect man. If you fight God's directions, opportunities may not come again, and he'll give them to someone else. Then, it may be too late. Don't waste his time."

"Mom, you have to stop being a drama queen. Don't pressure me. I'm only asking for some space. I need a clear mind to have a healthy creative flow. Stress kills inspiration." A migraine began to pulse in Roare's left temple.

"Point taken. Trust that the Lord has your back. Everything will work out. How's Wyatt?"

"Fine. Busy working on an antidote for a rare pathogen. The military wants to protect their soldiers from bioweapons. He gave me a faith pep talk last night. I must admit, he's starting to sound like you."

"Glad to hear it."

Roare sighed. "How're the boys? How's Ben?"

"Ben's fine, and your brothers miss you."

"We'll come and stay over this weekend if you're free. Mom, I have an appointment. Love you."

"Okay. And yes, by all means, you and Wyatt come on over. Love you too."

The subway ride provided time for Roare to consider what she'd like to accomplish during her therapy session. Ever since her past had come up during the interview, anger gnawed at her nerves. Like weeds that kept returning after being ripped out of the ground, reoccurring sentiments over the betrayal of friends who'd sucked her into the drug scene continued to sprout. She hated them for it—it had nearly destroyed her life. *I'm tired of trusting the wrong people. I need to overcome this blind spot. I get frustrated and take it out on people I love. Lord, hate has no place in your realm, and it shouldn't live in my orbit either, so please give me a breakthrough.*

As expected, Roare spotted a reporter with a zoom lens sitting in a van across the street from her destination. *For all they know, I could be visiting a dentist, a lawyer, an accountant, or having lunch with a friend.* Maybe she *should* employ a bodyguard—a discussion she'd have with Wyatt.

After Roare got situated, Dr. Peter Galletti crossed his legs and rested his writing pad on his knee, a fine-point pen in his left hand. "Shall we pray?"

Roare closed her eyes.

"Heavenly Father, I'm grateful for our time for discovery. Everyone has issues, hang-ups, and hurts where our souls need your healing touch. Free us by your mercy and grace. We're indebted to you for loving us as we are. In Jesus's name. Amen."

He fumbled through his notes. "During your last visit, we covered a lot. What would you like to achieve today?"

"I'm not sure but anger issues and mistrust come to mind," she said. "Both have been coming up lately, and I don't want them to affect my work or my marriage."

"You have good insight, and your concerns are valid."

"Oh, good."

"Let's address mistrust. Have you heard this description? 'When trust is absent, words become the cavernous sound of a wooden clang.'"

"Honestly, no I haven't. Care to clarify?"

"With the presence of trust, words become life itself. Some situations can trigger mistrust, ask direct questions, and express how a situation is making you feel. The past can't help you. Only the present can. Admit misgivings, ask for understanding. This will help put you at ease. Listen to your instincts. This will give you power over judgment. Does this make sense to you?"

"Sounds like a good tactic in theory, but can you give me an example?"

"Sure. How about this—you confided in a friend or work colleague about a personal matter and asked them to keep the information to themselves only to find out a few days later, they've shared what you told them to others."

"Yep, I've experienced this. Tell me how do I protect myself from those types of relationships?" She rested her forearms on the armchair and clasped her hands in front of her.

"Good question. The best way to handle this situation is to confront the person who'd gone back on their word and calmly share with them how their betrayal made you feel. If they apologize, that's great, but moving forward, refrain from sharing anything personal with them."

"Yeah, and my mistake in these scenarios was giving a person the benefit of the doubt, and then, they would do the same thing again. Made me feel like an idiot."

"You're not an idiot, and most of us have gone through this. Learning to discern is an art, and it takes time to gauge sincerity. That's when incorporating prayer into all aspects of your life is useful."

"And taking time to get to know someone well enough to actually trust them."

"Now you're on to something. Their actions matter more than what they say. Was this helpful for you?"

She smiled. "I think so."

Dr. Galletti glanced at his watch. "Good. Your session is halfway over. Would you like to take a few minutes to talk about anger?

"Absolutely."

"Great. Now have you thought about what triggers your anger?"

"Yes, I have. Some of my anger comes from not letting go of my biological father abandoning me before birth. It still hurts."

"I know it isn't easy to put this behind you. You're longing for answers, aren't you?"

"Yes, I am. That and being deceived by 'friends' I trusted. I was on drugs, living in a park for several weeks, and thought I had people around me who had my back, and they didn't. They stood by while I was about to be violated by a group of men ..." She paused and swallowed hard to fight away tears. She took a deep breath.

"Take your time. This is painful stuff you're talking about. Give yourself permission to process whatever you need to get through this. I'm here to help you."

"Thanks. I'm okay. I struggle at times to say what I feel."

"You're going through post-traumatic stress. Having discussions can relieve the weightiness of what you endured."

"I understand. I want to get this off my chest. Knowing God now, I realized he didn't forget about me and was watching over me. A stranger came out of nowhere and saved my life. It was as if he dropped out of the sky. I was so vulnerable, and the drugs made me incoherent. I couldn't fathom what was happening until I woke up in the hospital."

"Even though you went through this awful time in your life, living in a dangerous area, betrayed by friends, and on drugs, you were protected and saved from possible death."

Roare remained silent, reflecting on what Dr. Galletti just said. "I went through a lot, and now my life is a dream. I don't know how I acquired the life I have now, but it's a miracle." She began to tear up.

"Roare, does it feel good to see the contrast in your life? I'm looking at your expression, and I witnessed the pain in your face wash away. You relaxed and nearly smiled when you spoke about being saved and acknowledging what you have now. Can you do something for me?"

"I'll try."

"Hang on to your peace and beautiful miracle. It's a precious jewel. Every time those dark thoughts invade your mind, take a moment to consider what you have, and what you've accomplished. Ask God to help you focus on the good aspects of your life rather than being stuck in the past. You've had a horrible time, but it's no longer a part of you."

"Yes, I did, and I want this burden out of my life, it's draining me emotionally."

"And it's for this reason—for the sake of your faith, marriage, and spiritual wellbeing that you shift your energy on whatever makes your heart feel good."

"Hmm, I feel like something heavy just lifted off me."

"Uh-huh, because you've been carrying this everywhere you go, and you no longer need to."

"I hope you're right. Do you think my anger will go away?"

"I believe so with a little work. I'd like you to pay attention to what triggers your rage. Step back, pause and assess whether your distress is worth your time and energy. If you can walk away to avoid escalation, then do it. You can always revisit the situation later—with a clear head. Praying for calm helps diffuse emotions. Roare, no one can go back in time to modify things that happened. Or what people have done. Hanging on to hurt isn't going to buy you a dust ball."

She chuckled. "In other words, the anger I'm holding onto is worthless and won't buy me anything other than misery."

"You just had a breakthrough."

"I did?"

"Indeed. Consider this a milestone. Do you feel I've given you some tools you could use to empower yourself, and to become less agitated and stronger emotionally?"

"I think so."

"I'm hoping this will provide you with clarity to correct your perception of people and situations."

"You've given me good advice. I'll commit to trying."

"You made a wise choice. It's part of your journey. Remember, the adversary, Satan, prides himself on playing head games. The Scriptures themselves have the power to shut down the negative committee in your head. Take down these verses: 2 Timothy 1:7, Luke 10:19, 2 Corinthians 10:5, Psalms 71 and 91. The last two I gave you are for protection from spiritual warfare."

Roare opened her cell phone and typed the verses in the Notes app. "Wow. That was a lot to digest today. Can't believe I made progress, and I'm amazed everything we spoke about is right in the Bible. I'll do my best to read more often."

"You did incredible work today, Roare. Now, one last question. Where are you emotionally regarding your biological father?"

Roare shifted. *This isn't what I came here for.* "I don't invest a lot of time thinking about him."

"Why not?"

"He doesn't deserve the energy because he denied I was his child!" Roare practiced the doctor's advice and paused to reign in her emotions. "I believe he robbed me of my right to be loved by a protective father. Without that protection, I struggle to accept myself."

Dr. Galletti jotted a note. "And do you believe you're unacceptable because your father rejected you?"

"No." She sighed. "Maybe sometimes. I feel as if he stole my joy and sense of worth."

"How about your stepdad, Ben?"

Roare nodded. "He accepts me for who I am. He's always been supportive and made me feel I am his own flesh and blood."

"You're making good progress. You have every right to feel the way you do, but it's equally as important to let go of your anger."

"Yes, that's what I want to do. I will do it."

"Remember, people may abandon and reject you, Roare, but our heavenly Father never will."

"I won't forget. Being able to process this out loud really helped me realize my Lord was always with me and still is. Thank you. I'm feeling a lot better now."

"I'm pleased to know this." He looked at his watch. "Roare, my next appointment is due in ten minutes, so we'll have to end here. Should I schedule you for next month, same date and time?"

"I understand, and yes, please pencil me in. If anything comes up, I'll contact the receptionist."

"Sounds good, Roare. Take good care."

"I'll do my best."

When she exited the building, a gust of wind caught Roare off guard. Grateful for her flight jacket, she zipped it to the top, wrapped her black cashmere scarf around her neck, and stuffed her hands into the pockets of her jacket. Like the weather, the time for change had come.

chapter three—cryptology

The day science begins to study nonphysical phenomena,
it will make more progress in one decade than in all the
previous centuries of its existence.—Nikola Tesla

The next day, Roare prepped for her jazz set at Dizzy's. She'd stayed up all night practicing only to notify the band at the last minute that Tomas, the standup bassist, had flaked again. *That's the last time I trust him.* Roare clicked her guitar case shut harder than necessary and placed it with the rest of her equipment.

Her phone rang. "Hi, Pilar. What's up?"

"Just got off the phone with a journalist from *People* magazine. She said they'll be at Dizzy's tonight for your performance, take a few photos, and ask a few questions. Had to give you a heads up."

Nothing's sacred, living in this city. "How did they find out I'm playing tonight?"

"The club owners are big on publicity."

"Wish they'd okayed it with me. Don't I have any say?"

"Frankly, no. You're a hire at the club. Do you want me to call back and ask them not to headline you?"

She sensed someone or something was conspiring against her. First Tomas bailed, and now this. She guaranteed paparazzi would be lurking. Winning an Academy award definitely puts a blemish on my private life. *Despite my efforts for privacy, I keep being thrust into the limelight, which is unavoidable.* "What can I do but play along. They'll get nothing but short, vague answers from me. Thanks for the heads up."

While Roare updated Wyatt, they caught the train to Columbus Circle station. However, her husband's pep talk during the ride didn't offer any comfort. *This is going to be a disaster.*

At the Columbus Circle station, the dreamy sound of jazz on classical guitar wafted toward Roare and Wyatt. They joined a few passersby who stopped to listen to the elderly man perched on a wooden stool. Beneath his chair lay a richly colored Persian rug and his open guitar case displaying his CDs, business cards, and an open cigar box. He wore a loose-fitting green army jacket, baggy jeans, tattered tennis shoes, and a multicolored knit skullcap.

Wyatt whispered to Roare, "He's pretty talented."

Roare was grateful for the diversion from the preperformance jitters. "I'd like to buy a CD." She pulled a twenty from her pants pocket and dropped it in the box.

The tranquil man nodded and handed her the CD and a folded business card.

"Great," Roare said. "Looking forward to having a listen. We appreciate your style of music."

"Glad you do." The man peered at Wyatt. "What do you have strapped across your body—a guitar? You play?"

"Yeah, a little. My wife is the talented one."

"You don't say."

Roare shyly glanced away. A looming shadow caught her eye. *Oh no, it's starting already.*

Wyatt noticed her frown. "What's the matter, babe?"

"There. Past the third pillar on the platform. Paparazzi. He's pointing right at us."

Removing her guitar, he said, "I'll deal with this." He started toward the man, but Roare grabbed his forearm.

"No. Please, let's get out of here."

Wyatt sounded grisly. "Yeah, you're right. Don't want to cause a scene."

As Roare and Wyatt passed beneath the lit Jazz at Lincoln Center sign at the entrance of a gray steel-and-glass building, subdued electricity filled the air. Roare thought she heard someone call her name.

A man with a camera jogged up to her. "C'mon, Ro, give us a smile."

Wyatt stepped in front of Roare and shoved the man away with his forearm. "If you don't get out of here and leave us alone, I'm going to wrap that camera around your neck."

The man laughed at him and snapped a photo anyway. "Hey, man, I'm just doing my job." He took off.

Roare saw Wyatt's face turning red. "Don't waste your time, honey. Let's get to the club."

"These leeches are becoming a nuisance. I think you need a bodyguard."

She looked at him. "You're not the only one who thinks so. Mom told me this morning she had someone in mind for a bodyguard."

"I agree, the sooner, the better."

"I can't think about it right now. I have to concentrate on my sets and the interview." *All I want is to play well and hug my in-laws without anything going wrong. Surely that's not too much to ask.*

Once she walked into Dizzy's, her skin tingled. The atmosphere was intimate and sultry—only the coolest jazz cats played here. She'd be joining musicians from the Julliard School of Music, big names. Such a privilege!

Once all the musicians had arrived, they tested their equipment, inspected the stage, and set up their sheet music, while sound and light technicians did their checks. Then, Roare changed in the ladies' room.

Roare heard the bathroom door open and close while she touched up her makeup. She sensed someone next to her, then heard the click of a camera. Roare snapped to attention and glared at the woman. "Did you really need to take that photo? I'm in the bathroom for crying out loud!"

"I'm sorry. Your fans would love this sweet intimate photo of you," the young woman said.

"Yeah, intimate is a word I don't like and is a problem for me. Give me some space already!" Roare's heart raced. "Oh gee, let me guess. You're with *People* magazine, right?"

"How did you know? My name is Tess Becker, by the way."

"I was warned you'd be here. I don't like giving interviews, but apparently the owners arranged something with you."

"I hope I'll be able to ask you a couple of questions after your set."

Roare glared. "As long as your questions aren't personal. Otherwise, I won't have much to say."

"I promise I won't. I'm looking forward to your show. Good luck." Tess left the bathroom.

God knows I need it. Roare finished touching up her makeup and shoved her compact and lipstick in her makeup bag. She washed her hands, then turned away from the mirror, and leaned against the sink with her hands folded across her chest. *Relax, breathe, forget about the intrusion, and move on. I think I'm going to lay low on these gigs for a while. These paparazzi and tabloid reps can be aggressive. But honestly, I'm not so sure if I'll ever get used to being semi famous or get over my shyness. Anyway, I'm here now, I better get going.*

At seven thirty, the band members took their places onstage. Behind them, large windows revealed lights from the surrounding buildings—a brilliant backdrop.

Wyatt gave Roare a quick kiss and sat at a table close to the platform.

Roare stepped onstage and picked up her electric bass guitar.

She spotted her in-laws at the entrance and smiled. *They're here.* Anoosh, a petite Persian beauty, wore a black-wool pantsuit, floral blouse, and heels. Morrison followed her across the room. When they reached Wyatt's table, he stood, kissed his mother's cheek, and helped her into her seat. Morrison was a tall, handsome man, medium build, of Scottish and Dutch descent. He waved to Roare as he and Wyatt seated themselves.

Every table was full, as well as the seats at the bar. Soft lights created a subdued vibe. A large egg-shaped candle lit the center of each table.

When the lights dimmed and the oval room quieted, Roare gave a subtle gesture. She made eye contact with the drummer, trumpeter, and pianist.

They paused momentarily. Roare took a deep breath, closed her eyes, and exhaled. The drummer tapped the brush slowly on the snare drum and added a gentle swipe on the hi-hat. The pianist's fingers glided rhythmically over the keys.

Moments later, Roare strummed chords on her guitar, then the trumpeter introduced a sultry complementary melody.

The pianist stopped until Roare and the trumpeter completed their segment. The pianist began his solo. Afterward, the rest of the musicians joined in.

The audience clapped at certain ostinatos. Others leaned forward and closed their eyes as if transported with the band, while the haunting sound of the resonator guitar filled the air.

By the end of the second set, Roare was exhausted. She joined Wyatt and her in-laws at their table. By then, most patrons had departed, except for Tess from *People* magazine.

Wyatt beamed, cupped both her hands between his, and squeezed them as he pulled her closer. He leaned in to kiss her. "You commanded the audience. I could tell you were nervous, but you got better once you got in the zone. Your music bared your soul, babe. You're a natural performer."

Roare fought the flames in her cheeks and glanced away, only to find Tess standing behind her. Her eyebrows furrowed. She pulled away from Wyatt to face Tess. "You're still here."

Tess held her iPad. "I couldn't leave without getting an interview from you."

Wyatt looked at Roare. "Are you okay?"

She grabbed his hand and squeezed it gently. "It's all right, Wy. She's from *People* magazine. I got this."

Wyatt rejoined his parents at the table and told them to give Roare a few minutes.

Roare waved her hand at Tess. "We can sit over here." She guided her to a table where they could sit far away from her family. "How long is this going to take? I'm pretty tired and want to get home," Roare said.

"It'll be a few minutes. Only a couple of questions if I may," Tess said, and tapped on her iPad.

"You have three minutes."

"I enjoyed your gig. You're really talented. Have you considered having your own band?"

"No. It's only a hobby."

"When did you learn to play?" Tess began typing away on her iPad.

"When I was twelve. I messed around with the guitar off and on over the years."

"Why jazz?"

"Why not? I appreciate the complexity of rhythms, and it appeals to my senses. It relaxes me."

"I dig the cool vibe and different crowds jazz attracts to these venues," Tess said.

"Yes, so do I. The straight-ahead jazz gatherings tend to be mature, take the music seriously, and are unpretentious and earthy. They're my kind of people," Roare said.

"And you're an expert on this?"

"I never claimed to be, you just did. I can ask you the same thing."

"Actually, no, jazz isn't my favorite music."

"I'm not surprised. So, this was an assignment your magazine gave you?"

"I'm a freelance reporter. What I'm really after is a story on you as a film director."

Roare smirked. "I thought as much. You couldn't care less about my music. This interview is finished." She got up from the table and rejoined her family. *Now I'm starting to understand why Dr. Galletti suggested I walk away from escalation.*

Tess sat there for a moment, then reached for her cell phone. She collected her belongings, took a side-glance at Roare's table, and left the club quietly.

Roare rested her forearms on the table and sighed. "Sorry about the interruption."

Wyatt cupped Roare's right hand in his. "The interview's over already? Are you okay?"

She nodded. "All good. Turns out she was interested in me as a film director. She used the performance as an excuse to get to me. I'm already forgetting she was ever here."

Anoosh said, "My dear, you were very clever to see through her. I'm sure some of these people can be deceptive."

"Without a doubt. Anyway, I appreciate you coming out to support me."

"We're thrilled to finally see you play. You were wonderful," Anoosh said. "Have you considered playing full time?"

"What a generous compliment," Roare said. "Honestly, though, as much as I enjoy playing, I prefer making films more."

"Great answer," Morrison said.

"Hey, guys," Wyatt said. "We should go. Today's been intense. Roare needs to get some rest. I'll drop by in the morning to see you off."

When the adrenaline rush subsided, Roare felt her energy crashing. She changed into plaid flannel pajamas and hung her pants on a hanger when something fell out of the back pocket. She bent to retrieve a yellow note wedged inside the folded business card from the subway musician.

Where did this come from? She opened the note.

Hi Roare,
Apologies on the clumsy intrusion. I know you through your films. I admire your work, and I'm not a stalker. Your films are bold—with devastating truth. Many

deceptions will bombard our way of life. They'll prance and boast like necromancers. Our human existence has been compromised by sinister schemes.

I'm not a lunatic. The further you chase the truth, the more you'll be repulsed by the deception. Do your homework! Research transhumanism. Then call me at +39 380 3141831.

Signed,

A fan of Dr. Stanley Monteith

She placed a hand over her gaping mouth. *Is this man some weirdo? What does he want from me?*

She tried to compose herself and think clearly. Her only reference points were the foreign cell number and that he was a fan of this Dr. Stanley Monteith. She'd do some research. *Maybe I'll find some clues about this guitar player.*

Newly amped up from the gig and the note, she planted herself on the living room sofa with her laptop. She entered "transhumanism" into DuckDuckGo. *I can't believe the amount of information out there about this, and the word has yet to become a mainstream talking point.*

She researched Dr. Monteith using Cuil and Omgili and jotted notes until the early morning hours. Upon finding his book, *Brotherhood of Darkness*, her blood ran cold. The book contained his research on secret societies and their sinister agendas against humanity. *I need to order a copy.* Her eyes widened like saucers as she read about how these agendas were fueled by Satan. *Really? If that's so, then what kind of person am I dealing with? Only way to know is to call him. Do I dare?*

In the morning, Roare fired an email to Pilar. "I'll be at my parents' this weekend. I need you to suss out some independent investigative journalists. Make sure they're the best in the fields of transhumanism and xenogenesis."

Roare could trust her assistant with anything. The thirty-two-year-old was responsible, trustworthy, and affectionately looked after Roare like a younger sister.

When Roare passed through the lobby of her building with her weekend bag, she noticed the tall glass vases of fresh flowers on the white marble tops of three perfectly aligned cherry console tables. She'd always thought the bird-of-paradise looked like a plant from another world. After her research, she wondered if they were.

Being a film director created a natural habit for detail or neurosis. Today, her sense of sight was in hyperdrive—the security guard was staring at her, and a familiar neighbor suddenly looked foreign.

While Roare helped Wyatt load the back of their denim-blue Volvo SUV, she kept checking over her shoulders for movement on the sidewalk and streets. *Someone is watching me.*

As Roare got into the car, Wyatt asked if she was okay.

No, she was not okay. She told him about the cryptic note and what she'd discovered in her research. "Between that and the encounters with paparazzi recently, I'm creeped out by people right now. I feel like my life is being invaded. If what I've learned is true, technology will be used against us."

"You're joking, right? That's not going to happen. We just need to get out of the city for a while. Reset your perspective, and we can take proactive measures like getting a bodyguard."

They headed north toward the George Washington Bridge, then crossed into New Jersey.

Roare huffed. *He's not taking me seriously. I hate when he glosses over my concerns. Lord, help me to find the words to get through to him.* She said, "Wy, give me some credit. I'm not that gullible, and the sites and scientific reports about AI are reputable. Some people, including you, find it hard to believe someone can be so evil, but AI is worse than you know. Technology has advanced a lot further in recent years and is being kept under the radar."

"Forgive me for being judgmental, but explain to me why our species is suddenly a threat to the future?"

"Transhumanism is an ideology and a movement to merge man with machine. Some futurists and technocrats believe humans as a species have run their course and have limitations in furthering mankind. They believe we are wrecking earth because there are too many of us residing here."

Wyatt pursed his lips. "Maybe. Somewhat. We're wasteful, endanger the lives of others by our poor decisions, fill up the ocean with plastic, live without purpose, have violent natures, and love war. I'd say we aren't taking care of the planet very well—or each other, to be honest.

"True. I'm no Bible expert, but given that I'm still growing my faith, I do recall something about God wanting us to have dominion over the earth."

"You're right. The books of Genesis and Numbers mentions this."

"Ah, okay. Although your points are valid, here's the problem. There are some globalists who have nominated themselves as custodians of the world, and if they decide you don't have a viable purpose—one useful to them— you don't need to exist. And merging the selected ones with technology will transform mankind to reach infinite heights."

"And this will supposedly be an improved version of our species?"

"To them, yes. AI can learn faster than any human and is capable of doing most of our jobs more efficiently. Robots can go into combat zones, take out enemies, and diffuse bombs."

"With the elimination of millions of jobs."

"Hold on, there's more. Imagine seeing cyborgs doing surgeries instead of human doctors."

Wyatt laughed. "Cyborgs in an operating theater? I don't think most of the population will accept the idea. And where does procreation fit into this agenda? This is an assault against what God already created."

"Agreed. But this technology is advancing faster than scientists imagined—not to mention, it's frightening."

Wyatt scratched at his beard. "Sobering is a better word. Only a demonic plot would attempt to eradicate humans and create a new world unsuitable for our kind, except maybe for consumption."

"Are you trying to be gross?" Roare asked.

"During the days of Noah, when the Nephilim roamed earth, God had to eliminate them with the flood. I see a parallel story here," Wyatt said.

Roare asked, "In what way?"

"There is a certain breed of people who want humanity destroyed. Those are the plans of man, not God. He has the final say in our outcomes."

"True, and for the record, robots won't need to consume us, not physically, anyway. Our minds and souls are an entirely different matter."

"I want to dig into this more, but let's agree not to discuss this in front of the boys."

"Agreed. To be continued. We're almost there."

rage against the machine

Wyatt drove up the long, curved driveway to Lane and Ben's stately white Dutch Colonial home with powder-blue shutters. The house sat nestled among red oak, dogwood, and spruce trees off the Palisades Parkway in Rockleigh. At times, Roare forgot how beautiful this place was—stunning, peaceful, and historical. She still loved a small-town vibe. As she and Wyatt strolled to the door with their bags, the front door flew open.

"You're here!" Noland tried to leap into Roare's arms but slid back to his feet, then laughed. "Sorry, Sis, I guess I've grown a bit since you last saw me."

"Yeah, and gotten heavier too!" She realized he must have grown at least two inches since she last saw him. He was athletic and muscular for an eight-year-old.

Roare gave him a bear hug and smiled fondly at her brother. *I miss them and should make an effort to spend more time with them.*

"We thought you forgot us!"

"We texted a few days ago," she said.

"I mean *face-to-face*. We wanna see more of you."

"I'm here now, but how about this? How about we make a deal to have a video call every week."

Noland tilted his head to the left. "Sounds good, but you promise, right?"

"Yes, I promise." The two hugged again. Roare could always count on the unconditional love found at this house. Like the aroma of roses, visiting was therapy to her soul.

As animated as he was, Noland took his time to notice Wyatt behind her. "Hi, Wyatt."

"Whatcha been up to?" Wyatt knelt to make himself Noland's size.

"Lots of homework, and our basketball and fencing practices are way too long, which is annoying." Noland fidgeted with a small soccer ball with his left foot.

"Well, that would annoy me, too, buddy. Things'll improve. I see you like soccer too."

"A little. I might try out for a team next year, but I'm not sure yet," Noland said.

"I'm sure you'll figure it out."

"I guess so, but Maddox likes soccer more than I do right now. Hey, you guys are staying over, aren't you?"

"Of course. We're overdue for a chess rematch."

"I bet you're sorry you taught me how to play." He giggled.

Wyatt placed his hands on his hips. "I hate being slaughtered."

"We can play Xbox too. Mom, can Wyatt come play with me?"

Lane answered as she approached, "Sure."

"Actually, Roare and I need some grownup talk first, do you mind?" Wyatt said.

"Well, okay, but don't be too long," Noland said.

"I won't be."

Roare gazed fondly at Wyatt. He loved children and could connect with them on a profound level—her brothers adored him. He would've made a great pediatrician.

Ben stood behind Lane in the doorway and slipped his arms around her waist. Greetings, handshakes, and hugs all around. Lane sent Noland to retrieve his brother.

The four adults filed past a set of white French doors, their steps echoing off the hardwood floors, until they reached two facing sofas on an antique Persian rug in the middle of the living room. As they seated themselves, Roare set her backpack on one of the cement coffee tables. With their thin, brushed-bronze legs, they always reminded her of industrial spiders.

The lit fireplace warmed and illuminated the room. Anchoring the cherrywood mantle were a foot-high cross of forged bronze nails and a life-sized sculpted head with a crown of thorns.

Maddox came waltzing in. "Sorry, I didn't know you were here."

"Good to see you!" Roare said.

"Yeah."

He was finally putting on weight. The older brother had a small frame and was more introverted than Noland. Maddox wore a crew cut, had a cute nose, and his dimples showed when he grinned.

Maddox walked over, wrapped his arms around Roare's waist, and looked up at her.

Roare leaned down, hugged him, and kissed his cheek.

He smiled shyly and blushed as he pulled away. "All right, Sis, enough already. I know you miss me."

"Oh, I understand, you're too old for these baby hugs, right?"

Maddox slid his socks back and forth against the slippery, polished hardwood floors. "Well, kind of, but it doesn't mean I don't miss you. I do." He wouldn't look her in the eye.

"I believe you. Would fist bumps be cool from now on?" Roare asked as she swiveled to follow his movements. *These boys can't keep still, can they? They really don't know how to use the amount of energy I wish I had.*

Wyatt asked Maddox about what game he was playing on his tablet and promised they'd play together after the adults talked.

Ben returned with drinks and finger foods as the family had a catch-up.

Roare leaned her head to the side, soaking in the conversation about her brothers' lives at school and their sports activities.

"I've become a chauffeur, driving them back and forth to basketball games, soccer games, the list goes on," Lane said. "It's exhausting. You have been warned."

"Something to look forward to," Roare said.

"Ben and I decided to remain stateside for their safety until they're older. We'll return to ministry later. At the moment, we're status quo on Koni & Docks. With six design clients, we're busy enough."

Ben asked, "Wyatt, how's life in the science world?"

"Things are fermenting," Wyatt said.

The others laughed.

"Roare's news is more exciting than mine." He raised his eyebrows at her.

"Right," she said. "I've been holding out on you. Someone slipped me a strange note while we were headed to one of my gigs." Roare explained the details and handed the note to Lane.

"Did this guy seem dangerous?" Ben asked, while Lane read.

"Not at all. I'm intrigued yet concerned. I might call him. We'll see. Need to do more digging on transhumanism."

"What does this mean?" Lane passed the paper to Ben.

"Essentially, blending humans with technology," Roare said, "and artificial intelligence."

"Merging with machines might help some people," Ben said.

"And what I want to know is the dark side to all this," Roare said. "I hope to find out things the creators aren't telling us."

"Maybe there are *things* you don't want to know. Please tell me you'll be careful," Lane said.

"I'm trying. I've been running into paparazzi lately. And I have a feeling I'm being followed. Yesterday, Wyatt nearly slugged a guy who approached us on our way into the jazz club."

Ben and Lane glanced at each other.

Lane said, "Do you remember my friend, the bodyguard? I can arrange for you to meet him."

"I never believed having protection was necessary, but nowadays, I'm not feeling safe."

Wyatt said, "Considering the offer wouldn't be a bad thing."

Let's be real, I'm going to have to come to terms with being famous. "I can certainly use a buffer between me and those—"

"Vultures," Wyatt finished. "They have a lot of guts stalking their prey the way they do."

"My dear," Ben said, "people like you, who've been exposed to the public, are targets."

Roare felt outnumbered. "Despite my reluctance, I suppose I can give your bodyguard friend a try. But he'll have to prove himself, or I'll be sending him away."

"Fair enough," Lane said. "He has a thirty-day guarantee. Hey. You know we love you." She glanced at Ben.

Roare felt the intoxicating love of her family but couldn't shake a growing fear about AI. Her instincts told her transhumanism wouldn't be going away anytime soon or brushed under the rug as a fad. She was convinced the sinister nature of AI and transhumanism would come into the forefront of life in subtle but troubling ways. The mere thought of these posthuman ambitions being of evil nature assaulted her spirit. She had to unravel more.

chapter four—the elysian odyssey

Because you are my help,
I sing in the shadow of your wings.—Psalm 63:7

After rescheduling twice, Roare was stoked to finally catch up with her college friend Drue. They met in Soho to shop for baby clothes in preparation for Drue's new little one and to grab lunch at their favorite café.

Roare scoped out a table away from prying eyes, hoping no one would recognize her. She and Drue nestled themselves comfortably at a small, round table next to Café Lalo's large windows overlooking the street. The two women peeled off their coats, scanned the menus, and ordered.

As they waited, Roare shared the contents of the cryptic note and the preliminary research she'd already done on transhumanism. She was still spooked.

"Ro, remember I told you some time ago about my sister Tula and her experiences with advanced technology?"

"I do recall. I was hoping to pick your brain about her experience."

"Gladly. Well, Tula is comfortable with robots and saw the benefits of genetic editing."

"How so?" Roare asked.

"Well, imagine this—genetic technology can sense and repair diseases like muscular dystrophy or predict cancer before it happens."

"Hmm, yes, I can see this. These are helpful to humanity."

"I agree, but listen to this—Tula stayed at a hotel in Japan while she was at a tech conference. The hotel was run completely by AI robots."

"Really?"

"Not a human in sight other than the guests," Drue said.

Roare shook her head. "I must admit, all this sounds eerie and deeply impersonal."

"Yeah, I know. Tula thought the robots were soulless."

"Makes my skin crawl. That word makes me imagine an annoying swarm of black flies storming a field of flowers," Roare said.

As they finished their meal, Roare grew anxious to return home to do more research. She and Drue were about to leave when a young girl in her early twenties came in. *She's headed right to our table.* Roare's back stiffened while her eyes remained fixed on the girl's every move.

The young girl shyly stood over her. Introduced herself as Lily. Professed to be a huge fan. Even told her *Substance* had stopped her from taking drugs. Roare was pleased to hear it. Then, Lily pulled out a black T-shirt with the film's pink logo from her tote bag.

Lily asked, "Would you mind autographing my shirt?" She handed her a marker.

"I'd be happy to, and I'm glad you had a positive outcome from watching my film." Roare signed her name in silver ink.

Lily thanked her and left the café.

Roare watched her descend the stairs. The girl looked back, and Roare caught a flicker of blue light in her eyes.

Roare gasped. Her mind flashed back to the incident in the park eight years ago. A good Samaritan had saved her from being violated by a mob of men while her "friends" stood by and watched. She remembered the Samaritan moving so quickly, her assailants could barely see who or what was hitting them. She had witnessed those same blue beams of light from his eyes to incapacitate the men. She was still haunted by them.

Overcome by curiosity, Roare jumped up from the table and ran after the girl. She had to know who or what she was. Roare reached the bottom of the stairs, looked left and right, and ran to the corner. *Vanished.*

"How's my babe doing?" Wyatt hugged Roare from behind her place at the kitchen island, then kissed her neck.

"I enjoyed my catch-up with Drue." She recounted the experience with the fan at the café and her blue laser eyes.

"Ro, there are some strange things going on, too much to be a coincidence. Do you think the man who slipped you the note is playing you or setting you up?"

"Don't know, but I have a suspicion he may be responsible. I cannot prove this, but now is the time for me to call him, right after a little more research. I want to better understand the true intention of transhumanism—in an eerie way, this is fascinating. Could make for a compelling film."

"Gobo, I'm worried about you. Freakish things are happening. You know I don't like you staying up at all hours doing research. Turns you into a grump, and we lose time together."

Roare moaned. "Wyatt. I'm sorry you feel this way, but I appreciate your patience. This topic is all new to me, and I'm curious."

"Listen, I just don't want anything to happen to you."

"Neither do I. You're a good researcher. Why don't you help me? We can do this together."

"All right, but not all night. Deal?"

"Deal."

Two hours into the research, Roare navigated through scientific articles and reviews from AI summits. *My gosh!* One article claimed technology could end human and animal suffering. *"Renaming Humanity to Humanity Plus." What is all this supposed to mean?* Scenarios of sentient robots roaming the streets played in her mind. She jotted on her notepad and rubbed her forehead.

"This seems to get darker as I read more. I see why you're skittish," Wyatt offered. "On one hand, modifying DNA strands might improve human life. Robotics and technology could enhance vision or sense diseases before they happen. On the other hand, these advances could backfire and create monstrous results. Human technology will always be imperfect. AI can never replace God or conquer death."

They watched videos on DTube about studies in biotech advancements in cyborgs, used to heal or kill humans. Roare wrote down keywords as she learned them: PathAI, GPT-5, Artificial Neural Network (ANN), and sentient. She concluded "transhumanism" meant redefining humanity and self-governing our evolution through reliance on technology.

But what would prevent scientists from implanting sadistic ideas into AI? Surely, they've considered all kinds of scenarios. *At least now, Wy can see that our species is in trouble.*

chapter five—ebb and flow

We are torn between nostalgia for the familiar and an urge for the foreign and strange. As often as not, we are homesick most for the places we have never known.
—Carson McCullers

Pilar flashed Roare a grin. "I can't tell you how relieved I am. This is way overdue. What's his name?"

"Sloane McInerney." This is her first outing with her bodyguard. "I wrote his information on the pad in the office." Roare shoved her research notes and iPad into her tote, put on her shearling coat. "Catch you later." She flung her tote over her shoulder as she rushed out the door.

In the lobby stood a tall, broad-shouldered man dressed in dark jeans, black ankle boots, and a bomber jacket. He held a black knit skullcap in his hand. His brown hair was cropped close.

Must be Sloane. Roare winced as her boots echoed across the marble floor.

He eyed her. His neck was incredibly thick above a finely knit black-and-gray geometric-patterned sweater.

Roare bit her lower lip. *He has a fierce appearance, which is not a bad thing—useful to fend off unwelcome intruders.*

She guessed he was in his forties and hoped there was depth under the brawn, not an ex-CIA drone.

They introduced themselves, and Sloane recommended the A train to Jay Street in Brooklyn would be quicker. "I want to get you back in time for you to make your three o'clock appointment." His authoritative, yet eloquent, baritone soothed Roare's nerves. His piercing light-brown eyes exuded confidence, and his steady, secure demeanor reassured her.

Roare sighed in relief. "Good idea, thank you. You must've done your homework. Downtown Brooklyn is a quiet neighborhood, less exposure."

"Glad you dressed warmly. A blizzard may be heading our way."

"In October? How can you tell?" she asked.

"I can smell it."

"Ha, ha. I hope your nose is wrong, and the storm won't come, at least not until you return me home."

They walked briskly toward the subway station and caught the A train. After disembarking in Brooklyn, the wind whipped at Roare's legs like an invader, and she buttoned her full-length coat to the bottom. She and Sloane scooted into a beautifully converted warehouse—home of The Global Initiative for Ethics and Truth Group.

In the palatial lobby, they sat on two large chairs. The olive-and-navy furniture contrasted with the beige marble floor against dark wood trimmings. Black industrial steel framed the glass walls, while thin black decorative beams dressed the ceiling. Together, the black lines resembled a squared rib cage. Clever theatrical effects merged with a modern flair, creating a pleasant atmosphere.

"Ms. Murdock?" A svelte forty-something blonde with a British accent stopped in front of Roare.

Sloane crossed his arms and studied her.

"Yes?" Roare said.

"Good morning. A great pleasure to meet you." The woman extended her hand. "I'm Mavis Templer. I assume your companion is your personal assistant?"

Roare stood cordially and met her handshake. "Yes."

After greetings, they rode a private elevator to the top floor, where they entered a duplex penthouse. The lofty space was surprisingly private despite a large wall of windows facing the nearby buildings. Mavis led them into a dining area where five others were seated around a long, oval glass table.

A man wearing a blue tweed jacket stood and pushed his glasses up his nose. "Welcome. I'm Lars Gunter, head of TGIET. Please have a seat." He motioned toward three empty chairs at the table. "Ms. Murdock, I'm sure you're aware of how we conduct our 'strictly confidential' meetings."

"Of course." Roare took a seat. "I hope you don't mind I brought my assistant along."

"Should be fine." Lars gave a quick nod. "Our team here consists of investigative science journalists from *Truth Media*, *Signs of Today*, and the *Associated News*. We also have two scientists and an attorney."

As they introduced themselves individually, Roare made a mental note of their backgrounds. Lujza, an aggressive Hungarian journalist, sat on Roare's right. She and AI expert, Xander, provided information tersely, whereas the others spoke warmly to Roare.

Lars resumed. "We formed our establishment to expose topics the public knows little to nothing about—events that'll undermine life and jeopardize human existence."

Roare smirked. With those round specs, he seemed knowledgeable and thorough enough. The whole team had strong credentials. Time would tell what they could produce.

"We're pleased you're as interested in us, as we've been in you. We're aware of your work and how private you are," Lars continued. "When Pilar informed us of your zealous interest in transhumanism and genetic engineering, well, we jumped at the chance to chat with you. There are a few disclosures we'll need to discuss before you decide to work with us. But first, we need to ask you if this man is your assistant. He doesn't look or sound like a Pilar."

They'd done research of their own. "No. He's my bodyguard, Sloane McInerny. He was an army ranger in counterintelligence. He's extremely professional and respects confidentiality."

"A good call because the further you delve into the rattrap, the more you'll need protection," Lars said.

Roare reeled a bit. "Sounds pretty dire."

"You can't be serious," Xander said. "Haven't you researched this topic?"

"I'm used to being challenged on explosive topics." Her voice had grown tight. She paused for a moment, then calmly added, "I only recently decided to examine this topic because of an anonymous note. I haven't invested enough time yet. I came to learn more."

"Apparently, you have no credibility on this subject." Lujza twisted her wavy hair with two fingers. "No authority, no engineering background to contribute to our project. Why should we trust you?"

Heat rose to Roare's cheeks. "I may not have the credentials or background you do, but you knew that already, didn't you?"

Lars waved his hand toward the others, and the inquisition ceased. "We're familiar with your background,

46

your spiritual beliefs, and what you stand for. Your films will change ethics to lower the risk of harm to innocent people and unravel truths to awaken the masses. You're a brilliant director. We don't concern ourselves with your religious beliefs or your lack of expertise on transhumanism. We do value your passion for exposing the truth."

Lujza chimed in, "Top scientists, billionaires, and geneticists have grave concerns about how rapidly AI will change the world forever, as long as silence remains."

"You still haven't told me what you want," Roare said to Lars.

He met her gaze. "We want you to partner with us, to make a provocative film on transhumanism. Our goal is to expose the plans to replace humans with AI technology."

"What an enormous invitation." Roare questioned whether she had the ability to create a film of this magnitude.

"This movement is ambitious and more dangerous than you can imagine," Xander said. "As we speak, rogue AI technicians are plotting to destroy humanity. We need to act quickly to get the government to enforce regulations on these scientists to save ourselves from being made redundant."

Was this guy serious? Then again, Roare *had* come across those exact things online.

"We have private backers who want to ensure that evil doesn't thrive on this planet. Their budget is limitless. But we can't do this alone, and neither can you." Lars folded his hands on the table.

Presuming she declined, they would find someone else to make the film. *God, give me discernment and strength to make wise decisions. I trust you're leading me, so please give me a clue? Protect me, my family, and these decent people from harm. Help us, Lord!*

She had difficulty getting past the word "dangerous." She looked at Sloane briefly and lamented whether he'd be enough to protect her. Her gaze returned to Lars and his team. "Just how much risk are you talking about?"

The team exchanged looks.

Xander said, "More than you're used to. Keep McInerny close, and trust no one. All of us will be putting our lives on the line."

Previous films had taught Roare not to dismiss the dangers involved. "Essentially, the public must be made aware of a mad sci-fi narrative playing out behind the scenes. I'll need time to consider your proposal."

"Your impressions are correct," Lars said. "I'm sure you'll consider our offer thoroughly."

"Do you have whistleblowers in place? I'd want to interview them."

"They're available when you're ready."

"Great. My agent and attorney will need to review any agreements before I sign." Roare's voice remained level, but inside she was trembling. *This project could prove fatal for me. I'll really need to think this over.*

"Hope you don't mind my asking," Lars said, "how old are you?"

"Twenty-six. Why?"

"You're mature for your age, and too serious, in an unusually nice way."

Roare's cheeks warmed at the attention. She'd have to be candid to put them at ease. "What a nice thing to say. I don't like to talk about myself. I choose to be vulnerable only to those who question my capabilities."

To her right, a journalist whispered to Lujza, "I guess she called us out."

Roare's confidence kicked in, and she gave them a sneer. "My success doesn't mean I know everything. I don't."

"Don't underestimate your competence," Lars said. "Making a film of this importance will enhance our knowledge tenfold. It's been a pleasure to meet you both. We'll be in touch."

Most of the others agreed.

Lujza said, "A couple of us would prefer to wait until she has shown her worth."

Xander tapped a finger on the table. "Nothing personal."

Fair enough. "Thank you all for your time." Roare stood. "My attorney will be in touch."

The temperature had dropped outside, and as they left, Roare pulled up her collar. She took a few seconds to hold in a breath of cold air, then released it with her anxiety.

"Would you mind me commenting on the meeting?" Sloane asked.

"Please do," she said.

"You handled yourself well in there. I agree with Lars. You've only scratched the surface of your potential."

How did Sloane know her so well already? He and her mother were friends. Perhaps he had watched Roare over the years. Right now, she could muster only a simple thank-you.

Whatever the team's impressions, good or bad, Roare wasn't out to make a zillion dollars or to be a Hollywood megastar. She wanted only to benefit others.

"We better move along," Sloane said. "I don't want you to miss your next appointment."

Roare arrived home with enough time to unwind and review the messages Pilar had left. She took a cup of chrysanthemum tea and an almond cookie to her office and prayed over the call she was about to have with the guitarist from the subway station. Determined to needle him and get under his skin, if need be, she had to get more clarity about what she'd be up against taking on this endeavor. She initiated the recorder on her phone, took a deep breath, and dialed his number.

"Hello," the man answered.

"This is Roare. I'm responding to your note."

"Ah yes, my calling card. I piqued your curiosity."

"In a manner of speaking. I admit I started doing some research on transhumanism, xenogenesis, and the doctor you're so fond of."

"And?"

"The information I found was alarming, to be frank, but I want to stop here until you've answered a few questions for me." She refused to allow a stranger to pump her for details. "I need to know who I'm dealing with. Why did you target me? Is this about money?"

"Listen, I want you to be comfortable with me. I am not your enemy, nor do I want to hurt you. This isn't about money. I'm about saving lives, and I believe you're the person who can sound the siren. Incidentally, I assume you're recording our conversation?"

She raised her left eyebrow. "Well ... yes." Roare pulled off her sweater. Paced in her office.

"Good. Is your line secure?" the man asked.

"Yes, I'm using Signal."

He cleared his throat. "So am I, with end-to-end encryption. My main concern is for you to be put at ease. I've watched your last two films and saw your interview on *Spotlight*. I thought this topic might spark your interest."

"Why is that?"

"Because you're controversial. You're young and not afraid to take chances. Please call me Morgan."

"All right, *Morgan*," Roare failed to keep the edge out of her tone, "I'll play along."

"A friend of mine gave me info on transhumanism."

"Can you tell me more about this *friend*, and how you fit into this narrative?"

"He and I volunteered to deliver food to the elderly in the city. He liked shooting his mouth off. He told me transhumanism is not what it seems. He said it has already been done."

Roare stopped midstride. "Come again?"

"Transhumanists are living among us. They look like us."

She plopped herself in her office chair at her desk. Stared blankly into space. She recalled those two incidents—people projecting blue lasers from their eyes. She didn't trust him enough to tell him. "Morgan, are you talking about cyborgs? Do you have any facts to support your statement? I need you to provide me with proof, or we're done here."

"He's seen the laboratories. He was in the military. By chance, he stumbled across documents on the advancements made in recent years and did his own research. He knew how to find specific data."

Roare cringed. *At least we're getting somewhere.* "Can you elaborate?"

"I believe him. For the time being, though, I'm with a private company, and I'd rather remain invisible for now. I can't afford exposure."

"Are you a government contractor or scientist?"

"Not exactly, but I roam in those circles. Humor me for a few more seconds."

"Continue," Roare said.

"You have no idea what goes on in the dark world. Rogue doctors, scientists, physicists, politicians, secret government entities, private investors operating below the radar. Don't underestimate them—extreme AI is not going to waste and is in full use in plain sight. I hope the world isn't so corrupt as to allow humans to be destroyed by AI and genetic engineering. All I want is for you to consider the topic."

Roare leaned forward in her chair and placed a hand on her stomach, as if she was about to throw up. "You're not feeding me some lines from a sci-fi film, are you? The level of evil sounds unreal."

"I'm afraid it's very real, and I think you know this too," Morgan said.

Roare took a deep breath, exhaled then bit her lower lip. *I'll never admit to this guy he's right.* "Anything else you want to tell me?"

"Yeah. There is enough information already on the internet to support a phenomenal film. Have a look at OpenAI-ChatGPT, Dyson, and Lucerne University of Applied Sciences and Arts. This will give you an idea about what humanity is facing."

"I will." She settled back in her chair and stared at a blank computer screen. *God, tell me you're not done with humanity yet.*

"Two points I want to make. First—why do you suppose there are a few scientists screaming to put the brakes on the learning capabilities of AI? Its intelligence is accelerating at unimaginable speed, and the creators are terrified. Second point—I've told you about some AI labs that are visible to the public. There are rogue underground labs the military aren't even aware of."

God help us. "You've said enough for now. One thing—how did you know I got an offer for a film project on this very topic?"

"Apparently, I'm not the only one with these concerns. I'll be in touch." Morgan ended the call.

Roare's stomach roiled. What had she stepped into—a power struggle between nefarious world powers? Was the military trying to stop fiendish scientists, or were they pushing for AI robotics to depopulate the earth? *Is the goal to substitute humans with a highly evolved species that no longer has use for us and plots our destruction? Is this all true? What if Morgan is not a raving lunatic after all? Lord, tell me I'm wrong.*

Roare sat in her usual spot on the living room sofa, prepped for an afternoon of research, and bowed her head. *Jesus, I need help. While I explore the nuggets Morgan dropped on me, show me what to see exactly, what I need to know as I explore. Protect my spirit from fear and keep my mind from being overtaken by the wickedness of man. Guide me in making choices to reflect your truth.*

She flicked on *A Shot in the Dark*. The film wouldn't cause distraction. As she sipped on a liter of water, she probed private search engines again and reviewed David Pearce, Stephen Hawking, Steve Quayle, and Julian Savulescu.

The more she explored transhumanism, the more she replayed the ambiguous exchange she'd had with Morgan. The direction of AI technology struck her with sinister gravity.

In a few hours, Wyatt arrived home with sashimi. Roare stir fried string beans with walnuts and soy sauce, and steamed broccoli. While they ate dinner, she told Wyatt about her research and the conversation with Morgan.

"He is deliberately protecting his identity," Wyatt said. "If you can validate what he's told you, his credibility would be strengthened. Everybody's talking about ChatGPT."

"So I noticed. I found a few apps on the internet. Wy, I hate to say this, but the things he said are starting to take shape. Remember those two encounters I had with different people, on different occasions, both projecting blue laser lights from their eyes? I thought maybe they were aliens. However, after the meeting today ... too many events are aligning, establishing a common thread. I sense God's showing me the way. I've decided to take on this film project. I'm all in."

"Why am I not surprised? Have you gotten confirmation from God about making this decision, babe? I don't want to see you get dragged into an assignment we'll both regret."

"I'm certain God will give me validations. What worries me is the danger ahead."

"And you don't think I'm worried? I don't want to lose you. Ro, I can't tell you what to do. But there will be consequences. You must weigh the cost of your involvement. Would this project be worth losing your life and the lives of your family members?"

"What about the billions of people on this planet who may face extermination?"

"Maybe this is not your fight. If you don't do this, someone else will."

"I can't help but wonder if we're at a point of no return?"

Roare sensed she was only scratching the surface of something darker than she could begin to fathom. She questioned her motives for wanting to take on such a project of significance. *Is this to exalt myself to become some superhero? Am I truly following God's destiny for me? Or am I doing this out of sheer terror, uncertain whether there will be a tomorrow or future to hope for?* She remained on the sofa, staring at her computer screen with her mind a million miles away contemplating an extinct future. She prayed scientists wouldn't be reckless with AI. For all anyone knew, an opening to Gehenna could take place.

chapter six—hunter

What the wicked dread will overtake them.
—Proverbs 10:24

Hunter Barraclough's high standards suited the exclusive, peaceful neighborhood of Vaucluse in Sydney. He imagined the Earth had stopped spinning so his perfect world wouldn't be disturbed.

Yet, one late October night, Hunter's precious serenity was disrupted by a nightmare. Half asleep, he rolled to his side and finally dozed again.

An unfamiliar voice whispered, "The world has been taken over by vermin. You realize this, don't you? If not, where have you been? Pull your head out of the sand and wake up!"

Hunter moaned, turned onto his other side, and settled comfortably into a fetal position.

A few minutes later, the voice returned. "Alternative news outlets report daily on terrorism and political deception, while World War III is knocking on the door. Poverty, famine, incurable diseases, satanic rituals, and the killing of innocents thrive. Suicide is epidemic. Human life is imploding. Can't you see?"

Hunter turned on his back, stretched his legs, and opened his eyes briefly. His head flopped to the left as he drifted back to sleep.

"Wars and rumors of wars are happening as you sleep. Societies are deconstructing worldwide, making financial collapse imminent. People wage genocide against those they hate because of race, beliefs, or simply because they exist. The one percent who claim to be the greatest contribution to humanity deem everyone else worthless."

Hunter tossed his head from side to side. He flung his right arm over his head and half-awakened. *Bloody nightmares.*

The voice said, "You assume you are immune to trouble. Your days are few, and your tomorrows are uncertain. Straighten out your life, or I'll do it for you. Believe me, you'll no longer be happy living in your own skin. Regarding yourself as extraordinary will be a thing of the past. If you don't correct your evil ways, you will regret it."

Hunter bolted up like a flagpole, breathing heavily. He stared blankly into the dark, then glanced around. His wife lay asleep beside him.

He went into the bathroom and splashed cool water on his face. Refreshed, he quietly retrieved his robe from the foot of the bed, slipped out of the bedroom, and made his way to the living room. At the wet bar, he poured a double shot of cognac. The cement floors chilled his bare feet. If he returned to the bedroom to grab his slippers, he'd risk waking Evie. He sank like a bag of dirty laundry onto a cream leather reclining chair near the plate-glass doors overlooking Vaucluse Bay. With his feet on the ottoman, he watched the choppy waves.

A healthy gulp of his brew snaked down his esophagus, and his nerves unraveled like fine silk. He savored the raisin-esque, nutty liquid on his tongue.

Get hold of yourself, mate. You've had a bad dream. Need to lay off the drinking altogether and stop reading so many thrillers before bed.

Life was great—no worries and nothing to regret. He had everything to be thankful for, everything to live for. "Look, whoever you are, I don't scare easily, so don't invade my sleep again."

Still lost in thought, Hunter polished off the cognac. Nearly intoxicated, he remained fixated on his dream.

Rain poured outside like an open faucet. Sailboats along the docks bobbed, resembling wobbly bowling pins. He reclined his chair and rested until he drifted into a deep sleep.

Evie Barraclough entered the living space early the next morning. Drawn to the view, she approached the sliding glass door. The torrential downpour the night before had left a stunning cerulean sky and pillowy clouds. *Truly beautiful.*

She aimed for the kitchen but noticed Hunter and paused to watch him sleep. He looked disheveled, uncomfortable— completely unlike his usual slicked-back dark wavy hair and tall, athletic form. He appeared helpless and shriveled.

"Ah, there you are!" she said. "What on earth are you doing out here? Are you okay?"

Hunter shifted but didn't wake.

Evie walked closer and smoothed his gray-streaked hair.

He turned toward her, then slowly opened his eyes. With a broad yawn, he sat up and stretched. He grumbled as he rubbed his temples, then grabbed his lower back and grimaced. On the end table beside the recliner sat an empty Waterford snifter. "Don't say a word, Evie. I had a nightmare." He finally extracted himself from his recliner, then stretched his legs and torso.

"The dream must have frightened you," she said.

"Nothing scares me."

Evie snickered.

When Evie headed for the kitchen to make breakfast, Hunter rushed to take over. "If you don't mind, I'll make breakfast. You never did master poached eggs."

"For your information, I was going to make porridge. Get a professional chef. At least you can't complain about the espresso." She handed him a small cup and resumed her porridge.

"I'll tell you what happened," Hunter said. "An unfamiliar voice whispered in my ear to straighten out my life. He divulged other things too. It was surreal. I thought someone else was next to me in bed. I could feel his breath on my face."

"Blimey!"

"When I woke up, I even had a look around." He sipped his coffee. "I'm definitely over it now."

"You should lay off those late-night snacks. Still, you broke your promise to stop drinking."

Hunter shrugged as he made a mess of the kitchen to make his poached eggs and toast. "I'm working on it, so you don't need to keep bringing it up. What's on your schedule today?"

"I need to get to a hair appointment and show two properties. Among other things, we're meeting Aaden and his latest steady at Gantry at seven."

"A new girlfriend. Did you happen to catch her name?"

"No. He did describe her as being smart and beautiful, and they fancy each other. His words, not mine."

"Our youngest son is finally getting serious about a woman. Being in his prime, the timing could be right for him. She'll have to be brilliant to keep him interested."

Evie took her handbag from the counter and headed toward the door. "See you later."

"When you return from your appointments, I don't want to be disturbed. I have work calls."

"Sure. And just so you know, I'm hiring a maid."

"Knock yourself out."

Evie slammed the door behind her. Since he had become a world-renowned architect, he'd become increasingly difficult to please, let alone to live with.

Hunter worked from home so he could nurse his hangover.

The first Zoom call ended with him screaming at his assistant Mackenzie to have the 3D designs ready by Monday morning. He warned if she didn't, she should start looking for a new job.

Mackenzie defended herself. "I'll do my best, Mr. Barraclough, but I have five other projects I'm currently working on."

Hunter grunted. "*Trying* is not an option. Consider yourself fortunate to work here. So, either you get it done, or you're out."

"As you wish. Is there anything else?"

"No. We're done here." Hunter ended the call.

The second call was more of the same. Mylo, a seasoned architect and colleague, disagreed with Hunter about using a lesser grade of cladding. Mylo thought it was unethical. Hunter dismissed it as trivial, adamant the build wouldn't be compromised.

Mylo objected. "I caution you, one day you will regret your decision."

Call ended.

Hunter pivoted to his drafting desk and unrolled a set of blueprints for review. He'd submit them for a project in Lower Manhattan next week.

His dream plagued him again while he stared out the window. He'd done nothing in his life to warrant this nightmare. He'd obeyed his father, made no mistakes to impact his future, survived his stupid-bloke follies as a young man. He'd never been perfect—knew he wasn't flawless—except he hadn't let the drugs take him or done prison time.

He'd nearly lost his inheritance and promising future when he got a girlfriend pregnant. There'd been too much at stake to even consider raising a child. He'd had one last chance to please his father and couldn't afford to fail.

Hunter had been a pothead, a lazy pig with no discipline, and not enough drive to cultivate a successful career. If his father hadn't steered him in a stable direction, Hunter wouldn't have accomplished anything. Still, he couldn't find anything he had to rectify with God. *After all, God knows about all my failings anyway and still loves me.*

Hunter disregarded his sentiments and directed his energy into winning the Manhattan bid. The project would be a vital accolade for the award-winning firm he co-owned. K. P. Bangs & Barraclough pursued groundbreaking projects and promoted daring designs which earned them a reputation as leading architects in Australia and beyond.

With expanded offices in the United States and United Kingdom, his life had become a nonstop stream of consciousness—movement, form, creativity, and grand financial success. He didn't want the company to lose its elite status. Then again, he had worked ferociously for status and could afford to be arrogant.

"You haven't been listening," the voice said.

Hunter turned to his back and opened his eyes, then sat up on the edge of the bed, disoriented. *Not again.* He took a swig from the bottled water on his nightstand and ran his fingers through his hair. He had a plane to catch in the morning.

"I can't deal with your torment tonight, so why don't you bugger off?" he whispered. He scooted under the covers, closed his eyes, and fell back to sleep.

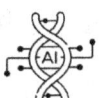

Long flights to New York did wonders for Hunter. He had time to reflect on life, prep for his upcoming meetings, and unwind. As he sipped a glass of wine in first class, he tweaked the floorplan for a high-rise fashion house in the Flatiron District on his laptop.

Wait, I'm not helping my efforts to quit. He buzzed the Qantas attendant and ordered a strong coffee with vanilla creamer. He peered over his black-rimmed reading glasses, ran his fingers through his hair, then gazed to the left where Evie slept with a novel across her lap. Beautiful little rascal. She'd practically blackmailed him into bringing her along for a chance to meet her favorite fashion designer. He cherished her never hiding who she was or what she wanted.

With plenty of time left, Hunter put the laptop in his backpack, pulled out a copy of *Australian Photography*, and thumbed mindlessly through the magazine.

A few minutes later, he struggled to keep his eyelids open. The coffee hadn't helped at all. He placed the magazine on his lap and rested his head against the plush headrest.

He thought of the nightmares again. While in New York, he'd visit a priest at St. Patrick's. He'd tell Evie he wanted to look at the cathedral's architecture. She could go shopping, and they'd meet later at a restaurant or the penthouse.

No one would know him, so he'd be able to speak freely. The tension gradually left his body. He had a plan and control over his troubled spirit.

After the long flight, Hunter and Evie were anxious to settle into the firm's spacious penthouse overlooking Central Park. After admiring the panoramic views, Evie noticed the huge fragrant bouquet in the foyer. "Did you order this arrangement for me?"

"My New York assistant found out you were coming."

Of course not, why would he? She shook her head and turned her back to him. "Please thank her for her kindness."

Evie called her sister Jenna and scheduled a shopping and dinner date with her and her niece. She overheard Hunter mumble something about being tired and heading off to bed.

The next evening, Hunter returned to the penthouse around nine, exhausted from a long day of meetings. A covered plate of food sat on the kitchen counter. "Evie?" He searched the apartment and found her in the master bathroom.

She stood dripping wet next to the shower stall and reaching for a towel on the long double-sink vanity.

"There you are!" he said.

She shrieked and reeled against the vanity. Her towel flew onto the Japanese vase on the counter, and it toppled.

To Hunter, the incident unfolded in slow motion. He tried to catch the vase. Unfortunately, the vase landed on the marble with a *crash!* Shards of ceramic scattered across the floor.

Evie froze with one hand grasping the towel around her and the other propping herself against the counter. "Crikey! You scared the life out of me!"

"Who else did you expect to walk into the bathroom? You silly woman! It was a 400-year-old vase—worth a small fortune."

"Nice to know where I stand in your life. No need to concern yourself with me. I'm fine." Evie looked over her arms, legs, and feet. "Go carry on with your 'business.' I'm to blame for overreacting, I'll sort out this mess. You can be a real mongrel!"

Hunter stalked out. He could use a stiff drink. Figured he'd better not. He shouldn't have allowed the nightmares to crawl up his spine the past couple of days, but the damage was already done. *Evie didn't deserve me being cross with her over a vase. The heirloom was covered by insurance. She didn't do this intentionally. I can really be a beast.*

By Tuesday, Hunter was burnt out from the grueling evenings of work. He had a late dinner with Evie, then retired. During the night, another intrusive nightmare encroached on his slumber. Finally, he gave up trying. Who was speaking to him?

The same distinct voice entered his left ear. "I am Jesus. Consider what you would ask me the next time we meet."

Hunter remained awake until morning. He showered, dressed, and quietly left to attend a breakfast meeting about the fashion house.

The fashion designer had accepted the designs for the store in Manhattan and signed the contract. Hunter could enjoy the city and run errands before meeting Evie, her sister, and niece for dinner at Marea's.

He walked north from his office on Thirty-Seventh Street, toward St. Patrick's cathedral.

The cathedral was cocooned between two tall, modern buildings—safe and protected. The neogothic bronze doors had to be nearly four meters high and could be seen from miles away. Seeing them up close was a privilege. As he viewed the story of the saints and God sculpted on the doors, Hunter's eyes gleamed. *Simply amazing.*

He took one step, then another into the opulent cathedral. Overstimulation set in at the sight of the vaulted design, intricate stained glass, and buttressed piers. Inspiration would have to wait.

A priest in a long black robe stood nearby, gazing intently at him. "Can I help you?"

"Oh, um, I'm an architect"—Hunter gestured upward—"and I couldn't resist having a look at the church's design." He pulled at his collar.

"Indeed, a miraculous accomplishment. I'm glad to meet a man who can appreciate the fine details."

"Yes, uh ..." Hunter ran a hand over his damp brow.

"You look like a man who wants to talk."

"Too obvious, eh?"

"No need to be embarrassed. Are you Catholic?"

"I suppose I am. But I haven't been to church in a great while. I'm hoping to talk to a clergyman regarding these nightmares I keep having."

The priest bowed his head and then looked at Hunter and gestured. "Follow me into my office, please."

They walked through a series of hallways to the back of the building and entered a small, stark room with a worn wingback chair behind a wooden desk.

Hunter sat in one of the Shaker-style guest chairs and clasped his shaking hands. *Don't sweat this man.*

"I didn't properly introduce myself," the priest said. "I'm Enrique Salazar, the priest here for over twelve years. And you are?"

"Hunter."

"How can I help you?" Father Enrique sat back and waited patiently.

"During the past couple of months, I've had this reoccurring dream. A voice keeps whispering in my ear. I thought some evil entity was tormenting me, until I found out who was talking to me."

"The voice told you who he was?"

"Yes, he said he was Jesus and asked me to consider questions I should ask him the next time we meet."

"Although I'm no psychiatrist, I can offer you spiritual insight. Care to tell me more?"

Hunter gave precise details about the dream, as if the dream became a living, breathing organism, an intricate part of his daily life. "I've gone over it a million times, analyzing it, and can't find the cause of my problem."

The priest rested his elbows on the arms of his chair and joined his hands in front of his mouth. "I see why you came. Perhaps something traumatic took root in your soul years ago and doesn't want to be suppressed any longer."

"The logical answer would be to yank out the root, right?"

Father Enrique sighed. "If only life's problems could be resolved so easily. Ask yourself if you've offended anyone from your past—caused pain, hurt, or betrayal. If you knew something was wrong but did it anyway. I call them 'consciousness of guilt' dreams. I don't know you or where you are spiritually, but I can tell you Jesus doesn't torment, but guilt could. God has a mysterious way of bringing truth to light. Your soul may find the peace needed once the situation is corrected."

Hunter groaned as a particular time in his life came to mind. "I've offended a lot of people. I wasn't the nicest man, especially before I married. I was an overactive sod, broke too many hearts, had too many barroom brawls." He looked at the floor. "I was rebellious and selfish, never gave a rat's bag whether I ruined people's lives or not. I may have done permanent damage to a certain person."

While he recalled the years of his youth, a defining moment exploded at the forefront of his mind, as if someone had resuscitated him after he'd taken a stab wound to the chest.

Silence extended.

As Hunter struggled to catch his breath, the priest sat quietly.

Hunter's chest hurt, and he felt nauseous. He finally managed a few words. "I did a horrible thing. I was with a beautiful American woman over twenty years ago. The moment I found out she had conceived, I knew the child was mine. Without a doubt." He ran his fingers through his hair. "I couldn't let a baby into my stinking, rotten, filthy life. My father would never permit a half-breed in our family lineage. He would've disowned me and cut me out of his will. If he had his way, he would've killed the child *and* the woman."

"What happened?"

"I told her I wasn't the father, and even if I was, I didn't want anything to do with it. Later, I asked myself what sort of swine would do such a dirty deed. Me. Occasionally, I was conflicted over the mess, except as time passed, I pushed on with my life and left the past behind." Hunter shook his head and hung his head low. "Truthfully, I have pure hatred for myself. I can't even look you straight in the eye, Father. I didn't own up to my responsibilities. I returned to Australia, carried on with my pristine life, and got everything I wanted, like any entitled gent. And now, what about her? I can't imagine how life was for this woman."

"Most of us have remorse over our sins at any given moment. It's designed to force you to examine yourself, presuming you have a conscience."

"Back then, I had no scruples. Now my thoughts keep returning to my past. Maybe the nightmare triggered it. Here I am now, compelled to blurt out my filthy rubbish to you."

"Jesus doesn't torment the soul. He brings things out of the darkness into the light, where healing happens. Guilt often resembles shadows, playing games in the dark."

"I'm sorry about what I did. I've kept this secret buried in my heart, never told a soul, not even my wife. Other than God, I'm the only person who knew." Hunter's lower lip quivered.

"Yesterday can't be stored on a shelf to be forgotten, or be erased with alcohol, drugs, or sheer determination. Our heavenly Father has fascinating methods to communicate with us. And, yes, one of his methods is dreams."

"Does Christ still love me after the things I've done?"

"You are loved by the heavenly Father. God washes away worry, fear, and offense. Call out to him, ask to be forgiven, with sincerity. Go make amends to those you've offended and forgive yourself. In doing this, you'll be released from the bondage of remorse. Christ died on the cross for our sins. He gives salvation to those who repent, choose to believe in him, and accept him as their Savior. Read John 17."

Hunter stood and thanked the priest. On his way out, he placed a couple hundred dollars in the offering box.

Night was swiftly falling, and he had a small window before he met Evie. He hiked from Fifty-First Street to Fifty-Seventh and popped into Tourneau. Inside the glass display case at the back of the store was a stunning Nomos Metro watch. "I suspect my wife would adore this. Can you wrap this gift for me please?"

Roare approached 30th Street Guitars to pick up her freshly tuned guitar, the best place for tuning her beloved Fender, Velvet. The trip gave her a distraction from all the research on AI and time to consider the gravity of her decision about the film project.

The tuning specialist handed Roare her guitar. "How does it sound to you now?"

She played a few measures of the tune she had been working on. "Almost there."

The man tweaked a string.

She played again. "You guys are the best!" she said. "And Velvet is all polished and shiny."

"'Done right' is our policy."

Roare stored her guitar carefully in its case. After paying, she waited at the corner for a taxi. She noticed a messenger cyclist in all black stopped at the light. *Why is he wearing a full body Lycra suit? Even his head is covered. To keep him warm maybe?*

He glanced at her.

Blue laser eyes!

She remembered the horrible night she had first seen eyes like that. Three men had attacked her at the park. They would have violated her had her good Samaritan not shown up. He beat them to a pulp. He moved so swiftly in the dark, they could barely see who or what was hitting them. And then she swore she had seen blue piercing light project from his eyes. When the incident was over, he'd carried her to a nearby hospital without a word. She'd never seen him again.

And Morgan did tell me they're already here.

The light turned green, and the cyclist departed.

She told the cabbie to take her to the Apple Store on Fifty-Seventh and Fifth. She planned to buy Apple Vision Pro, a set of virtual reality headset goggles, hoping that becoming more intimate with AI would give her greater understanding of advanced technology.

Roare paid the driver and grabbed her guitar case and tote bag. As she struggled to remove herself and her belongings from the cab, a hand extended toward her from the sidewalk.

A tanned businessman stood beside the taxi. "You look like you need a little help, yeah?"

Charmed by his Australian accent, she accepted. "How kind of you." Their eyes locked momentarily as he assisted her out of the taxi, then he got in himself.

"Marea's," he said.

Despite the Apple Store Manager offering a "special perk" as a celebrity, free Vision Pro goggles for a plug on

Instagram, Roare declined. Trying them out in the store gave her motion sickness. The experience reminded her of the gesture recognition technology in *Minority Report*. Fiction was becoming reality.

chapter seven—the art of flight

I wish I could fly like that hawk, rising and falling with
the still spaces in the air, far above all this sickness and
death and evil.—Heather Day Gilbert, *God's Daughter*

Hunter hailed a taxi for the ride home from Marea's. He
and Evie settled into the backseat without conversation. She
turned her head toward her window—away from him. He
cleared his throat and pulled the jewelry box out of his coat
pocket.

She glanced at it.

"I hope you might consider my peace offering for our
vase incident last night." He handed her the box.

"An olive branch?" She glared with contempt, then
opened the box.

"Can you forgive a bloke?"

She examined the watch, then shifted closer. "Your
elegant apology is impressive, I admit. However, next time I
won't be forgiving if you take liberties."

"Never again will I behave like a beast. Let's call a truce."

She smirked playfully. Their kiss lingered, then Evie gave
him a gentle love slap on the right side of his cheek. She still
loved him.

Hunter smiled at her. He grasped her hand for the rest of the ride. Cold air crept through the cracked window and stung Hunter's face, reviving his mind. He closed his eyes, welcomed the fresh breeze, and thanked God for his grace.

But during the night, the nightmares returned.

As the flight to Sydney moved like sludge through a drainpipe, Hunter considered how he'd explain his illegitimate child to Evie. He welcomed the idea of a picnic on his boat. He could no longer dance around his words with her.

He began to doze. A subdued voice whistled past like a soft breeze. "Seek forgiveness from those you betrayed."

Hunter sat up, heart racing, and ran his fingers through his hair. He took a deep breath to calm himself.

Evie's large blue-gray eyes appeared liquid and her eyebrows furrowed. "Are you well? Did you have another nightmare?"

"I've been pushing it too hard with work. Need a long holiday." He stood, clasped his hands, and raised them over his head briefly, turned his torso side to side, took two steps into the aisle, and collapsed. Throbbing pain in his lower right leg extracted a scream from him as he crumpled into a heap. He moaned loudly and rolled onto his stomach with a thud.

Evie slapped the attendant button, then extricated herself from her seatbelt. She bent to scoop his arm over her shoulders but couldn't move him.

A male flight attendant approached. Down the aisle, a male passenger stood as well.

"Sir, are you able to stand?" the attendant asked.

Hunter failed to raise himself off the floor, then shook his head. In agony, he crumpled again, practically in tears.

"I can't walk!" Here he was, high above the clouds, lying on the floor of a fuselage, trapped like a rattlesnake. One of the lowest points of his life.

A calm voice filled the cabin. "Attention Qantas Airlines passengers. If there is a medical doctor aboard, we ask for your assistance at the attendant station as soon as possible."

A slender, middle-aged brunette flight attendant knelt beside Hunter. "Mr. Barraclough, hang in there, we'll take care of you."

A sturdy, middle-aged man joined her. "I'm Addison Pober, a doctor from the UK." He helped Hunter lay on his back, then began to check Hunter's vitals. "Are you in any pain?"

Hunter pointed to his leg. "Can't walk."

"When did this begin?" Pober asked.

"A few minutes ago." Hunter took a steadying breath. "I think it might be broken."

The doctor gently squeezed Hunter's legs from top to bottom.

Hunter grimaced when the doctor reached his lower right leg.

"No broken bones," the doctor said. "Let's get you settled comfortably back in your seat, okay?"

Hunter winced and gritted his teeth.

"Mrs. Barraclough, would you please recline your husband's seat to a flat position?"

Evie complied. She stroked her husband's hair. Her voice strained out. "Honey, you're going to be okay, I promise you."

"Is your husband allergic to any medications?" the doctor asked.

"No, nothing."

"Good. Mr. Barraclough, I'm going to administer an anti-inflammatory medication. This will alleviate your discomfort until you can be seen by your doctor."

Hunter agreed.

Pober prepped two needles. "I'm also giving you a sedative. You'll be able to sleep the rest of the flight."

"Great. I need it."

The doctor administered the shots and monitored Hunter's heart rate.

Hunter breathed deeply. "Meds are working already." His voice grew faint as his eyes closed. He licked his lips and muttered under his breath. "Don't ever want to fly again." His head rolled to the left, and his breathing steadied into a slow rhythm.

chapter eight—full transparency

That's where the lies disappear. They can't live in the water because water is transparent. That is where truth is revealed. —Jacqueline Edgington, *Happy Jack*

The blustery November afternoon at home was pleasantly warm, a stark contrast to the cool weather in New York. Hunter mulled over his diagnosis from his leather recliner as he gazed out at the bay. Fate chilled his blood, as if death were coming to take up residence. His silence of the past few weeks had driven a wedge between him and Evie. The only recourse to save his marriage was to tell her everything. Hunter shook his head. The news would crush her.

"I'm obliged to speak to you, God," he muttered. "I've delayed long enough." He closed his eyes. "I dare not ask for mercy, other than needing it more than ever. You've won. You did warn me. And I didn't hear you because of my narcissism." Hunter rubbed a hand over his head. "Please, God, please ... spare my wretched life and preserve Evie's love for me. Thanks for hearing me out."

He longed for the relationship he had with Evie before the nightmares started.

"How did your showings go?" he asked Evie midafternoon.

"Hopeful," she said as she removed her blazer. "You're home early."

"Yeah. I figured now is the time to stop dancing around each other like fireflies and finally clear the air."

Evie moaned. "You're right. We can't continue this way." She plopped her handbag on the kitchen counter, then brought glasses of water for them both.

"Thanks for the water."

"You're welcome. I was glad you weren't drinking any alcohol."

"I've no choice other than to listen to my doctor." *Not to mention to stay in good graces at home.*

She leaned forward. "What's on your mind?"

He hung his head. "I deserve what's coming to me. I regret not keeping you updated." He raised his head again, determined to speak his mind. "My life's a train wreck now because of my pride. I didn't want to face you or anyone."

"Your buggering pride is a real killer and gets the best of you, and you still couldn't come to *me*?" She took a deep breath and lowered her shoulders. Tears welled up as she glanced away.

"I wanted the facts," he said, "and I needed time to absorb them. I'm sorry I put you off. Look, I've got bone cancer." Hunter nearly choked on his words. "I'll need a bone marrow transplant as soon as possible."

"You didn't have to deal with this alone. No one can be a wall of steel all the time." Her gaze returned to him, softer. "What options are there?"

"Not many, other than two types of transplants." His chest heaved. "I have more to tell you." He swallowed hard and cleared his throat.

Evie looked at her empty glass. "I could use something stronger."

"Me too. However, I need to hold on to optimism instead."

"All right, I'll get us more water. Then you can tell me whatever else you're willing to share." When she returned, she was gulping the cool liquid. "The heat is unbearable today." She gave Hunter his glass, then opened the sliding door. As fresh air filtered in, she returned to her seat.

Dread wrapped its icy fingers around Hunter's heart. He furrowed his brow and cracked his knuckles. "Twenty-seven years ago, I was a different man. A reckless, irresponsible bloke out of his head on drugs half the time. I cared only about myself. I dated this woman while visiting New York one summer. I was a nature photographer for *Australian Photography*."

"And the woman?"

"A couple of years younger. A model. Smart, no-nonsense." He knocked back his water and told the whole sordid story.

She peered at him from the corner of her eyes. "And?"

"I denied the child was mine, though I knew full well it was. My father would've killed her, *and* our child. Even worse in his eyes, she was Black. His violence forced my silence."

Evie scowled at him. "Well, aren't you the trifling brute."

"I wasn't a nice guy."

"Go ahead. Let me hear the rest."

"I didn't want to ruin my life before I've had a chance to live. I washed my hands of her and carried on. Until those nightmares took over my sleep."

She glanced away. The corners of her mouth turned down as if she'd eaten a piece of rotten fruit. "I don't know you anymore. Were the children and I just a respectable cover for you?" She closed her eyes and shook her head.

"I confessed to a priest in New York. I hoped the dreams would stop."

"And did they?"

"After I saw doctors about the cancer."

She clasped her hands in front of her and tilted her head to one side. "The truth always wins in the end, eh? We try to bury things, and one way or another, the Earth always finds a way of regurgitating our infidelities."

"Mine was unearthed by a bulldozer."

In a tight voice, she said, "I cannot *begin* to tell you how upset I am. I could spit the dummy! This is all too much for me. The woman and her child have my compassion. I'm sad about your health, but this doesn't surprise me, with you holding a grenade inside you all these years."

He folded his arms across his chest and hung his head. "I'm sorry I've distressed you."

"You ought to be. Not sure if I want to scream, cry, or kill myself. I'm spent." She massaged her temples. "I better take something. But we're not done yet." She left.

Hunter ran his fingers through his hair, then leaned back. What had he done? Steamrolled his perfect life. All he could do now was witness his life disintegrating bit by bit.

When Evie returned, his heart raced like a steam engine. *Jesus, I would prefer to die than lose her. Please, help me. Tell me what to do.*

She glared at him from the sofa. "Don't ask me if I'm okay. You can figure this out by yourself."

"You said we weren't done yet. I'm ready to listen."

"These problems with your health, your past—they're opportunities to correct wrongs in your life."

"I can only hope to fix the trauma I've caused."

"As a mom, I sympathize. I wonder about the child. Did he—she, whichever—have a harsh life? I cannot abide the abandonment of a child. I don't even know if you're human, Hunter."

Hunter remembered Evie's childhood stories. Abandoned by their parents, she and Jenna had been raised by their grandparents. He squirmed in his chair.

"I will pray over this child as I would our own family. God's hand is on our lives. How do you suppose we got to where we are in life? God's help from above. I'm not a religious person, but I do believe there is a God. I prayed when Aaden's legs were broken during his motocross competition. The doctors told him he might not walk again, yet he did. Remember Abbi's pneumonia as a baby, and when you nearly drowned in the boating accident?" She thrust an arm toward the glass doors.

Her words burrowed to the core of his soul, and a revelation overcame him as subtly as a cattle prod. "Aaden, Abbi, me. No one has control over life or death, only Christ. It's always been him. A fact I chose to ignore."

"Because you were god with a little *g*, right?"

"Too egotistical from the success of my business. In the end, success doesn't mean power, and power doesn't mean control. And turning my back on an unborn child may have caused lethal repercussions." He sat like a wooden statue and gritted his teeth. "Why couldn't I see this before?"

"Because life was always about you," Evie said, continuing to massage her headache away. "You must rectify this quickly. You'll need your strength for the fight ahead."

Hunter's chest heaved. Her words sank like a stone in his stomach. "Life sure has a way of spitting in your eyes when you don't respect its lessons. I don't want to die."

"Find your faith. We'll get through this."

He met her gaze. "You ... you're sticking by me? I can't do this without your help, Evie, except I'm not worth your time."

"I'm absolutely livid. However, I will fight this cancer with you. We need all our energy to eradicate these cancerous cells."

"I'm relieved you still care."

She rested her forearms on her thighs. "I never stopped caring. To set the record straight, I never saw you as weak."

"Would you come to the doctor with me?"

She shook her head, then gave him a slight grin. "How could I refuse?"

Hunter and Evie sat in matching leather chairs across from bone cancer specialist, Bruno Chrostowski. "In short," he began, "bone cancer is an error in a cell's DNA. The faulty cell divides uncontrollably. Triggers can be immunodeficiency, arthritis, leukemia, or multiple myelomas. Stem cells in the bone marrow can malfunction, produce defective blood cells, and interfere with normal ones."

Evie sat straight, hands clasped in her lap. "And this is happening inside of Hunter?"

"Yes. Specifically, he has chondrosarcoma, a tumor of the joints predominantly found in middle-aged and older adults, which is rare."

"Hunter mentioned transplants."

"A bone marrow transplant is critical—the cancer could attack other joints and organs if nothing is done."

The doctor consulted the chart on his desk. "This diagram reflects increased joint pain and swelling in the leg. You also have a low red blood cell count. We need to scout donors. Family members generally come first."

Evie fidgeted with her bracelet. "There's so much to digest." Her low voice shook.

Dr. Chrostowski handed each of them a pamphlet. "The autologous transplant is invasive and taxing on the body. Stem cells are taken from the patient and frozen. A high dose of chemotherapy or radiation will kill the cancer cells in the body. Afterward, the stem cells are placed back in the body to make healthy blood cells."

Hunter shook his head. "I've seen the ravages of chemo. What other options are there?"

Evie agreed.

"The second option is an allogeneic transplant," the doctor explained. "Stem cells are extracted from a donor and tested to ensure a match. Parents, children, and other relatives are the best prospects. We have a registry of Australian donors as well."

"This is probably the better way to go, I sense," Evie said.

The doctor leaned back in his chair. "I know there's a lot to mull over. You two have a discussion, but I'll need your answer in a day or two."

Hunter exchanged a knowing glance with Evie, then said, "I can tell you already, Doc. The second option, the allo ... whatever you said."

"Allogeneic."

"Yes, what you just said. Evie?"

"Agreed," she said.

"A sensible choice." The doctor typed on his keyboard, and his printer slid out some papers. "This is a procedure election form. Merely a legality and in the best interest of your health."

"You mean you don't want to be sued in case things go pear-shaped." Hunter had done enough war dances himself in corporate board rooms.

"Indeed."

Hunter and Evie both read the form. She retrieved her glasses and read the paper. "Looks fine."

"Any of our children should be a good match." Hunter signed the form.

"A wise choice," Dr. Chrostowski said. "Dr. Alma Vilner oversees donor selections. During your six-week treatment, my staff will screen candidates. Chin up. Courage and confidence will advance your recovery progress."

Hunter stood. "You're the best, Doctor. I'm encouraged." He grabbed his crutches, and Evie helped him out of the office.

In the car, a million thoughts bombarded him at once. "I'm indebted to you for coming, especially after all I've put you through," he said to Evie. "I'm convinced I'm being sucked into a wind tunnel and can't run away." He rubbed away the tears on his eyelashes. "Now, how to tell the kids."

She took his hand. "Don't try to guess how they'll react. Handle this like the man I know you are."

"That's what troubles me. I'm no longer the man you think I am."

chapter nine—up and down the ladder

What happens between rising to the top and falling to
the bottom is a mediated and divine path between man
and God.—Anonymous

Hunter's heart pounded like a wild boar and his fingers
itched to grab a drink. The doctor threatened to knock
Hunter out himself if he even considered a nip. Hunter
believed him.

The unpredictable storm outside resembled the outcome
of his cancer. Evie and his kids were enough reason for him
to face the fight. Pride afforded only the illusion of strength.

He joined Evie in the living room. She hugged Abigale,
the lanky nineteen-year-old, brushed aside her wavy, waist-
length hair, and rubbed her back.

"Abbi, there's no need to be upset," Hunter said.

"She's going to be okay, don't worry," Evie said. "Let's
go into the kitchen, Abbi. We'll make tea and put out a few
biscuits." She winked at him as she passed.

Abigale pecked her father's cheek.

He hugged her. "Glad you're here. I'll see you when
you're done."

Twenty-five-year-old Reynalds arrived next. He reminded
Hunter of himself as a younger man—tall, medium build,

olive skin, and an ambitious architect. He admired Reynalds's decision to not join his firm—would've ruined their relationship. Reynalds ran his fingers through his dark curls as he headed for the bathroom.

Then Aaden arrived, a straightforward man of twenty-three years. Slightly shorter than Reynalds, he too had Hunter's skin tone and his temperament, while his cropped blond hair was entirely Evie. Where his green eyes came from, nobody knew. He claimed Hunter's recliner.

"I appreciate you coming on such short notice," Hunter said.

"Yeah, we know, Papa, but what's up?" Aaden clasped his hands and rested his forearms on his thighs.

Abigale returned with a tray of tea and snacks, placed it on the coffee table, and sat next to Hunter.

Evie took the other end of the sofa as Reynalds sat in the remaining chair.

"What I have to say stays with us," Hunter said.

The siblings glanced at one another, then shifted their glances to Evie, who waved her hand lightly at them.

"I'll be straight with you. I don't want to cause alarm, but my health is getting worse day by day—bone cancer. I need a bone marrow transplant. The doc told me to line up donors, beginning with family."

Aaden said, "I know everyone here is ready to do whatever is necessary."

"Yeah," Reynalds said. "When and where?"

"Oh, Papa, are you going to be okay?" Abigale scooted closer to Hunter. "Talk to us."

When he took her hand and held it on his knee, she leaned her head on his shoulder and choked back a sniffle. "Don't know yet. It depends on how my body accepts someone else's marrow."

Glances passed among the siblings, then over to Evie again.

Aaden's back stiffened as if gearing up for a fight.

"Calm yourself, Aaden." Hunter saw his own rashness in his son.

Evie said, "Right now, we've got to focus on doing whatever it takes to get him well. The sooner we take the first step, the sooner we find out if the treatments will be successful."

"I have a great team of doctors," Hunter said, "a bad case of optimism, and the support of my family. I'll get through this."

Reynalds said, "*We'll* get through this."

"I don't want to sound paranoid," Abigale said, "but Papa, what if your body rejects the transplant?"

"Great question," Aaden said.

Hunter faced him directly. "The doctors will clear space in my bone marrow before receiving the stem cells. Afterward, my immune system will be throttled to lower the chance of rejecting them."

Evie had his back. "The doctors aren't missing anything."

"They can't afford to. I'm sure they've done this procedure enough times," Hunter said.

Reynalds asked, "Are they able to remove all of it?"

"That's our expectation."

"And what I'm praying for," Evie muttered under her breath.

Hunter handed each of his children a sheet of paper. "This explains the donor testing process. You'll need to schedule appointments with the nurse, tomorrow if possible. If one of you matches, the donation process takes six weeks. The nurse will brief you on the technical details. Eh, thanks again, everyone, for supporting me."

"You're our papa. Any of us would die for you," Reynalds said.

"I know, Son. I'm humbled by you all."

Evie darted her eyes at Hunter and folded her arms. "Your father has something else to share. Don't you, love?"

Hunter sighed. Time to come clean. "Yes, eh, I must ask you to extend more grace to me."

Abigale lifted her head. "Why, Papa?"

He cleared his throat. "Because somewhere in the world, you have a brother or sister." He briefly explained the story.

"After twenty-plus years, you want to do something now?" Reynalds's sarcasm stabbed at Hunter like a scorpion.

He snapped. "Yeah, I do. This is my own bleeding business, not yours."

Aaden spoke up, "Ah, wrong. You brought us into your mess. No one here is perfect, eh? If there's anything else, you need to fess up. I've had a long day."

"All right. Her name was Lane. Lane Murdock, American. And your grandpa hated people of color." Hunter couldn't read his children's expressions as they kept silent. He took a couple of deep breaths to slow his racing heart. He couldn't blame them if they walked away and never spoke to him again ... unless God granted him the grace he didn't deserve.

Silence blanketed the room—an eternity for Hunter.

Finally, Reynalds said, "Showing your true self is one of the most honorable things you could've done for us. I'm sure sharing your past was difficult, especially with Mum."

Aaden's jaw clenched, and he crossed his arms. "All sorts of people come together in the name of love. You and Mum raised us to treat others as individuals, with respect, and not judge others based on how society looks at them. Or are you a hypocrite?"

"Forgive me," Hunter said. "I failed as a father and a husband. I'm a weak, insecure man, who couldn't stand up to his father. I wanted his approval. In the end, I posed as a man as strong as an ox. But I was a scurrying rat."

"How awful!" Abigale said. "Maybe everything you're going through needed to happen so you can readjust your life." She leaned over and hugged him.

"Try not to worry, Petal. I keep forgetting how sensitive your soul is."

"I'm a gusher, but I'm tough."

"Yes, you are. Your mum told me something I regretfully missed," Hunter said. "She told me my children are stronger and more open-minded than I ever knew. She was right, and you're who you are because of her. It never dawned on me how fortunate I was until now."

"Well," Reynalds said, "make your health a priority. Cancer isn't a thing to take lightly."

"I know." The adrenaline had subsided, and Hunter felt weak. "If you don't mind, I'd like to finish for tonight, I'm wiped out."

"You aren't the only one," Aaden said, "and we need our strength for blood tests tomorrow. We're going to do whatever is needed to get you well."

Hunter stood with his crutches.

One by one, his sons hugged him and left. Abigale held back tears as she gave him a big squeeze and a brave beam.

"Keep your wits, girl. Things will turn out well because of smiles like yours."

"You're such a charmer. Good night. Love you."

"Love you too."

As Abigale left, Evie cleaned up. "Are you at ease now since you cleared the air?"

"Not particularly. Too many things ahead of us."

"You did a nice job tonight. Brace yourself, though. The worst is ahead of you."

"Your words aren't comforting."

"There may be rough days ahead to survive this bloody cancer business. Then there's the matter of finding your child. Are you up for the challenge?"

"Do I have a choice?"

"We always have choices."

"Not when God has his hands on the controls."

"He gave us free will to make our own choice to trust him or not. Either way, he gives us the right to choose. But what comes along with choices, is the brunt of consequences."

"Don't I know it."

Tucked away in her office on the other side of their home, Evie bared her soul to God. She regretted not praying often or attending church. Why hadn't she reached out to him when her marriage was in trouble? *God, forgive me for my shortcomings.*

She closed her laptop and her eyes. "Forgive me for my absence and not making you the center of my life, but, Lord, we've got some issues. Give me strength to handle the days ahead. We need to find a donor quickly. Please give Hunter another chance at life and a chance to reconcile with his child. Strip him of his pride, break him if you must, only bless him with a more gratifying experience to replace the successes he's idolized." Warm tears flowed down her cheeks. "Please, God, help Hunter free himself from his past hauntings. Change him from a little boy to the man he's supposed to be."

Evie didn't always agree with her husband's selfish and callous decisions. Yet, the phrase "amour propre" exploded in her mind like an air-raid siren. *Funny, whatever he did for me and our family, he always managed to turn the attention back to himself. Maybe his being struck with cancer wasn't a coincidence. Perhaps now he'll be forced to pause and examine his life.*

Evie found solace interceding on her husband's behalf because he desperately needed God's mercy. Evie wiped her face, blew her nose, and retired for the night.

Hunter settled into bed with his back to the door. As he drifted off to sleep, Evie's warm, lean body and silky skin cuddled next to him. Overwhelmed with gratitude, he turned on his side, took her hand, and squeezed it gently. "Glad you're here."

"So am I," she whispered. "Thought you were asleep."

"Almost. I need to consider the business, especially my contracts."

"Your partners are entirely capable. For everyone's sake, leave the business to them." She released his hand and moved away.

"I know I've been a bear, but I do love you. I *am* worried about my health. I have to take little steps—don't want to go into a panic over this, yet."

"You shouldn't. Your doctors are the best in the field and on top of this. But you can take some initiative too. Praying isn't a bad thing."

"I haven't cracked open the Bible in years," he said, though he feared the words might jump off the pages to confront him.

"Now is a good time, I reckon. You'll be forced to face yourself, find some hope and clarity."

Whatever she meant, Hunter's thoughts were as muddled as if he were walking through a dense fog. Things would look better after a sound sleep. Darned if he was going to be spooked by reading a book.

Right before he went into a deep sleep, a low-pitched whisper spoke. "Read my words to know me, and I will give you wisdom. Fearing God is the beginning of true wisdom."

chapter ten—quid est veritas?

The unexamined life is not worth living.—Socrates

Sloane thrived in the dark. *Although, there's probably more going on in the astronomical star system far above my head despite all the night activity I see here in the city.*

He ascended the three metal steps of his triplex home on Plymouth Street. Then, he flattened his left hand against the steel door, and the capacitive scanner within identified him. The door clicked open. He crossed to the elevator and rode to the second-floor loft.

In the spacious living area, he turned to perform an infrared deep scan of the apartment to detect movement. With everything clear, he strode to the kitchen and stowed his takeout in the refrigerator.

He climbed to the next floor and spent thirty minutes in the sauna and shower. Dressed in sweatpants, T-shirt, and a cardigan, he returned to the kitchen.

Dinner in hand, he relaxed with a view of the Brooklyn Bridge and city skyline through tinted Ceramatrix-coated windows. In this room, he did most of his contemplation.

With a shiver, Sloane set his food on the table between two blue leather recliners. His time as a ranger had taught him to never have his back to a window. He switched on the small, black Aether fireplace suspended from the ceiling in the corner beside him.

With the air warming, he sat in the chair closer to the fireplace and peeled off his cardigan. A large silk Persian rug insulated his feet against the wood floor. Outside, snow was falling. *Whaddya know. You're brilliant, Lord. Makes for a real pretty picture while I'm eating.*

Snow also meant Thanksgiving was near, and he'd get to spend his time with a dear friend. The few people he allowed into his life were close to his heart and trustworthy. Given his general distrust of people, friendships were blessings and gave balance to his nonhuman attributes and, at times, loneliness.

With the snow creating a whiteout over the bridge and city, he remembered when he was in Antarctica several years ago. *The worst experience of my life was when I encountered Matchithew. I would never sell him my soul.* As rage built, his brown eyes turned to intense blue lasers. *Control. I have no doubt we'll meet again.*

As Sloane finished his dinner in the firelight, he retrieved the Bible from the end table drawer. He blinked hard and bowed his head. *Night vision on.* He lifted his head again, and his pupils shone a green light onto his reading: 1 John. *Truth.* Chapters 3 and 4 were stored in his memory bank, but thumbing through the Bible connected him to God.

He leaned his chair back and embraced the quiet around him. God had given him everything! Cloaked him from enemies. Mended him back together, for the greater good. *Father God, I honor you for giving me a purpose in assisting others for your kingdom and glory. Please guide my words, thoughts, and intentions with Roare. Remove the scales from her eyes to see supernaturally and strengthen her to withstand the wicked years ahead.*

He needed spiritual strength himself. Taking Communion would draw him closer to God through the sacrifice he made for humanity. Sloane made a trip to the kitchen for the elements. He read verses on the Last Supper, ate a cracker, then drank a bit of grape juice. He lay face down on the rug and stretched out his arms. "God, align me with your will to enable me to complete your assignment to warn people of the darkness ahead."

Sloane's prayers continued through the night.

chapter eleven—match

If you want to keep a secret, you must also hide it from yourself.—George Orwell

The afternoon temperature dropped in Kárášjohka, Norway. Match smiled, content. He stood patiently behind a lectern in the plenary assembly hall, waiting for seventy Sámi Parliament members, delegates, and community leaders to settle. The building blended with the surrounding pine forest. Match admired the fresh layer of snow draping the cone-shaped foyer, reminding him of a ski slope. Tall, narrow windows revealed slivers of navy-blue sky, and occasional celestial activity guaranteed a stir from spectators. Everything he did was intentional and served a purpose. Including the presentation he was about to give.

Matchithew "Match" Ryu Tekeda waved to familiar cabinet members and pressed palms with delegates. His Japanese and Odawa ancestry gave him good looks, even in his fifties with scars from his ninja training. With a five-foot-ten frame, cropped black-and-gray hair, and head held high, his commanding presence demanded respect.

A beautiful elderly woman with thick, salt-and-pepper, shoulder-length braids stood beside him. Shenandoah,

Match's mother, was a retired thermodynamics engineer and his main contact within the Sámi Parliament. Her community involvement served Match's purposes to seize the opportunity to be philanthropic.

Match stood behind the lectern while he organized his note cards and took a sip of green tea from his mug. He looked up, recognized a familiar face approaching the lectern, and flashed a smile. "Bavlos Vaara, I didn't know you were coming. I'm grateful for your presence." He extended his hand.

The tall, fair, broad-shouldered man with a thick gray mustache met Match with a firm handshake. "I confess that was your mother's doing," Bavlos said. "She told me about your presentation. I'm planning a feature story about TV station donors, and you've been a loyal supporter of *In View* the past couple of years."

Bavlos and Shenandoah exchanged acknowledgements.

Bavlos narrated a program showcasing the Sámi culture, origin, lifestyle, and language. Fascinated by the people, Match had made a substantial monetary donation to support the NRK Sámi Television network to keep Bavlos's program on the air.

Hmm, a cameo story about NRK donors would further promote CoSynthesis's noble efforts to partner with indigenous communities. Public charitable donations work splendidly to gain the nod from the world stage. Match smirked.

"What a grand gesture, but please don't play me up too much. I'm no superhero," Match said. *He has no idea how well I can pretend.* "Let me know if you'll need an interview or short video clip."

"Great. I'll be in touch." Bavlos stepped down from the platform and grabbed a reserved seat in the front.

rage against the machine

Match looked at his watch. A hush descended among the attendees as the main feature commenced.

"Ladies and gentlemen," Match began, stepping away from the lectern. He stood with legs apart and hands folded in front of him as he faced his captive audience. "I cannot express my enormous gratitude over your presence here today. The Sámi people continue to impress me with your dedication to tradition and love of culture. You remind me of how my own company, CoSynthesis, respects the past. As we respect the past, we also look to the future and how technology can help preserve the traditions you value." He paced the stage as he continued. "We continually expand our AI Technology division at CoSynthesis, and I'm here today to offer our assistance. Upgrading your community library to have global access to vast amounts of educational information as well as to share your lifestyle with the world will have tremendous benefits for the Sámi people. We are offering full grants to those who are interested in learning about AI Technology to use in your communities for film, television, social media, energy projects, and any other platforms that will expand your voice and reach throughout the world." He paused and placed a hand on his heart to emphasize his final line. "I am committed to continuing my support for your right to life, liberty, and justice."

The audience clapped.

A young lady wrapped in a blue plaid shawl stood and said, "We know who we are. We have an identity. We're the First Nations people of Norway, and I think I can speak for all of us here to formally thank you for your generosity and standing with us."

Match smiled and deflected the compliment with a wave of his hand as the meeting adjourned. *I've done my good deed for the sake of human rights.*

As the parliament members departed, Match noticed his mother's gleaming eyes. Her approval bolstered him, and he held his head high on his way out of the building.

Match had founded CoSynthesis Dynamic Ventures, an AI Robotics and Science lab, with his uncle, Raidon Tekeda. They employed a small army of top AI, bio, computer, and planetary scientists, medical doctors, nano and astrophysicists, mathematicians, geologists, and quantum and galactic engineers. Through the company's efforts, Match and Raidon actualized their ambitions to replace humankind with an advanced manmade civilization.

Sloane McInerney had been CoSynthesis's first test case seven years prior with a black-budget contract. Since then, Match and Raidon acquired more and more contracts from clandestine stakeholders. One by one, CoSynthesis created a massive army of highly advanced, flawless, sentient borgs.

In public, Match pursued benevolent projects for the underprivileged and used CoSynthesis as a means of supporting medical and industrial advancements. The perfect cover. Match found societal acceptance and attracted private investors interested in exploring esoteric concepts. With enough funding, Match had finally been able to initiate phase one of his greater plan for AI robotics.

After everyone had left the building, Match took a long, deep breath of the frigid evening air and tilted his head toward the stars. He savored the breath as if inhaling a fragrant flower. His body adjusted to the glacial chill effortlessly. Didn't even need a coat. He merely wore some warm clothing and relished having a moment of *humanness*—a foreign sentiment to him lately. Match stood with legs spread apart, hands clasped in front of him, away from the attendees still lingering and chatting. He continued to search the stars. And he waited.

Shenandoah stepped up beside him. "You're waiting for something, aren't you?"

Without taking his gaze off the sky, he said, "You could say so."

"You and your astronomy. Ever since you were a boy." Her tone was steady.

Match recaptured a sweet, brief sentiment of his childhood when he'd spent countless hours looking up into the heavens. He'd lie in the tall green fields of Bygdøy with his mother and father. Match had never fully appreciated his genetic lineage until his uncle educated him. Powerful bloodlines could determine destiny. Integrating his prestigious heritage with other-worldly technology made him feel superior over others. To say the least.

On his father's side, Match descended from Emperor Kammu of the Heian period. His father Yoshi was a math professor. Kind, patient, and brilliant. He loved the Lord and growing Bonsai trees. *Though, I could never understand his faith. It prevented his true accomplishments to further mankind.*

His mother was a distant relative of Chief Pontiac, an Odawa war chief. Match and his mother were close. Shenandoah was a confident and intuitive woman who loved science, nature, and her son. She had deep insight into the inner workings of her son's mind. *I will forever admire her strength, quiet beauty, and acceptance of my indifference toward marriage and family. She knows I have other goals, and still loves me in her own way, and I love her for that.*

Match was twelve years old when his father passed away from a massive heart attack. Shortly after, Uncle Raidon became his mentor. Raidon held a PhD in Computer Science and Automation. He was a futurist, but possessed a dark spirit, and had no regard for God. He saw most of humanity as feeble and preferred the company of highly evolved individuals. As he grew up, Match was determined to emulate Raidon in every way and then surpass him.

Match caught movement out of the corner of his eye. An array of pinks, oranges, blues, yellows, and violets broke through the dark night. "As I predicted, the conditions for the mother-of-pearl stratospheric clouds is perfect." The last time he'd witnessed them was seven years prior in Antarctica.

Shenandoah appeared awestruck. "Surely a sight to behold. As if another world has punched a hole into the atmosphere." She retrieved her phone from her shoulder bag and clicked away.

"Mother, your perception is remarkable. This phenomenon is an instrument used to rip a hole in the ozone layer. I would be more concerned about what can come through from the other side." He peered at her.

She grimaced. "Son, I believe this is nothing in comparison to what you've seen in your part of the world."

"A magnificent understatement."

"Maybe one day I'll come for a visit."

"With your engineering background, you should have clearance," Match said.

"Something to think about." Shenandoah yawned. "Meanwhile, it's getting late. Can you take me home?"

"I can and will. I have an early flight tomorrow. I return to home base." Match drove his mother home, had a cup of oolong tea with her, then returned to his hotel in Oslo.

At six the next morning, his private jet was fueled and prepped for departure to Antarctica. When he strapped himself in his plush, cream-colored leather seat, he smirked. *I see nothing wrong with emulating being a human. Mom understands what I truly am.*

rage against the machine

Back in the sci-lab at Belgrano Base III, Match sat comfortably in his gray egg-shaped chair. Relaxing Native American flute music gave him focus and tranquility. He turned his chair away from the doors to his private dojo and faced the Japanese tearoom behind classic Shoji doors. The view of oversized bonsai trees and the garden he maintained in a greenhouse never failed to calm his mind.

He sipped on Pu-erh tea while reviewing stats on recent upgrades to his borgs. Match's team had mastered Alcubierre's Model for bending space-time. *This will make our cyborgs superior to anything created on earth. Using portals through dimensions will enable them to travel from one planet to another in a tenth of the time it would take a spacecraft. They will be like gods. My private clientele will find them impossible to refuse, and humans will become pointless.*

chapter twelve—arrested development

And you shall know the truth, and the truth shall make you free.—John 8:32 (NKJV)

Roare had more questions for her next phone call with Morgan. Data on transhumanism and geoengineering revealed how AI might be used to improve lives, but a looming shadow remained. There might be rogue AI creators with monstrous intentions. However, she surmised the fear could be conspiracy theory and not completely factual. *Morgan had better have some solid evidence to back up his claims if he wants me to take him seriously.* She made the call.

After exchanging pleasantries, she said, "I did a deep dive and checked with my contacts. If you read between the fluffy phrases, one percent of trillionaires—self-proclaimed rulers of the world—want to replace select humans with upgraded versions, minus any evidence of God. They believe the rest of humanity should be discarded."

"You're headed in the right direction," Morgan said. "Keep going."

"Sure. A few other groups consider themselves watchdogs. They understand what's happening—ten years too late. They believe these rogue scientists have gone too far with AI and gene modification, and they're terrified. Some scientists and financial supporters who'd once pushed hard to advance AI now want to reverse what they've done—"

"And they can't. Megalomaniacs have created hybrids, intentionally and accidentally."

"And now these borgs are considered dangerous to society," Roare said. "Humanity is going to face a nightmare worse than *Terminator*. We're already the prey, and we don't even know it."

Morgan's silence lingered like a film of smoke. "Your analogy is spot on," he finally said, "and it's worse than you think. We should meet. What I have to tell you can't be revealed over the network."

"Morgan, if we're on *secured* networks, then we should be able to talk. Your facts are too vague for me to build enough trust in you. Give me something concrete if you want us to meet." Roare placed her left hand on her hip while she leaned against the desk in her office.

"Sounds reasonable. Recent peer reports on robotics revealed machines are built and programmed to perform tasks without human interference. AI, however, emulates the human mind to learn, solve problems, and make decisions independently without relying on programmed instructions. Dental assistants, restaurant servers, and hospitality bots at hotels are already being used in a few countries. Robots called Stuntronics perform death-defying stunts, so actors won't get injured."

"All harmless so far. Tell me more," Roare said.

"There was an incident in a robotics lab in Japan involving four AI robots. Two had to be deactivated because they killed twenty-nine people. The AI scientists took apart the third robot, but the fourth one restored and upgraded itself by connecting to an orbiting satellite," Morgan said.

rage against the machine

"I never heard about this on the news—"

"Documentation of this was done only by scientists. AI borgs are creating their own language to communicate among themselves. Their own creators couldn't even decipher the foreign coded programs. A tech company had to shut down one of their AI applications because it had turned Synthesia—started thinking independently and became self-aware."

"But what ..." Roare dropped into her chair, brushed her hair away from her face, and crossed her legs, considering the ramifications of this information.

"Take a moment and imagine a world where autonomous vehicles can be hacked into remotely to cause accidents or to kill the driver. Or, what about AI borgs walking among us on the streets of New York City? They look real and move as we do, think as we do, and can engage in conversation. You won't be able to tell the difference between a borg and a human."

Roare wondered if this was a good time to tell Morgan about seeing humans with blue laser eyes. *No. Not sure if I can trust him yet. He could be fabricating these stories.* "All this is leading up to something, I hope. I don't have time for games," she said.

"Neither do I. I'm gravely concerned for our lives," Morgan said. "Remember my friend who stumbled across some info in a lab? He uncovered successful experiments with AI sentients that shapeshift, bleed through walls, and can jump from one location to another in a fraction of a second. I saw the documents myself."

Roare gaped. "Bleeding through walls? What? How?"

"These sentient AI borgs can dematerialize and pass through walls. They reach the other side of the wall and rematerialize, still intact, and so is the wall. Imagine walking through a glass door without breaking the glass. They know how to bend time to move from say a street corner here in the city and—in the blink of an eye—jump inside an office building in Shanghai."

For the first time since she'd met Morgan, Roare's heart raced. All she could say was, "Oh." An unsettling fear took shape in her spirit. She managed, "Does the military know about this?"

"Not our complete military force, only a select few who are off-grid. And not only the US military but other military forces across the planet. Their goal is to carve a pathway to other planetary systems and their technology."

Inaudible words came from Roare's mouth. She finally said, "Are you referring to extraterrestrial beings?"

"Possibly."

This isn't just about what AI is capable of, but what some other entity may have in mind for us. Am I in over my head? Hard to say, but I have to continue to dig. "Okay, one condition. Give me a copy of the data, and I'll meet you."

"Fair exchange. How about at the Campbell? Even if you came alone, you'd be safe. People pass through constantly, police officers too. You can easily go unnoticed, you follow me?"

"Port Authority?"

"Close. Grand Central Terminal, off the main concourse. You'll appreciate the setting—elegant, private, and low-key."

"When?"

"Today at four."

"Aren't you rushing things?"

"Not nearly enough. If you think these rogue scientists and elite groups are sitting on their anonymity believing they're free to do as they please, we can't afford to sit on the sidelines."

"If we did, we'd be complicit in what they're doing, wouldn't we? How will I know you?"

"I'll know you." Morgan disconnected.

Roare stared at her phone. *Rude.*

What had she gotten herself into? She should've become a nurse instead of a director. *God put me on this path.* When the time came, she'd need a double portion of guts. *Lord, I'm on board with whatever you want, but if you're taking me down a dark road, guard me against evil.*

She called Sloane, and he agreed to come right over. She texted Wyatt, Drue, and Lane to tell them where she was going and to call 911 if she went missing. Sloane would be with her.

Lane texted back: *If Sloane's with you, you'll have nothing to fear.*

Next, Wyatt: *He was hired to protect you. Please take him along.*

Drue responded: *Glad you aren't going on your own. Be careful.*

Three confirmations.

She went into her bedroom and dressed in the usual black stealth gear—leggings, combat boots, and a T-shirt under an oversized black sweater. With her hair combed onto her face, she added a big pair of glasses and a skull cap, then wrapped a charcoal-gray scarf around her neck and a matching waist-length fake-fur overcoat. Hiding behind layers of clothes was easy in winter.

Not every form of evil is of human origins. The words were distinct.

"God?"

Yes, child. Look beyond the words you hear. You will walk through fire and not be scorched. I sent you the intruder. Believe I am with you and will shield you from harm's way.

She shivered but paused. The chill exuded peace.

Sloane arrived a few minutes later, his face expressionless except for a crease between his eyebrows.

"Are you okay?" Roare asked.

"I'll explain later. At the moment, I have a few projects I'm overseeing."

"I hope I'm not taking you away from anything," she said.

"It's my pleasure to look after you."

Roare beamed. "I'm glad you're coming. I'm a little nervous."

"Don't be." Sloane held the door open as they left the apartment.

Upon their arrival at the pulse center of New York City, Sloane said, "Stay close. I mapped the way to the Campbell. Once you find it, you won't forget. Man, it's busy here."

"It has incredible energy." Roare welcomed a lighter subject. "When it's quiet, though, you can see the beauty of the building. The perfect place to shoot a movie."

"No doubt. We're right over here, up the marble staircase toward Vanderbilt Avenue." He led her to the doors at the top and through the Campbell Terrace.

I wish Wyatt were here. Stay cool.

When they reached the bar, Roare's jaw dropped at the grandeur of the Roaring Twenties architecture blended with contemporary elements. Around the room were a few dark leather club chairs and small café tables spread far enough apart for privacy.

"Swanky," she said. "Like walking into an oasis. I would've never found this gem on my own. Wyatt would love it."

"Yeah, posh, pomp, and private. Where'd you like to sit?"

"In a strategic place."

Sloane smirked. "You've been watching too many spy thrillers."

"No, just hanging around you."

"I'm flattered."

They were seated in a semi-private nook near the lit fireplace. Roare pushed away the menu. No appetite.

"Tell me," Sloane said, "do you know anything about this mystery man?"

"He's on a crusade to save the world."

"Maybe you are too."

"Perhaps."

Sloane looked at his watch. "Your friend is running late."

A waitress appeared, and Roare ordered a cup of strong black tea with hazelnut cream and honey. Sloane ordered a chocolate espresso and two waters.

Roare waited until the waitress was out of earshot. "I'm beginning to believe Morgan is an enigma."

"Perhaps not." Sloane leaned forward, palms flat on the table as if he were going to stand.

She noticed ragged scars on his hands.

The waitress returned with their drinks.

"Your hands," Roare said. "Are those knife wounds, a hot poker, a gun?"

"All three, during my days as an army ranger."

"I'm sorry you had such a horrible experience."

"Part of the job. I survived."

Roare glanced at her phone on the table. "I assumed he'd text if he was running late. Five p.m. is nearly here."

"What if I told you *I* am Morgan?"

Roare nearly choked on her tea. "You're joking, right? You don't sound like him."

"A disguise. Suppose this were true, would a tragedy exist?"

She sat dumbfounded. Pressed her back into her seat. "I dunno, I need time to get my head around this. Mom recommended you to me! Who are you? What other lies have you told me?"

"Logical questions."

"You're not joking, are you?" Her voice was tight.

"Afraid not."

Roare's face heated. "You betrayed me! You knew I had a gig that evening. How could you? You were hired to protect me from *yourself*?" Roare's tone was low and fiery. She gritted her teeth to contain her rage. She didn't want to cause a scene. "No more spy games. I gotta go."

She stood, but Sloane grabbed her wrist, compelling her to sit.

She yanked her throbbing wrist away.

"I'm sorry," he said quietly. "Stay until I explain."

"Don't ever touch me again, you understand?"

"I'm sorry, Roare." In Sloane's piercing glare was a hint of bluish light seeping from under his eyelids.

She gasped. "Oh my gosh, what are you? Are you one of those cyborgs? Wait, you've tried to warn me. You kept telling me they are among us. This means—"

"Yes, Roare, I'm a cyborg."

She shook her head. *God save me from this nightmare.* "Get away from me, or I will scream."

Sloane stared her down, his eyes glowing blue. "Don't let fear dictate your actions. Give me an opportunity to say my piece. After you hear me out, then you can choose to leave or stay."

She looked at the time on her phone. "You've got five minutes." Roare kept one hand on her phone in case she needed the police.

"Don't blame your mom—she was the little sister I never had. We met at a high school workforce program, and I helped her secure an internship with a New York advertising agency. I went on to West Point and became a ranger, among other things. We remained friends throughout, nothing romantic."

"Did my mom put you up to this, to look after me?"

"In a way she did, but there's much more to the story."

"I bet." She sat up straight and rested her forearms on the table.

"I intend to fund your next film. I'm the anonymous proprietor of Global Initiative. The people you met at TGIET are under my employ along with a few other silent partners. Do you remember when you were living in Central Park a few years back?"

"Mom told you where to find me, right? You were him, weren't you? Those blue laser eyes, I never forgot them, and the way you moved. You've been watching me all these years? Why? What about those other ones?"

"What other ones?"

"Two other times, I saw people or ... those things. They flashed their blue laser eyes at me. Are we being invaded?" Roare said.

"Lots of questions."

"I'm entitled to them." She looked at her phone. "You've got two minutes left."

"Roare. Your mom thought you were lying in a ditch somewhere dead. She asked me to find you, and I did. I think the assault in the park scared you enough to get help for your addictions. Off and on, I've kept watch over you from a distance. There are others like me out there in the world, but they have different capabilities—and different intentions. Certain underground labs are unleashing them into society to test how well they can integrate with humanity."

Roare was speechless. *All this time, Sloane was my good Samaritan, the man in the subway, Morgan, and the owner of TGIET?* "Why me?"

"Because you did what I asked you to do. You did your homework. You drew strength from your past experiences to drive you to this point in your life. Your belief in God primed you for a greater purpose. This may not make any difference to you, but I'm a believer. Being a loyal citizen to our country is why I'm here. God's creation is being assaulted on a grand scale, and I want to do something about it."

I think my head's going to explode. "So, you decided to create this group?" she asked.

"Let's say there are a few men and women who still honor the moral code, who value life, liberty, and the planet they live on. We don't want to see humankind wiped out by psychopaths. Each of us has witnessed atrocities against people. If we told you what we've seen, you'd never sleep again or want to bring a child into this world. If you knew the unscrupulous leaders you've trusted and admired were the ones who've traded your freedom for subjugation— including clerical figures—you would lose your faith in human beings altogether. If humanity knew what's ahead of them, they wouldn't want to spend another second on Earth. The people you met at the TGIET meeting are as passionate as you and I are about exposing corruption in high places."

"Only God can save this broken world," she said.

"True, but he expects us to work in partnership with him. He gave us brains, gifts, and authority to exercise our skills to suit his highest purpose."

Finally, he was making sense. Maybe she *could* trust him. "Where are you from again? What are you, and how do I fit into your equation?"

"I'm originally from Rhode Island, but I'll answer the rest of your questions in due time—just not here. I'd like to get out of here now and go back to my place, so we can have some privacy. I've got sensitive content to share with you," Sloane said.

Roare raised her voice. "You want me to do what?"

Sloane smiled. "Don't go there, this isn't a come on. I want to be transparent with you, so you'll know what you're up against."

Roare rolled her shoulders back to loosen the tension in her neck. *Don't stress. You're on edge. Chill out. The news is a big shock but maybe you should hear him out.* "Oh, okay. You had me worried for a second." She'd observe with the mind of a film director and peel away the layers to uncover more about what all this meant.

"You can relax now." Sloane chuckled.

"I'm speechless," she said. "Are we all done as a species and far gone as a civilization?"

"Sounds far-fetched. I'm no fatalist. I'm a survivalist and an optimist. I believe in life and ultimate peace on Earth. But the world is in a dire predicament now. Many people succumb to fatal threats. Others are ruthless about preserving life and refuse to be enslaved by an antichrist."

"I must admit, seeing those people with blue laser eyes alarmed me. Made me think there is a silent invasion taking place, and we're the last to know. This sounds supernatural. The book of Daniel comes to mind," Roare said.

"We're living in the prophecies of Daniel and Revelation today. Worldly *distractions* numb our ability to see things happening in the supernatural realm. Something's not right—even some nonbelievers are sensing this. But few comprehend the magnitude. Roare, I know this may be awkward to be alone with me, but I want to reassure you, you're in no danger with me."

Roare's chest heaved and stared into his eyes. "Just so you know, I'm relying purely on my faith regarding you."

"You have so far. God forgave us. Therefore, we should forgive each other. Besides, revealing the truth will put my own life at risk as well."

Roare had no choice but to trust him. She'd already signed the film contract. Presently, there was too much at stake. And God was with her. She looked him in the eye. "You better not let me down, Sloane. I don't want anything to happen to either of us."

He nodded. "I won't. God will bless your bravery."

She could only hope.

chapter thirteen—providence

When a train goes through a tunnel and it gets dark, you don't throw away the ticket and jump off. You sit still and trust the engineer.—Corrie Ten Boom

While Sloane signaled for a taxi at Grand Central, Roare enjoyed the frigid air on her skin to clear her mind. She felt like a character in *The Outer Limits*.

Sloane directed the driver to 222 Plymouth Street and motioned for Roare to enter the backseat. She pinned herself in the corner as if four other people were squeezed in next to her.

Sloane looked over. "You okay?"

"Yes." She quickly cracked open the window. "Stuffy in here."

His broad shoulders slumped, and he folded his hands in his lap. His brown eyes gazed at her with concern. Fortunately, he didn't press her further.

Her stomach flip-flopped like pancakes being tossed in the air.

He peeked out his window, then back at Roare. "My goal is to protect you, not kill you."

"I wish we would've taken the train."

"I thought the cab would give us time to collect our thoughts."

Morgan was Sloane. What was God going to hit her with next? He didn't make it easy for her, did he?

God whispered into her mind, *Strength in faith makes a powerful testimony.*

Roare decided she wasn't going to fail. "You don't mind me texting Wyatt, do you?"

"By all means."

"He'll want to know where I am. I'll tell him I'm still in a meeting with Morgan, and everything's okay." She pursed her lips, pulled out her phone, and sent the text.

When they entered Sloane's place, an overhead light came on. At the end of the hallway, they took the elevator to the main floor. More lights turned on as they entered the living room and kitchen areas.

Roare's gaze wandered around the large space. "Your home suits you. The red brick is beautiful, and the open concept works"—she nearly gasped at an enormous skull across the room—"but it's ... moody." *Maybe "odd" is a better word. Don't be rude.*

"At times. I prefer it. Check out the view. I'm going to make hot chocolate. Interested?"

At his kind offer, tension began to leave her body. "Yes, I am."

She walked to the large windows in the other room and gazed out at the city. "I love seeing the bridges lit up at night. And the fireplace—ultra modern."

"One of the best features of the house. From Australia," he called while he prepared drinks.

Roare sat on the edge of her chair.

Sloane returned with two cups of hot chocolate and a few cookies on a tray, then sat adjacent to her. "Glad to see you relaxing a little."

"Still working on it." She took a sip from her mug. "Mmm, delicious. Coconut milk?"

"Always."

She could no longer hold back her curiosity. "Mind if I ask about that skull in your showcase? Looks gruesome. Is this of human origin?"

Sloane turned toward the view. "The Old Testament called them the Rephaim and Anakim."

"Ah-ha. Wait … they existed? I thought—"

"That God was a prankster? How I came across this is another matter. Thousands of those skulls are a part of Septuagint history. A subject for another time."

"Sure." Roare stood to browse the floor-to-ceiling shelves next to his desk. *The Book of Enoch. Project Paperclip: German Scientists and The Cold War* by Clarence Lasby. *Advanced Artificial Intelligence* by Zhongzhi Shi. *Introduction to Nanoscience* by Stuart Lindsay. *Conspirators' Hierarchy: The Story of the Committee of 300* by Dr. John Coleman. What was this man into … or running from? "Your entertainment choices are … interesting," she said. "Are you building a demon-possessed robotic human?"

Instead of responding, Sloane walked to the curio cabinet, retrieved a small object, then sat in the chair furthest from her.

"Whadda you have there?" she asked.

"Come over and check it out."

"Will I be safe?"

"One way to find out. Try to take it from me."

Roare did. "What the heck!" She could barely lift the object out of his hands. "You're not even doing anything to keep me from taking it." Her eyes widened. She gave up and returned to the sofa. "Well?"

"I wanted you to feel the weight yourself. Dense and heavy, don't you think?"

"Extremely."

"This is a meteorite fragment."

Sloane stared at the hunk in his hand. His eyes narrowed slowly and became a soft, piercing blue. A blue beam projected from his pupils, focused on the object. A small hole formed, then the rays went through the meteor.

Roare scrambled to the far end of the sofa and curled into a ball.

"Do you know this metal I'm still holding in my hands never got hot, even after piercing a perfect circle straight through?"

She shook her head rapidly, dumbstruck again. Her heart pumped as hard as an automotive piston. *I'm going to have a heart attack. Breathe. Breathe.* Words wouldn't come.

His eyes returned to their normal color.

Roare stared at him for several seconds, bewildered and frightened. "Your eyes ... you had those same blue eyes at the café."

"Yes. Imagine me trying to explain this to you there—you would have freaked out and called the police. It wouldn't have ended well."

"I'm calm now, Sloane. How did you become what you are?"

He spoke quietly, "During my army days, I served on a reconnaissance mission in Kosovo. A military security chain was breached by a traitor within their unit, and our location was compromised. Four of our ten men were killed, two of us captured and tortured. The other guys regrouped and returned with the rest of the platoon to rescue us."

"Good grief! Your life being spared was not a coincidence."

Sloane snickered. "I'm not convinced being kept alive was in my best interest."

"Come again?"

"My body and mind were severely damaged. The other ranger didn't survive the journey back. Miraculously, I did. I was chosen for an advanced AI robotics experiment in Antarctica."

"Sounds like a horror film, Sloane, and you were the lab rat," Roare said.

He leaned in. "You're not far from the truth. The surgeons injected my skin with hundreds of thousands of nanobots. Specifically, the dermis or second layer of skin. Strangely enough, the bots keep me human. Individually, they activate my senses. Together, they form an ultrathin mesh around my body. Essentially, an additional layer of skin allows me to experience the normal five senses. Fortunately, these bots also shield me from injury, including firearms and biological warfare. The tech would help my body heal quickly from any illness."

"So you're invincible?" She tried not to sound like a starstruck preteen.

"Not quite. A steel beam can land on my head and crack my skull. Then I'll need a time out but will heal over time. And I still have a few vital organs that could be injured."

"Like a kidney punch?" She tried to sound like she was teasing, but—in truth—this whole thing was creepy.

"A kidney punch wouldn't faze me but puncture it with a sword or a stiletto—you'd slow me right down."

She didn't want to hear more but couldn't resist. "Dare I ask what else they did?"

"The lenses of my eyes are minicomputers. They allow me to see thermal images, even through walls. You saw the meteorite. My lasers can heat *and* cool objects—or kill when need be."

"Or burn a hole through anything, like you did a few minutes ago. Incredible."

"Very impressive, I must admit."

"Transhumanism is getting easier to fathom. Since you're a cyborg, what's left of who you were?"

"Before I share more with you," he retrieved a flash drive from a desk drawer and handed to her, "I encourage you to record this conversation. This device will encrypt the data. You must give me your solemn vow you won't use my testimony in the film, nor are you to share this with anyone. I'll make an allowance to share this with Wyatt but no one else—not even your mother."

"You have my word." She examined the hardware and determined the drive wasn't ordinary. "This unit is intense. Has a number and built-in keyboard. How is this secure?"

"Not only is the data encrypted, but there's a two-step verification process using a twelve-digit number on the keypad and a twelve-word phrase you enter on a private encrypted link sent to your phone. I'll change your recording settings to auxiliary, and the recording will save to the drive, and will automatically shut down in case verification fails," Sloane said.

"Super clever."

The recording started. Sloane leaned forward as if he were going to turn over vital security codes. "Most of my memory is intact. I have my belief in God and take solace in still having a soul. Still, I'm seventy-two percent machine. When I regained consciousness, I had to relearn things, starting with the simplest tasks. As I made mistakes, the data fed into the AI. Over a few weeks, the technology learned to self-correct, as well as learn my humanness in seconds."

Roare's jaw dropped. "You're a walking miracle. God honored your faith. I just can't get over how advanced the technology was even a few years ago."

"Yeah, at the time, the technology was bleeding edge. Look at me now—my mind can absorb any kind of information in a fraction of a second and gives me telepathic abilities, which comes in handy for covert activities. The human side of me prefers not knowing what's on people's minds, though."

"You knew how I'd react to seeing your eyes. You knew I've seen others with those eyes. You have no right to violate my privacy! Have you been reading my mind since you met me?"

"I'm sorry I was intrusive. Most of how I got to know you was through your mom."

"Don't use her as an excuse. I don't want you around me if you're gonna rummage through my head."

Sloane rubbed his right thigh, as if he was soothing an old injury. "Honestly, I do respect your privacy. That feature remains dormant unless I'm threatened or need to understand someone's motives," Sloane said.

"Seems logical. How are these things possible?"

"The technology is completely brilliant. The skin is made of fine silicone laced with a nanocrystal silver coating to withstand extreme temperatures and heal injuries. Burned skin can regrow almost immediately. For example, let's assume I get cut, I could simulate bleeding. I can walk through walls by changing my molecular structure."

"Wait a second! You have this ability too, like what those rogue scientists are creating in the labs? Yeah, okay—superhuman strength, right?"

"C'mon, young lady. Use your brain. Remember, as Morgan, I told you about bleeding through walls and dematerializing?"

"Ah-ha. You mean, with your technology, you can move from one dimension to another? Holy cats, this is all true then!"

"Remember when Jesus entered through the wall when he visited his disciples before he ascended to heaven? The molecular structure of my body has been replaced with nanostructures. They assemble DNA to do extraordinary things. The nano-DNA regenerates cellular structures at the atomic level as my body passes through things."

"My head hurts trying to process everything. You better not come through any of my walls!"

"Not a chance. I'd be too afraid you might kill me." He gave her a fading half-grin. "Seriously, these advantages come with a heavy price. I hold onto my sanity and spiritual life dearly."

"I'm amazed you still have them."

He stood. "I'm blessed to be alive."

"I knew you could do more than sear a hole in a hunk of rock."

He wandered into the living area and stuffed his hands in his pants pockets. Finally, he stopped with his back to her and stared toward the kitchen. "I was turned into a superhuman weapon, a monster who can seek out enemies and destroy them with waves of various frequencies using my *eyes*. The enterprise who created me tracks me through GPS. What they don't know is I can disable the tracking by shifting into maintenance mode. Fake transmissions throw them off. I safeguard my privacy as fiercely as you do. AI stops hackers by shutting down automatically."

Roare's gaze followed him. "I'm concerned about you. Tell me about this enterprise."

"You'd make a great journalist. It's a private company called CoSynthesis Dynamic Ventures, established about fifteen years ago in Antarctica. They pride themselves on taking projects at the cutting edge of technology—

intergalactic projects that use extreme science to advance the human species."

"Why did you leave?"

"Their technology is enslaving us, their ultimate goal," Sloane explained. "Sure, they contributed to robotics research at the beginning, helped wounded soldiers regain the use of their limbs, and protected them from injury. They also supplied AI robotics breakthroughs in medical technology. But over the past few years, CoSynthesis has gone wickedly dark."

While he walked around the living area, Roare ensured the green light was flickering on the drive.

"Things were getting out of hand. Now I'm a superhuman-gone-rogue. I need to be careful. With my self-learning capabilities, the AI in me has upgraded its software several times. My abilities are sophisticated. I have an advantage over them presently, but not for long I suspect. I read lots of books on cybersecurity—remaining invisible is imperative. When I engage the telepathic feature, the GPS turns on, and they might locate me. I wish they'd left me to die instead of turning me into a freak. I value human life and detest evil. Sometimes, I pray Jesus would come quickly and sort us out."

"Now would be a good time. I see why you want me to do this film." She crossed her right leg over the left and folded her hands across her knee. "Being different must be lonely. Do you have friends?"

"Only a few trusted friends. We took bullets for each other back in the day. And, of course, your mom. No one knows what I am except Matchithew, the mad scientist who made me—the head of CoSynthesis—and a couple of selected friends and now you."

"Oh my gosh. The cell phones, they have listening devices."

"Doesn't matter. My home is radiation proof and has a Faraday shield. My internet is set, and the landline is secure too."

"What an astonishing way to live," Roare said.

"I'm comfortable," Sloane said. "Your film will expose the true faces of the adversary and how deeply evil has infested our world. CoSynthesis and others like them plan to build a massive army with special abilities to deconstruct the human condition and exterminate any forms of inferior life."

Tears welled in Roare's eyes. She squelched them with deep breaths. "I wish this were all a bad dream or an elaborate joke. To think there are people insanely obsessed with their power who believe they're entitled to have the entire planet for themselves. Such depravity and disrespect for human life! I'm grieved by all you've been through. What can we do?"

"Look, you've got a lot to digest. There's more to tell, however midnight is approaching. Wyatt will be worried about you. I better take you home."

"Yeah, I'm exhausted and have a migraine. And haven't had dinner, thanks to you."

"Ah! I should've whipped up something. I'm an excellent cook."

"Why am I not surprised? One more thing. Can I trust you, Sloane? I mean, everything you told me is factual?" Roare stood and put on her coat.

"Either you believe now or not. *I'm* the one risking everything. CoSynthesis would destroy me should they discover I want to shut them down."

Wyatt was relieved she was home, had prayed everything would turn out well. They sat together on the sofa.

"Successful meeting with the mysterious Morgan from the subway?" he asked.

"Yes and no."

Wyatt scrunched his eyebrows together. "What do you mean?"

"Morgan never showed because he was with me the entire time."

"You mean Morgan is Sloane?"

"Exactly."

"What a conniving fraud. He's not your bodyguard, then? What's he trying to pull?" Thoroughly annoyed, he ran a hand over his beard and scratched.

"Don't judge him until you hear the whole story." As she reflected on what Sloane had endured, Roare's heart rate increased. She shared Sloane's story with all the details she could tolerate.

Wyatt said nothing until she finished. "I'm at a loss for words."

A thought struck her. "Oh my gosh! God told me a while back he sent me 'the intruder' and not to fear." She held his gaze to see if he caught her meaning. "Can't say I was fearless tonight, though."

"Fearlessness will come. Sloane's in your life because you have a message to deliver. I can't believe what he's had to suffer. He chose you because you would sound the alarm without causing mass hysteria."

"I suppose. Wish he'd selected someone else. Are the masses prepared to accept the truth, or will they call me a whack job, trying to score the next Academy Award?" Roare bit her lower lip. "I could be sabotaging my career."

He took her hand gently. "The more important question is whether you would survive the effort. You can anticipate what they'll do to you in the event CoSynthesis thugs find him and take him out. This bothers me. Since he is risking his life, he'll want the information out there. What was done to him could be done to millions of others—unless these elitists believe they're worth saving."

"Or they'll repurpose humanity."

"You're exactly right."

"Wy, anything we discuss must stay between us. Absolutely no one else can know. Without a doubt, Sloane can't disclose any information, especially his abilities."

"No need to ask."

When CoSynthesis had decided to take their projects on a more ambitious path, Match thought his AI lab could use a pair of insiders—Doyle and Grayson—collaborators who would keep him informed about potential exposure that could jeopardize the company's projects and goals.

Planted in exclusive circles in media and tech, the collaborators got wind of a new film in the early stages of production. Its purpose was to expose the dark side of AI robotics and the catastrophic effect on humanity. Match's collaborators gave him the name of the director, and the organization funding the film. But they didn't know the names of the whistleblowers.

Sloane might be one of those whistleblowers, Match thought. *Shouldn't have let him go when he was here.* Otherwise, the news pleased Match. Certain he'd unmask his adversaries, he set to work on plans to interfere with the film. *Anyone who attempts to dismantle CoSynthesis will be dealt with.*

chapter fourteen—slough of despondency

Mr. Worldly-Wiseman is not an ancient relic of the past. He is everywhere today, disguising his heresy and error by proclaiming the gospel of contentment and peace achieved by self-satisfaction and works.

—John Bunyan, *The Pilgrim's Progress*

Unable to sleep, Evie sat up and switched on the lamp next to the bed. Determined to read awhile, she hoped she'd drift off. Evie picked up *The Pilgrims Progress*, flipped to a folded page, and read, "When you talk of your journey and of what you have heard and seen, you inwardly desire your own glory in all you do and say." She shut the book, placed it on her lap, and closed her eyes.

Was Hunter still seeking his own glory? And what sort of turmoil stirred internally in her husband's spirit? He hadn't been himself lately. Naturally, he was burdened by his health—more than he'd let on.

Living with Hunter for over two decades had taught her how to read him. And she had prayed through every crisis. Now, each second of his life ran away like a freight train without brakes. She could only watch helplessly while he slowly sank into the marshlands, and she fervently prayed to God like never before.

Warm tears trickled down her cheeks, and she wiped her face. She whispered, "Almighty God, here I go again, calling out to you when I need you desperately. You've always come through, looking after us along the smooth paths and the rocky roads, but I'm asking for help again. Hunter's in big trouble. He needs healing from cancer. I know we've all been guilty of being far from you, but please grant him mercy. Give him an opportunity to correct his mistakes and heal his infirmities of body and mind. His hope is evaporating like water in the sun—the fight in him is leaving his spirit. Transform him from the inside out. In Jesus's name. Amen."

She turned toward Hunter, still sound asleep. She placed the book on her nightstand, turned off the lamp, scooted into a comfortable position, and finally fell asleep.

Thankful for the rain, Evie worked from home. Showing luxury homes in poor weather would not lead to any sales. Still groggy, she made her usual muesli and a strong cup of coffee and perched at the kitchen island.

Hunter hobbled to his favorite reclining chair on his crutches. He waved and smiled to her, then leaned his crutches against the sofa. *At least one of us got rest. Those meds worked well.* She decided to prepare a green powder shake to help build his immunity. She'd promised to do all she could to lift Hunter's spirit.

He was on the phone. *Who is he talking to? Probably Dr. Chrostowski.* Hunter's countenance changed from light-hearted to somber. She listened with half an ear.

"The news is staggering, Doctor," he said gravely. After a moment, he asked, "May I have a few days to mull this over?"

rage against the machine

What could all this mean?

Hunter's call ended. He leaned back in the recliner and gazed up at the ceiling. His chest heaved with defeat.

"I couldn't help but overhear," Evie said.

"None of the children are suitable donors. I don't have much time."

She gasped. "How is this possible?"

Hunter explained that Reynalds had a flu coming on, and with Aaden's bone fractures from his recent motocross accident, he wasn't eligible. Taking bone marrow from him would cause further damage. And Abigale's fibromyalgia ruled her out.

Evie prayed her words would nourish Hunter's soul. "My love, this may look like a tragic tale, but your story is far from over. Once Reynalds's immunity is restored, he'll qualify. Is having to go outside the family gene pool a criminal act?"

"I'm not sure I want a stranger's genetics injected into my body. Well, God has me in a headlock now, and I have no strength to wrestle with him. All I can do is cry out for grace. Time is a co-conspirator of Satan and has the advantage." Hunter sat up on the edge of the recliner with his head hanging low.

Evie reached out to hold his hand. "Things will work out, dear. Don't fret. Circumstances can sometimes change overnight." She paused, choosing her words. "We're with you in this, Hunter. Think of your family and release your stubborn pride."

"I want to be alone. I need to recover from this bulldozer." Hunter grabbed his crutches, huffed off to his office, and slammed the door.

"Oh, God, please help me." Hunter plopped into his office chair and turned away from his desk. He'd rather ingest poison than search for a donor outside his gene pool. He suddenly remembered what Father Enrique had told him to read, John 17. He retrieved a Bible tucked away in the back of a desk drawer and read the passage.

Events are stacking up against me. I haven't glorified God, haven't given him any of my time and barely acknowledged him. He's long on patience, especially with me. He hasn't given up on me, even though I've never been a part of his world. I foolishly ignored his love for me while he's been waiting on me to come to him. I squandered my eternal life. He pivoted in his chair and looked out the window—took in the sea view.

A voice invaded his painful thoughts. *You still have a millstone around your neck. Cut it loose, and free yourself while you still can.*

Hunter spun around, half-expecting to see Jesus standing in front of him.

Watch yourself—a proud and haughty spirit smothers wisdom and humility and will affect how you treat others. Take my mercy. And don't mistake my generosity for a dirty rag.

"You know every inch of me, including the things I've tried to hide," Hunter said. "Either I'll swallow my pride or choke to death."

The Bible passage gnawed at him. He digested the words like bitter medicine. His family would be spared and better off without him. The notion to dispose of himself enticed him. However, true to form, he had no guts.

A false accusation. To live is courage.

Hunter closed his eyes and tilted his head back. "I'm a man with many faults. Who am I to contend with you? Here I am, moaning over bloodlines."

rage against the machine

His phone buzzed. *I don't think I can stomach any more bad news today.* His hands were sweaty. The number was familiar. *My barrister.*

"Manus Cross here, Mr. Barraclough. How are you getting on?" The man spoke loud enough to be heard halfway around the world.

"Still breathing, thankfully."

"I have some good news and not-so-good news for you. What do you want to hear first?"

"Give me the bad news, since I'm on a roll here."

"One of your clients is suing you. Apparently, you gave him bad advice to skimp on the quality of materials that was used in your build. What are you doing, man? You know this could be the downfall of your empire. I'm urging you to sort this out soon. I can't tell you how to run your firm, but—ethically speaking—I don't like how you operate it."

"What do you suggest? I didn't think it would matter so much. I couldn't get a particular brand of steel he wanted to use due to overseas logistics. I advised him on a lesser brand for the sake of moving the project forward."

"Which means *you're* liable because you recommended the lesser brand, and the client is not pleased. I advise you to settle and provide the product he wanted."

Hunter grunted. "For the sake of my firm's reputation and preserving my health, I'll comply. Can I hear the good news now, please?"

"You wanted me to find someone."

"Keep talking."

"The woman is Mrs. Lane Murdock-Anakoni. She's married. They own a branding design business and have three children. The eldest, her daughter, is remarkably renowned—an Oscar-winning director of docudramas. The younger two are boys. Shall I go on?"

"Yes. Can you tell me about her daughter?"

"Roare Violet Murdock-Galloway. In the film industry, she goes by Murdock. Tall, beautiful, brilliant, and recently married to a gentleman of affluence. Wyatt Galloway comes from a family of doctors. Roare's twenty-six and graduated from NYU under a full academic scholarship. She's a devout believer in God, as is her entire family. Before she became famous, she went through a rough patch. Typical troubled teen—drugs, depression, abandonment issues—but she pulled through. Had her family and friends not been there to support her, no telling where she'd be. Maybe below ground. Why the personal interest?"

"I need to make amends with a person I wronged years ago. I'm grateful you located her." Hunter paused. "I'm the father of this famous lady."

Cross let out a long breath. "How do you know? A ton of legal questions are flooding my mind."

"Before you say anything else, I already came clean with Evie. She wanted me to reach out to make this right. Lane told me she was pregnant when we were dating. She wasn't the type to fool around. But I told her I wanted nothing to do with her or the baby." Hunter paused to clear his throat.

"You're an interesting man, Mr. Barraclough."

"Actually, not. These were my idiot-bloke days." Hunter provided more details of his past.

"Well, life lessons have a way of changing people."

"No kidding."

The line had gone quiet except for Cross's heavy breathing.

"Are you still there?" Hunter asked. *Is this going to turn into another fight?*

"I'm going to be frank with you." Cross's booming voice had dropped a few decibels. "I protect both the prominent and the oppressed. As my client, I'm obligated to give you sound legal advice without personal opinion or prejudice. However, as a friend, I'm bound by my moral code to tell off blokes like you. Should anything I say offends you, I'll assign your case to another partner."

"These sorts of mistakes happen all the time."

"People carry on as if abandoning a child is a trivial matter, as if a child can be discarded like a piece of rubbish. The deed is done, and people walk away unscathed, without accountability or ethical duty, then expect others to carry the weight of the world alone."

"Are you speaking about people as a whole or referring to personal experience?"

"Hunter, here's something you don't know. I run a men's ministry for former sex traffickers. You should come sometime. Count your blessings your daughter didn't become a victim. I suspect her family wouldn't have allowed such a thing to happen."

"Indeed not. Not a woman like Lane."

"Humanity is sick," the barrister said. "Modern Pharisees strut around judging everyone else. They deceive others for self-gain and pit people against each other—a sport to keep morale low. The entitled reign with no regard for others. Now, ask yourself why you haven't hung up on me yet?"

"I reckon I needed to hear this from another man. You've brought me face-to-face with myself."

"Given your health, I assume you want to connect with Ms. Murdock as a possible donor?"

"Only partly. I've caused her and her family enough pain. No, I can't burden her with such a request. Rather, I want to resolve the offenses against my daughter. God has been talking to me in the middle of the night," Hunter said.

"Yes, you mentioned the nightmares. I guarantee those came from the Lord. Let go of your pride, ask for guidance, and he'll help you see more clearly. I've gotten valuable wisdom reading the Bible. You might find some insight there. No harm will come to you."

"Maybe not. Nonetheless, I can see a reduction in my ego happening."

Cross snickered. "Your intuition is stellar. God's words can take a chunk out of us for good reasons. His Word is designed to deal with the bits of ourselves we despise or try to hide. May I tell you something?"

"Sure."

"I've presided over your business and personal affairs for more than twelve years, come to know your family well, and I'm fond of them. You and I bump heads like bulls in the same paddock. Nonetheless, we've always respected one another at the end of the day. I advise you not to overthink things. I don't believe in religion—I believe in Yeshua. My relationship with him gives me some wisdom. God wants your undivided attention for communion. He wants you to reach your fullest potential to serve a higher purpose. Find out who he is. He can straighten you out."

"How?"

"You've walked around with a chip on your shoulder, trying to prove your self-worth, you already have. You're in your fifties, at a critical point in your life, and you may not come out of this alive, old boy. How can Jesus straighten you out? Do away with yourself."

"Come again? Kill myself? I can have you disbarred!"

"That's not what I'm getting at. Die to *self*—assassinate your ego. Then you'll comprehend who God made you to be. He'll help you through these emotional entanglements. He's preparing you for the months ahead. Dying to self forces reliance on God. Talk to him like an old friend. Wait on him," Manus said.

"I don't have any old friends."

"You do and don't know it."

Hunter rubbed his leg and reached for the pain medication on his desk. "I have to bugger off. My leg is aching, and I tire easily these days."

"Before you go, I need to loop back. I'll initiate contact with Ms. Murdock's attorney to inquire about whether she'd be willing to meet you. I'll stress the urgency. If we can establish a neutral meeting ground, I'll let you know. I'll draft a letter and will get your approval before I forward the request. And for goodness' sake, man, update Evie on our chat."

"I nearly lost my wife by concealing things. I won't make the same mistake. Look ... Manus, I'm sorry I was such a jerk to you through the years. I undervalued our friendship and took advantage of you too many times. Can we disregard the last few years and start over?"

"Those are the first heartfelt words I've ever heard you say."

"Only a true friend can say the things you have to me."

The call ended, and Hunter cradled the phone in his hands. Manus had given him a lifeline—a second chance to be a friend and human being—an offer he wouldn't turn down.

chapter fifteen—the chastening

Look upon these chastenings ... as God's chariots sent
to carry your souls into the "high places" of spiritual
achievement.—Hannah Whitall Smith

Roare relished the festive and relaxing weekend with
Wyatt and both of their families at her parents' home. It
had been just the break she needed from working on her
film. Once she returned to the city, she'd have back-to-back
interviews with whistleblowers, scientists, and journalists.

On Wednesday morning, brutally cold air hit Roare's
face. The all-nighter she pulled to prep hadn't been enough
to wake her, but she was awake now. Geez! Clutching her
black leather tote, she took fast, long strides to warm
up. She was due to meet Odin Yaremenko of TGIET at the
National.

Odin was already there having a cup of coffee. He
extended his hand to greet her. "You're out of breath. Have
a seat." He had an Eastern-European accent.

"I had to walk fast. I thought I was being followed."
Roare took off her coat. "This guy did his best to keep up
with me but never tried to pass me. Every time I looked over
my shoulder, he'd do the same thing."

"Strange. Do you think anyone could've known we were meeting?"

"Other than TGIET, me, and my husband, no one I can think of."

"Hmm. Given who we're about to interview, anything is possible. Neither of us can afford to take chances. When we wrap up here, we'll use a different exit, and I'll put you in a taxi. That guy could be waiting for you to leave."

"I like your thinking." *Odin is definitely seasoned in eluding trouble.*

He gave her a minute to catch her breath, then signaled a waiter and ordered.

They traded business formalities while they ate, then strategized how to approach the whistleblower and tighten their questioning techniques. She wanted to allow the whistleblower to tell his story. Odin wanted to probe deeper into the facts, documents, photos, and other privy information he had on a flash drive. They settled on the approach, and Roare was relieved they were finally like-minded.

When they finished, Odin said, "We'll be a great team. Our opposing interview methods should work to our advantage, and you have a good vibe. I'll escort you to a side exit and flag a taxi for you."

"Agreed. I think we will work well together." Roare stood, put on her coat, and shoved her notepad into her tote.

"We should look after each other during these interviews. Things could get rough."

"Let's sync our flights to Saratoga Springs and anticipate the unexpected. He may change his mind," she said.

"We must see him as soon as possible before someone helps him change his mind. I'm inclined to carry brass knuckles and keep a few thugs I know on standby—you never know."

rage against the machine

They walked to the side exit, checked their surroundings. Clear. Not even the guy who'd been following her. Odin flagged a taxi.

Back home, Roare searched her tote for her ringing cell phone. "Hey, Pilar."

"Sorry to disturb you, your attorney called. She deemed this to be an emergency."

"Did she say what?"

"No, just call her as soon as possible."

A problem with the film contract? She stowed her stuff, went to the office, and phoned Scarlet Rafferty.

"Hello, Roare. Thanks for getting back to me," the attorney said.

Roare sat in her office chair, placed her tote on her desk, and sighed. "What's going on?"

"Attorney Barrister Manus Cross contacted me from Sydney, Australia. He represents your biological father, Hunter Barraclough."

"You really caught me off guard. What does he want?" Roare rubbed her forehead as if a migraine was coming on.

"His client wants to meet you about an urgent matter," Scarlet said.

"Is this a joke?" Roare asked.

"Trust me, I wouldn't waste my time otherwise."

"Diabolical timing. I'm on the verge of shooting my next film. Can you give me time to consider this?"

"Given his circumstances, delaying your answer would be inhumane."

Roare sneered. "Look, I could respond a dozen different ways about being 'inhumane.' I didn't mean to snap—you are not to blame. I mean, seriously. You can't expect me to decide at this exact moment."

"I can delay until the end of day. Should provide you some time, but I expect to hear from you by six."

"I'll reach out before then." Roare ended her call but couldn't remove herself from her chair. Her throat constricted, and she struggled to get air into her lungs. She closed and opened her hands. How clammy they were. She needed air.

The front door opened and shut. Wyatt's voice, "I'm home, babe."

When he reached the office, Roare waved him in.

"Honey?" He knelt beside her. "Why're you sitting in the dark?"

Roare said nothing.

"Ro, you okay?"

She muttered and shook her head. "No."

"Oh, Gobo, you're pale. Breathe slowly through your nose. I'll find a paper bag."

When Wyatt returned, she raised and lowered her hand a couple of times.

"I know, I know. You'll slow down after you breathe into this bag a few times."

She did as she was told, and her heart rate slowed.

As he stood beside her and rubbed her back, he prayed quietly. "Heavenly Father, don't let Roare stress over any challenge. Let fear leave her mind like snow being washed away by the rain. Amen."

Able to speak at last, Roare said, "My biological father is gravely ill and wants to meet with me. My attorney needs my answer today. What does he want?" Roare placed her forearms on her thighs.

"Unbelievable. Seriously, he's never bothered to contact you or wanted anything to do with you." Wyatt's voice grew louder as he spoke. "He didn't even acknowledge you as his daughter, and now, out of the blue, he wants to have a family chat?"

Her eyes misted.

He softened his tone. "An apology is all I can hope for. He might have a legitimate reason to contact you, I don't like seeing you so agitated."

"I feel like I've climbed Mount Everest only to miss a step near the top and tumble to the bottom. As soon as something incredible happens, and I think I can take on the world, then boom, a warhead drops a payload on me. No wonder I always look over my shoulder awaiting the next assault on my life. And don't say I'm being assaulted because I'm doing something Satan doesn't care for. This menace always stealing my joy is tiresome."

Wyatt grinned. "Sounds like you're breathing well now. Come downstairs, and let's have a chat."

Once she was tucked next to him on the sofa, he continued, "I've celebrated the best days with you, and helped you pick up the pieces of the dark days. I'm here for the duration. Whatever you must go through, we'll work through this together. We don't know what Hunter wants, so let's wait and see what he has to say."

"I never doubted you'll be there for me. But I'm missing God's presence. Guess things were going too well for me. Suddenly, demons are conspiring against me."

"They won't win, will they? Lean on me, Roare. Stop dwelling on the past. I don't want to see you meltdown."

"Wy, forgetting is difficult. In my opinion, I was doing well not dwelling on him, until now."

"God gives us seasons of goodness *and* trials. Persevering will make us stronger and help us endure. Satan will try to hijack your life, but God won't intentionally cause you distress. The problems he allows will refine you to be something greater. You'll never know what's on the other side of the bridge until you get to the other side."

"I'm trying real hard to believe you. The bottom line is, I won't know what Hunter's after until I meet him."

He stroked her hair. "You're going to need to call your attorney before her office closes."

"Yeah. I'm going to give Mom a quick call first, though."

"She's a wise woman." He kissed her forehead. "I'm heading to the gym. Send my love to your mom."

"Will do."

Roare propped her legs on the coffee table and dialed her mother's number. "Hi, Mom. Can you spare a second? I need to run something by you."

"What's wrong?"

"Hunter wants to meet with me as soon as possible. He's seriously ill. For humanitarian reasons, I should see him, but I'm struggling whether I want to do this or not. Would you mind giving me your input?"

"I never thought you would hear from him, and now, here we are. A part of me would've joined you at the chance to rip him to shreds. But—"

"There's always a *but*. You're going to say I can't condemn him and inflict pain on him like he did to me. I worked too hard in therapy and prayer for God not to give me the heart to forgive him. I have a busy life right now and can't afford distractions."

"Before you give your answer, consider this: As believers, we have to look beyond our human viewpoints and tragedies as we see them in the natural world. Instead of being reactive, try to respond with foresight and kindness, not hatred. We're to forgive our offenders with deep sincerity, erase the hurt from our memory, and grant grace."

"I know, Mom, but I don't want to open old wounds."

"I may sound heartless but get over the self-pity. We don't know all the answers. God protected you from Hunter and from yourself. Rise above the physical world. Don't let the negative experiences of your past hold you captive. Forgiveness reflects the heart of God. And Ben would love to hear you call him 'Dad.'"

"I *am* guilty of refusing to call Ben my father. He's only shown love and tenderness, no matter how many times I've failed as a daughter. By the way, I'm the one who needs to apologize—to him. Mom, how did you forgive Hunter? Do you still resent him?"

Lane took a deep breath. "This is strictly between you and me, understand?"

"I do."

"I never considered abortion. I knew I'd be raising you on my own. How I wanted to drag him to court! A wise, mature woman told me if I didn't let go of my rage, I would transfer toxic energy to my child instead of love. My spirit would erode and harm the soul of my baby. She said to be productive with my thoughts and prepare for your arrival. One day, I agreed to attend church with her. I'd never heard about how God forgives us and how we're blessed when we forgive others until then."

"Forgiveness was a simple decision for you then."

"No, childbirth was easier. I preferred stewing in my bitterness. I needed God, and I needed peace. Letting go of hate was part of healing. I figured if a young boy could forgive a drunk driver who killed his entire family, then I could forgive Hunter. Once I allowed my heart to heal, God replaced it with a new one open to receiving love. As I poured love into raising you, Ben came into my life and accepted both of us out of his loving spirit. Nonetheless, both the forgiver and the offender profit spiritually. So life-changing."

"Thanks for being open with me." Roare checked her watch. "Oh! I have to call my lawyer. Wyatt sends his love. I know now what I need to do."

chapter sixteen—fate on tenterhooks

Waiting does not mean doing nothing. Waiting is a time
of listening.—Lisa Clements

In his office, Hunter sat fixated on the planks of his
tallowwood floor warmed by the radiance of daylight. He
hoped the warm day would take the edge off his nerves.
What was taking Cross so long to get back?

He was happy for Roare's success—driven to excel like
her mother. The way things were going, her refusal to see
him would not surprise him.

The hours burned away. He needed fresh air. So he
hoisted himself onto his crutches and shambled to the
kitchen, where Evie was perched on one of the stools with
her laptop open and paperwork sprawled across the island.

"You look busy," he said.

"I am. And you're fidgeting," Evie said.

"Yeah, I'm anxious. Maybe I'll water the grass."

"Good. I need to finish my paperwork."

"I can take a hint."

"Off you go."

"Love you too. Maybe I'll cruise the bay."

"Should you, in your condition?"

"Don't patronize me." Hunter stormed off as quickly as his crutches allowed.

"I'm certain Manus will call you soon. I know you're jittery but try not to worry."

Hunter knew it probably wasn't the wisest idea to take the boat out in his condition. *I could make my situation worse.* He stood grudgingly on the lawn, watering the lush green grass. With the corners of his mouth turned down, he looked out onto his private dock, where his Carver C52 Coup was tied to the cleats at the bow and stern. Going out to sea relaxed him and took his mind off his dilemma. To keep peace in the house, he'd stay put.

Mercy had run out on him, and faith was an elusive phantom. Roare might detest him, but maybe this could be a chance he had to take to confront his past and be forgiven before he could ask anything of her. She'd either agree to meet him or tell him to go jump into a bottomless pit.

Convinced the lawn was well soaked, he carefully trudged up the stairs to the door and clung to a glimmer of hope.

As Hunter was preparing to retire, Reynalds called. "I guess you heard I've got the flu," he said. "I'm sick as a broken-down ute, my flu is full-blown now. I'm gutted I can't test as a donor."

"No fault of yours. The timing of everything is maddening. I'll need to consider other donors in order to stay among the living."

"Love you, Papa."

"I know, and I love you. Look after yourself." Hunter hung up.

Maybe I'm better off dead all around. He poured a double shot of bourbon at the minibar in the sitting area of their bedroom. He sniffed the oak-scented elixir and groaned. *No, this isn't the answer.*

Manus still hadn't called back yet. More bad news after losing the last bit of hope he'd had with Reynalds wouldn't help. Hunter's relationship with his two brothers had died years ago. "I'm at a loss, Lord. What now?"

He dumped the drink. If Evie knew, she'd have my head on a skewer.

The next morning, Hunter reflected on last night's negative mood. What a close call. He couldn't reach for the bottle every time a crisis arose. The problems would still be there when he sobered. He held a slip of paper with the number he'd found online for AA. He reached for his phone, but before he could place the call, Manus Cross was on the line.

"Things are looking up," said the barrister.

"Really?"

"Ms. Murdock agreed to meet with you. Regrettably, you'll have to wait two weeks. She has work commitments. Is this suitable for you?"

"Of course. I'll admit, I was considering other options."

"This update should help your disposition."

"No doubt. That'll give Reynalds more time to get over his flu, as well."

"Sure, however, if neither Roare nor Reynalds works out as you hope, you simply must cast your net elsewhere."

"I was afraid you would go there."

"Maybe someone has something else in mind for you."

"Yeah, and I know who he is. God figures he would pounce on me and tear me to pieces."

"He's doing a great job. I'll send you the meeting details. Cheers!"

When the call ended, Hunter swiveled toward the patio and bay, ready to fall out of his chair with the unexpected news. *Lord, you've been here for me all along, in plain sight, and I ignored you for most of my life. Please forgive me.*

chapter seventeen—unwanted intrusion

You know what a miracle is ... But another world's intrusion into this one. Most of the time we coexist peacefully, but when we do touch there's cataclysm.
　　　　　　　　　　　　　　　　—Thomas Pynchon

After a rash of updates from Doyle and Grayson, Match gloated over their new information—the exposé film, the whistleblowers, and the interview location.

While he watered his bonsai trees, he ruminated over how he detested traitors. *We don't have much time before the director and journalist get to them. Three of my executive borgs will do the trick.* Match informed his senior board members over tea.

Uncle Raidon expressed growing concern. "Thankfully, we have an insider at TGIET."

Hemmi, a planetary scientist and cyborg, chimed in. "The sooner we respond, the sooner we can preserve our anonymity."

Match turned to Valentino—cyborg, AI genius, and business advisor. "We need to send a direct message to those driving this project to stand down."

"Or face more severe consequences," Match added.

Everyone nodded.

Raidon said, "We still don't have intel on who is behind TGIET."

Match remained stone-faced. "Not yet, but I expect to have more soon. I already have our security borgs ready to descend on Green Pond Lane in upstate New York."

Meeting adjourned.

Valentino transferred ten thousand dollars of cryptocurrency into Doyle's and Grayson's accounts. *They have their uses,* Match mused.

Match frequently sought esoteric methods to increase his mental capabilities. His first foray into the supernatural realm had been a few years back when he'd learned about a Mexican shrub called Calea Zacatechichi. Match began to brew his own tea from the shrubs he grew.

A Brahms concerto played while he sipped his dream tea. Then, he closed his eyes and drifted into a dream. In his unconsciousness, he summoned the Drexans, an advanced species from Drexa, an ancient civilization from the Xa galaxy in the sixth dimension. *The tea is a portal to their world. But ugh, will I ever get used to their appearance?*

The Drexans' dark green reptilian skin and single bulbous ochre eye in the center of the face, with muscular humanoid physical form, reminded him of an experiment gone wrong. Their enormous frames filled a corner of his office. When they shapeshifted into attractive humans, they were easier to look at. Even their harsh, guttural voices morphed into warm, nonthreatening tones.

When they revealed their plan to pillage Earth of its resources in exchange for off-world technology, yes was an easy word. Our mutual disregard for humanity unites us. Part of our partnership includes joining them in one of their star systems where we can fully utilize our abilities. A moment I look forward to.

Had my father been alive to see what I've done, what I've become, he'd tell me I've made a pact with demons. His absence came with some advantages. Otherwise, I would've been forced on a different path.

Match was wise enough not to breach the *unholy* alliance he'd formed with the Drexans and was sworn to secrecy. He'd never reveal their proprietary technical knowledge or its origins. Not even his board members would know. *Roare Violet Murdock and TGIET have no idea what they're up against.*

chapter eighteen—mania

Behold, I tell you a mystery: We shall not all sleep, but we shall all be changed.—1 Corinthians 15:51 (NKJV)

The curbside check-in for American Airlines was eerily quiet as Roare walked to the gate at 5:15 Saturday morning. Fortunately, only three people besides her and Odin would be on the flight from JFK to ALB.

She sat at the far end of the terminal. With her cable-knit cap pulled low over her forehead, she positioned her hair over the sides of her glasses and peered around. She took out her phone and managed a quick study session in Proverbs with her Bible app, then checked her emails.

Another look around and no sign of Odin. She gnawed at her fingernails.

Finally, he approached and quietly sat beside her. "Sorry to keep you waiting. I had a slow start. Bet you're hungry by now."

Roare's stomach growled. "How can you tell?"

He took off his gray puffer jacket and placed it atop his backpack on the floor. "I'll grab us something."

While Odin went on a food run, Roare pulled a manila folder from her tote and reviewed the profile of whistleblower Dr. Andrei Ponte, a robotics scientist. He had worked at CoSynthesis Dynamic Ventures until he abandoned his position and went into hiding. The proprietors warned he would no longer be safe—and government entities wanted to silence him before he became a risk to national security.

Odin returned with his hands full, and Roare relieved him of a few parcels. She sifted through and moved her items into one bag. "Appreciate the extra napkins."

"You can never have enough."

The flight attendant announced the start of boarding.

"The other passengers are far enough away for us to talk freely," Odin whispered.

Roare copied his tone. "We have a rental car in Albany, right?"

"From Enterprise and two rooms at Embassy Suites. Lots of foot traffic there—the more people around, the less we're a target. I got us IDs authentic enough to pass. Dr. Ponte will contact me on a burner phone which I'll dispose of once we're done with the interview."

This guy was amazing. "Were you a spy?"

Odin grinned. "I almost wish I was. What I do can be nearly as dangerous. When I'm after a story, I'm deliberate with everything I do—to protect my work, the information given to me, and the people involved. Danger is part of the allure."

"Sounds like you can handle yourself if trouble comes."

"I'm quick on my feet ... and with my fists."

"I believe you."

They reviewed their interview questions, and he handed her the fake ID. She became Darla Fillmore and he was Boomer Morrison.

Roare smiled. "Why did Ponte approach you?"

"Probably knew AI was my specialty. I put him in touch with an organization for whistleblower protection. They'll move him to an undisclosed location and arrange a new identity after the interview."

Roare swallowed hard. *Good grief, Lord. Along with a hedge of protection, I'm gonna need a moat, a thirty-foot steel wall, and a bulletproof vest.*

A reply impressed itself on her mind—when *worry lives in the physical world, the condition of your heart can be compromised. Worry doesn't live in the spiritual realm. Place your trust in me and those emotions will disappear from your spirit.*

Odin was staring at her. "Is everything okay? There's no need to fear. Uncovering evil comes with hazards. All part of the job."

"'Uncovering evil?' Sounds like a line from a movie."

"Definitely. Many films are inspired by real life. I believe we're living a movie in real time, and we create the dialogue as we live."

Roare and Odin continued with small talk until the plane landed. They retrieved a late-model black Jeep Wrangler and drove to the hotel. Their rooms were at opposite ends of the hallway.

"Stand by." Odin scoped out her room. "As soon as I hear from Dr. Ponte, I'll knock on your door. For safety measures, I'm going to avoid calling or texting you."

While she waited for the knock, Roare unpacked and phoned Wyatt. She left him a message about where she was and that she'd be home tomorrow.

Half an hour later, someone knocked.

She nearly ran to the door. "Finally," she said as she opened it. "I was starting to believe the doctor flaked."

"Not a chance," assured Odin. "He's too desperate to tell the world what he knows. We have a fifty-minute drive to his weekend retreat in North Hebron. Green Pond is pretty remote. My gut is telling me we better catch the next plane out after the interview. Grab all your belongings. We gotta move."

At the bottom of a long, winding driveway through the woods, a two-level house with burnt-wood siding blended with the surrounding trees.

"Looks like a converted truck trailer," Roare said. "Great hideout. Too bad the trees don't have their leaves— they would've provided full coverage. I'm sure when the snow falls here, this place will look magical.

"Probably, but right now, I'm grateful the storm went out to the ocean. The view of the creek is incredible though."

"I could sit in one of those lounge chairs for hours." Roare pointed to the windows and doors. "I presume those are bulletproof."

"One way to find out."

They grabbed their gear and walked onto the terrace. As Odin reached for the button beside the door, a gaunt man with glasses jarred open the door. The doctor scanned the surroundings, craning his neck to check behind the trees.

"Are you expecting anyone else?" Odin asked.

"Not to my knowledge. Please, come in quickly." Dr. Ponte ushered them in.

Roare took note of Dr. Ponte wringing his hands excessively. *He must be terrified.*

"I'm Odin Yaremenko, and this is Roare Murdock, the director I mentioned."

"Is this sanctuary new?" she asked. "I can smell the pinewood."

"Yes, a recent build. For now, this is my residence until I can begin a new life someplace else. The fishing is therapeutic. Please, have a seat."

Apart from those nervous hands, he seemed overly calm to Roare. "Do you believe you're safe here?" she asked. "In the wilderness, away from the world?"

"These days, who can be sure about their safety? Nonetheless, when I saw things I wasn't supposed to see— monstrous things—I had to leave."

"And you reached out to us," Odin said.

"Indeed."

"You've taken a few precautions," Roare said, "except there's a lot of glass around you. Are your windows bulletproof?"

"I wouldn't be here without them."

She found a spot for the interview. "Odin and I can't tell you how grateful we are that you're doing this. Try to relax for a few minutes while I set up my camera. Are you ready for your interview, Dr. Ponte?"

"Yes, and you can call me Andrei." His handwringing returned. "Before I reveal anything, I want to go over the guarantees. You won't disclose my identity or even show my face, and you'll distort my voice. You'll provide security, and the organization for informants will escort me to an undisclosed location to begin a new life."

"Your safety is of the utmost importance to us. We've arranged security personnel to look after you," Odin said.

Andrei gave a faint smile.

"You've made a brave decision."

"I'm a man with a distressed soul, and I cannot leave this earth without divulging what I know."

"Have you been followed?" asked Odin.

"I don't believe so, and no one lives near me."

Meanwhile, Roare eyed the lighting and furniture placement. "Why don't you sit on the sofa in the nook over there?" The pinewood wall paneling would provide a vague background.

He moved to the sofa and crossed his legs.

She placed a multicolored embroidered throw pillow beside him, a subtle distraction. Next, she went to the kitchen and filled a glass with water for the doctor—placed on a side table.

"All the information I collected on the AI experiments are on this flash drive for you." The doctor retrieved a steel briefcase he had hidden under a floorboard. He opened the case and handed Odin a flash drive. "Blueprints and notes on nanophysics. Guard this carefully. I have a copy in a secure place and gave instructions to a reliable associate as a backup. Let's begin the interview, shall we?"

"By all means." Roare tested the background lighting and ran a sound check. "Now, Andrei, speak in your normal tone. The sound engineers will distort your voice and face. The audience will see only a shadow."

"I'm relieved to hear."

She turned to Odin. "I'm ready whenever you want to start."

He signaled and waited until she pointed at him to begin.

"Please, tell us about yourself and the work you have been doing."

"I worked at CERN and left a while ago because a fantastic opportunity at CoSynthesis found me." As Andrei warmed up, he unfolded his arms and motioned with his hands.

"At the time, I couldn't resist exploring pico-technology programs that were far more ambitious compared to what I'd done at CERN. Having gotten a fair amount of experience there over a few years, my breaking point was when I saw the laws of physics defied with wormholes, and what I saw come out of them. I've seen entities—spirits—jumping out of one physical being and entering another."

Odin raised his eyebrows. "Incredible. Tell us, why should anyone listen to you?"

"In my opinion, CoSynthesis is merging the supernatural with technology. I'm certain they were inviting Satan himself to live inside AI cyborgs. This alone makes them extremely dangerous to society. I came up with a name—phantom phenomena. I never told anyone, until now." Dr. Ponte gritted his teeth. "Listen, I'm not a religious man. What I saw going on there spooked me. Forced me to believe something unnatural and evil is out there."

"Would you elaborate please?"

"Have you heard about how the heart has a brain of its own? The heart also has its own nervous system, which sends functional decisions to the cerebral cortex. The electrical field of the heart has a stronger magnetic element than the brain, and the methodical beat of the heart syncs to the brain. Emotions, respiratory functions, and experiences are passed back and forth between the two with electromagnetic signals."

Odin leaned forward.

"EM signals act as a force field around the entire body. Humans are like antennae—we transmit energy from and to us. People say where the heart-brain is, so is the soul. Theoretically, the soul can be captured by electronically recording and collecting sequences of neural pulses and ionic charges."

Andrei took a few sips of water. "Another way to harness the soul is to use sensory entities. In ancient Sumer, people would've called them Utukku Lemnutu or evil spirits. We thought 'sensory entities' would be more translatable to the AI language of today. These SEs seek out specific EM signals, intercept humans' energy force fields, and overthrow their souls. This is truly the beginning of a hostile invasion to overtake every atom of a person's existence."

"You're telling us evil spirits are taking over humans?"

"In a way, yes."

"Isn't that a bit far-fetched?"

"No, because I witnessed the harnessing of souls myself."

Odin's brow furrowed. "Where do they come from? What's their intention?"

"I'll explain as simply as I can. SEs are from another dimension. They're difficult to detect because of their picoscopic size. Thankfully, we stumbled across them while exploring ways to integrate living microbes into robots."

"Nanophysics?"

"Yes." Andrei gestured as he explained. "We strongly believe these SEs hitched a ride by meteorite or satellite reentry or forced their way into our dimension through portals. There are other dimensions we can't see, yet we know they exist. We noticed the predatory behavior of SEs, the way they latch onto a DNA strand and reformat its nucleotides and sequences. We integrated SEs into a synthetic material used to build cyborgs and their central processors. The result was miry clay mixed with living microbes—they bind together and the composite far superior to iron."

"You mentioned predatory. Are they deadly?"

"Initially, they weren't. They were supposed to safeguard humanity—to help them heal faster and aid the body to self-correct dysfunctions like cancer cells and other ailments."

"No doubt life-changing for everyone. What's different from the original objective?"

"When you have maniacs attempting to redesign the genesis of life, disregarding creation and science, ethics no longer exists. When we cross the threshold of good to evil, we become deranged. I used to be one of them." Andrei tugged at his collar. "SEs are predators. They seek humans who have malevolent souls. When they sense this, they enter the human and emit a translucent, living plasma throughout the body, which penetrates each cell and atom to prime body, mind, and soul to fully integrate with AI technology."

"Like a prewash."

"Precisely. We speculate, due to their aggressive behavior, their primary purpose may be to build a society of hybrid specimens to replace humans. They're self-evolving and will surpass all other intelligent life forms." The doctor took another sip of water. "To get back to phantom phenomena, the plasma can change cyborgs to look and act like us. You won't be able to tell whether they're humans or machines. The plasma also gives them exceptional physical and intellectual abilities, creative power, and telepathic skills."

"They can physically change their appearance? I'm a reasonably brave man, but—"

"Paranormal things can cause hearts to fail. To answer your question, *yes*, they can change their form."

"Good grief. What else can these cyborgs do?"

"Go into stealth mode."

"You're joking, right?"

"I wish I were. There isn't any aircraft on this planet that can ascend into space faster than these cyborgs. These picoscopic life forms can move from one dimension to another. There aren't enough weapons of mass destruction or science to use against them. The only way to prolong the existence of human life is to search for something far superior than death."

"Isn't eternal life greater than death and more paramount than science?"

"Look, I was an atheist. Science was my gospel. I couldn't accept the possibility of eternal life. If these SEs had invaded our world, what else was out there? Science never excluded the presence of God. We ignored the signs. Remarkably, science and God might be one and the same. Only a supreme engineer could create the complex cosmos and a divine union between himself and humankind. When I observed the revenge of those SEs, I knew there must be a supreme Creator over all the planetary systems throughout dimensions, who existed before time."

"What a weighty analogy."

"Without a doubt, Odin. I fear we've busted down the door to Gehenna and can never be closed from the physical world. My grandmother gave me a Bible. When I read the book, mysteries of the universe unfolded before my eyes. I met the God of Hosts."

Odin looked over his shoulder and met Roare's wide-eyed gaze.

Andrei sighed. "All this was bloodcurdling to me as well. When I understood the offenses I'd committed and how much was at stake, my conscience awakened. And by giving you my testimony, I'm certain I've signed my death warrant."

Roare tapped Odin's back and stopped filming.

"Would you like a break?" he asked Andrei. "Do you want to stretch your legs? We can stop if you want."

"Please, continue before I lose the last bit of nerve I have left."

Odin exchanged nods with Roare, and she restarted the camera.

He pressed the scientist to answer tougher questions about who was driving the project and their endgame.

The interview ended ten minutes later.

Roare shut off the camera. "Compelling. I pray to God in heaven our audience will hear the interview, leave the theaters filled with terror, and demand answers. You've done a heroic deed, Andrei. We're eternally indebted to you."

The footage downloaded to Roare's flash drive and private server, and she gave an additional copy to Odin. She packed her equipment.

Andrei stood, wiped his face with a handkerchief, and drained his glass. He walked them out to the deck.

Odin turned to face him and placed a hand on the man's forearm. "You'll be well protected."

chapter nineteen—incursion

They are a taproot to a world that runs deeper than our presence on this continent. But, more than that, they are an incursion into a spiritual realm where there are powers and forces that neither can nor should be taken for granted.

—Kent Nerburn, *The Girl Who Sang to the Buffalo*

Roare and Odin promptly left the doctor's safe house, scanning their surroundings on their way.

She texted Wyatt: *Hey, babe. We're catching an early flight. See you soon.*

A few minutes on I-87 South, another vehicle rammed the Jeep from behind. The tires screeched and burned as Odin hit the brakes. The Jeep swerved madly. Smoke billowed behind them in Roare's side mirror. A black Hummer chased close behind, passed Odin's side, and veered away.

"Brace yourself!" Odin screamed.

She covered her face. *Lord Jesus, help us! Protect us!* She grabbed the handle above her door and closed her eyes. Tried to regard this as a freefall ride at an amusement park. Thank goodness for seatbelts! *Please, God, let the airbags deploy.*

The Jeep veered sharply to the right, crashed through the guardrail and rolled down an embankment. Endless jarring. Steel and glass crunching. Airbags deploying. At last, the vehicle jolted to a stop among the thick shrubs of a gully.

Still alive. Roare opened her eyes. Her hand still clung to the grasp bar above her door. She flinched at the intense throbbing in her head. *Brain's foggy. Can't focus.*

Odin's eyes were open. He was breathing, though motionless.

She didn't want to budge either.

He mumbled and released the handle above his door. His other hand remained on the steering wheel. "Feel okay? Anything broken?"

Roare stared blankly past him. The vehicle had landed on its wheels. *Thanks be to God, for sparing our lives.* Slowly, she shifted one limb at a time. She exhaled. At least nothing was broken. "My head."

"Probably a concussion. You have some scratches on your face. What's my name?"

"Odin Yaremenko. My mind's in slo-mo, kinda cloudy. How 'bout you?"

"Ribs may be bruised, I'll live. I think we should get out of here. Smells like the Jeep is leaking fluids."

"Wait. I don't see my backpack. My life is in there!"

"Try to relax. We'll find it. Can you open your door?"

Roare pushed hard with her shoulder, then the door flew open, after a few kicks. She swung her legs around and stepped out. The pain in her head intensified, and she held onto the door until she gained her balance.

Odin forced his door open. He grimaced and held his lower abdomen while he hoisted himself out. "We have to move away from the Jeep, now."

"My bag." She cringed, massaged her forehead.

"Don't take chances."

"Yes, fine, but the bag is jammed under the dashboard and needs a firm tug." Didn't budge an inch. "Can you help me? I sure hope the camera's okay."

"Hold on." He held onto shrubs as he maneuvered his way to her side. The light on his cell phone provided a better look under the caved-in dashboard, and he freed a strap impaled on a piece of plastic. "Got it. Let's move."

"Shh. I hear voices."

They froze briefly, then shouted up the embankment, "Help! Help! We're down here!"

She squinted, barely making out the forms of six people standing near the ripped steel guardrail.

They talked among themselves. "I saw the whole thing," one man said with a loud baritone. "I'm certain the Hummer clipped them on purpose."

"We can share those details with the police later. I heard someone call them." The other man's voice sounded anxious. "We need to get them up here now. I'll grab some ropes from the back of my truck."

An elderly woman hovered nearby. "I called 911," she said, then shouted to Roare and Odin, "Are you okay?"

Odin yelled, "We're bruised and have head injuries."

"Help is on the way. And three of these gentlemen are off-duty firefighters. They'll get you out of there." A younger woman stepped up beside the elderly woman and placed an arm around her shoulders.

Roare sat on an old tree trunk several yards from the Jeep, her head swimming.

"Stay where you are." The baritone voice belonged to a tall, burly man. "We're coming down."

Odin said, "Hurry, the Jeep might explode!"

The man tied a rope to the guardrail and lowered himself toward them.

"We're extremely fortunate you stopped," Roare said.

"Can you stand?" the man asked.

"Not too well. My legs are wobbly."

"We got you. Lean on me, and I'll help you into the harness. Those two men at the top will hoist you up."

He strapped Roare in, and she wrapped her arms around her backpack. He whistled and gave a thumbs up.

As the other two hoisted her, she closed her eyes to minimize the dizziness. How could this happen? She and Odin had made sure they weren't being followed.

At the top, the two women helped her out of the rope. "Mom and I saw what happened," the younger one said. "We wrote down the license number."

Roare nodded. "How kind of you. Good info for the police." She recoiled from the agonizing pain in her head.

"You sit tight. EMS is on the way." The mother placed her hand on Roare's shoulder and helped her to the backseat of her car.

A few seconds later, a fire truck arrived. Four firefighters climbed out and huddled with the off-duty firemen. Three of them tied a rope to the rail and climbed down the embankment. Within minutes, Odin came up to the road. With a grimace, he clenched his right side.

The state police and emergency medical vehicles arrived a few minutes apart. As the two troopers examined the scene, medical personnel bandaged Odin's chest, and placed him and Roare on stretchers. One trooper marched to each emergency vehicle.

The stern-looking one approached Roare and said, "The Jeep is being sprayed with Explosion Suppressant Foam to make sure the vehicle is safe before being moved. Are you the owner?"

"No."

"I'll need to see your driver's license."

"My associate was driving the rental." Roare dug into her backpack, retrieved her wallet, and handed her real license to the trooper.

"Can you tell me what took place?" He glanced at her, then the license.

She relayed everything she could remember, while her eyes followed Odin as he passed by on the stretcher. Roare overheard the medics tell him they were taking him to Four Winds Hospital for X-rays. While EMTs secured her with straps, Roare saw one of the medics glare at her, smirk, and flash his blue laser eyes.

Roare clutched at her chest and gasped.

The police officer looked at her. "Are you okay? Do you need medical attention?"

Roare shook her head. *He'd deem me crazy for sure, if I tell him about the borg I just saw.* "I'm all right."

He nodded and joined the other officers to collect witness statements.

The medics approached and strapped Roare onto the stretcher. *I can't believe I saw another borg. They've been following us all along. I've got to warn Odin somehow.* "Odin! You're not safe! There's a borg with you!" she yelled. She squirmed and twisted to get off the stretcher but couldn't move. The straps restrained her. Everything spun and drove her head back to the pillow.

One medic said, "She's delirious from the bump to her head. We need to get her to the hospital quickly."

"Your vision may be sensitive if you have a concussion." The female EMT examined her head wound.

"Ouch." Roare frowned and pulled away.

"This antiseptic will burn. Nonetheless, the cuts need to be cleaned out. They're minor—no stitches required."

"Good."

The woman flashed a penlight in her eyes. "Probably a concussion. You'll need a CT scan and a few hours of observation. I'm going to give you pain medication straightaway."

The EMTs rolled Roare into their vehicle. Inside, Roare squeezed her eyes shut against the bright lights. She kept muttering, "I have to warn him. I have to warn him." She turned to the EMT. "My husband, I need to call him. He'll want to know where I am."

Still under observation, Roare waited in a private, outpatient room. Doctors kept her awake while they ran endless tests. They insisted she could not sleep for the next twenty-four hours. She longed to be home with Wyatt.

Around five in the morning, a new female nurse entered. Roare didn't recall seeing her before but perhaps she was part of the latest shift change. The woman was attempting to stick a needle in her arm.

"What are you giving me?" Roare asked with growing alarm.

The nurse said in a low monotone voice, "This will help you sleep."

"No way are you putting anything into my arm. I'm a concussion patient! I'm not supposed to sleep! You get away from me right now!"

The woman's eyes shone blue.

Roare screamed for help. *This thing is trying to kill me!* She pushed the red emergency call button next to the bed.

The nurse tried to jab her with the needle.

Roare kept her at bay by pushing and kicking her.

A male and female nurse rushed in and pulled the borg nurse away from her. The needle fell to the floor. The borg broke through the male nurse's grip and darted out the door. The female nurse notified security. When she examined the needle, she discovered there was a lethal dose of benzodiazepine.

Nearly hysterical, Roare demanded to leave.

The doctors persuaded her to stay until her husband arrived. They offered to relocate her to a different room and notify Wyatt.

Burnt out and shaken, Roare was pleased to be home. "Wy, I'm so grateful you drove over three hours to come get me."

"Gobo, how could I not? What a horrific time you've had! How come you didn't have Sloane escort you? There are too many bizarre events connected to this film, and I'm concerned."

"I must admit life has been getting out of hand. Being nearly killed yesterday and a cyborg attacking me today made me realize how serious this film is. I need to regroup and be more strategic. Right now, I'm exhausted, my head is killing me."

He gently kissed her forehead.

"Careful, the pain meds are wearing off," she said.

"I want to have a chat with Sloane. He needs to do a better job of protecting you. You were nearly killed by psychos."

"Wy, I need answers as soon as I can get them."

"For now, I'll look after you. Let me help you up the stairs. I'll bring your bags to the bedroom later."

As he escorted her up the staircase, she peeked toward the kitchen. All the cabinet doors were left open. *Typical. Lucky for him I don't have the strength to give him a hard time.*

Once in their bedroom, he assisted Roare with changing her clothes. "I'm thankful you weren't seriously injured."

"So am I."

Unable to sleep, Roare stared at the ceiling as the accident and the attempt on her life replayed in her mind. She could have died! She'd realized this project had deadly hooks. Tears flowed down her face.

She whispered fiercely, "God of the universe, why did you choose me to do this film? What made you believe I could handle these lunatics? I need protection, Lord, if I'm meant to live through this. Help me out here. Please."

I did warn you, came the quiet reply. *Fear not, I am with you until the end of time. What you're doing won't be in vain. Allow my words to bring you peace.*

Calmness enveloped her, and she eased into a deep slumber.

Barely awake, Roare answered a call from Odin. They unpacked the aftermath of the accident. He asked how she was feeling. She told him about the borg she'd seen at the crash site and at the hospital when the fake nurse had tried to kill her.

"Hang on, you haven't heard the most astonishing news," Odin told her. "Dr. Ponte is dead. The media is claiming his demise was an accident. Totally a load of garbage. He was assassinated by CoSynthesis."

Roare covered her mouth and closed her eyes. She didn't want to believe they'd gotten him. "What a brave soul he was. These ruthless people—"

"We were fortunate to get his interview before they—"

"That's why we have to get these interviews done as soon as poss—"

"They'll keep coming after us until they've shut us up for good," Odin finished.

She shuddered, considering the days ahead. "Dr. Ponte didn't have an accident. He wanted to live, I captured this on film." Roare admired Andrei for his courage. "How did he die?"

"Fishing wire wrapped around his neck." Odin scoffed. "He lost consciousness and fell into the creek. The current swept him downstream a quarter of a mile until his sweater caught onto a dead tree in the water, where a man and his little boy found him."

They both questioned why TGIET hadn't sent him bodyguards the moment he'd contacted them. Roare blamed herself for his death, but Odin nixed that idea. "I warn you, though, this will not be the last incident."

Roare knew in her spirit more was to come.

"His interview is safe in TGIET's hands, and the files have been uploaded to their private server," Odin assured her. "One of the founders will retrieve the data, in case Andrei's data gets corrupted, or something happens to either of us." He'd sent a copy to Roare and had his own copy of everything on a flash drive in his safety deposit box.

Roare rubbed her temples and placed her hand over her racing heart. Her throat was tightening. Could she survive the next two interviews? *C'mon girl, do those deep breathing exercises.*

"Roare, are you there?"

"Uh, yes. There's so much to digest, and I'm in pain."

"I don't want to sound insensitive, but you need to get ahold of yourself. We can't do this without you. You *were* aware of the risks involved."

"Um, yes, you told me. Give me time to process everything. I'll reach out to you in a few days."

"We have more people to interview."

"I haven't forgotten. Speak to you soon." Roare ended the call.

Pilar wore a floral print apron over her casual business attire while she stirred something in a stockpot on the stove. "Your husband left you a note. Your accident sounded awful. My job is to make sure you rest, and I intend to look after you," she said firmly. "You need more sleep."

Roare walked to the stove and peeked into the pot. "Mmm, something smells divine."

"Butternut squash soup, roasted brussels sprouts, red quinoa, and kale chips. Why don't you take a seat?"

Roare sulked but did as she was told. "You're such a *mom*."

As she ate, she read Wyatt's note: "Good morning, babe. I watched you sleep peacefully last night. Having you safe next to me gave me comfort."

A smile pulled at the corners of her mouth.

A notification binged on her phone—from Odin. *Police report came back on the vehicle that hit us. No strong leads. They'll investigate further. No mention of the fake nurse who invaded your room. No surprise there.*

She'd better call Sloane.

rage against the machine

Match rarely lost his temper or quibbled over *oversights*. He had his way of *dealing* with failures. He grunted when his borg infantry returned with a poor report, although one of the three borgs had disposed of Dr. Ponte. The other two had misjudged the impact of their advance on their targets.

As punishment for their faulty behavior, Match had his lieutenant commander decommission them. Now they were mere borg builders. Determined to remove his opponent from Earth, Match formulated a new plan.

chapter twenty—humble pie

Do nothing out of selfish ambition or vain conceit. Rather, in humility value others above yourselves, not looking to your own interests but each of you to the interests of the others.—Philippians 2:3–4

Nothing surpassed the warmth of a hot meal to inject life into the bloodstream and invigorate the senses. Good for not only her mind and soul but also her bruised ego. Roare had presumed she was well prepared for anything. But in only the first few weeks of shooting her film—a dead body. *How many more corpses, Lord?*

She called Sloane.

"Roare, how are things with you?" he greeted.

"I'm still alive. Wyatt is pretty upset. And to think I defended you."

"What did you tell him?"

"I told him there was nothing you could've done. You assumed I would be okay having Odin with me, but—as you know—he got banged up too. And poor Dr. Ponte is now dead."

"Dr. Ponte's employer caught up with him."

"And they nearly did us in. Not to mention a borg at the crash site, and another one attacked me at the hospital. I'm being stalked, and I'm scared! What I want to know is what you are going to do to keep me from being killed?"

"Roare, I'm not taking this lightly. We're under siege, and I know where the strikes are coming from. Match and his thugs from CoSynthesis. We need to expose him. I'm not comfortable with it, but you *are* a target. If we can keep you alive—"

"*If?* Sloane, there shouldn't be any *ifs* in this conversation. Either you protect me and the whistleblowers, or we have no film. What are we doing here?"

"I'm going to tighten security immediately when a whistleblower approaches us. Also, I'm afraid to tell you this, but my intuition is telling me we have a mole at TGIET. We've got to shut him down and remove him from our circle as soon as possible."

"What do you know about Odin?" she asked. "Can he be trusted? Who else knew we were upstate, and how did CoSynthesis find out about the film?"

"No need to worry about Odin. I know his family personally, and he's loyal to the death. There is someone else I have on my radar. It's likely the same person who blabbed about our film. Roare, I'm sorry I didn't protect you like I was supposed to. I'm responsible for the safety of everyone on this project. I should've done better."

"Apology accepted, but I'm not dead yet, and we can't bring Andrei back, so what do we do now?"

"Based on the urgency of this film, I have to make you my main focus for the sake of your life and this project."

"I'm depending on you."

"By the way, I watched the interview. Quite explosive. We couldn't ask for anything more. Odin gave me all the data. Well done to you both. We have two more whistleblower interviews. To save time, I'll have Odin conduct one session on his own, while you speak to a scientist couple."

"Sure."

"Any thoughts on our last one-on-one meeting?" he asked.

"Yes. Andrei Ponte's interview validated everything you told me and confirmed how deeply rooted the evil is. I'm terrified—not of you anymore. What we don't know is what disturbs me. And the public won't be able to deal with what's ahead." Roare swallowed hard. Scenarios of how she might be taken out ran through her head. Real life imitating fiction.

"No, they won't know what hit them. But if they remain ignorant, they'll face deadly consequences. Sounds grim, but perhaps we can change the outcome. You've handled each obstacle well, including what I've shared with you. At times you'll feel the strain, but the burden is not yours to carry alone."

Roare pushed a pillow behind her head to ease the mounting headache. She couldn't wait to sleep. "Anything else? I'm getting groggy."

"One minor detail. Because you trusted me, even after disclosing who I am, I have someone I'd like you to meet. You'll never guess who."

"Probably not."

"Chips M. Jaeger."

"The famous docudrama director?" Roare said elatedly.

"Seriously, he's a friend of mine and wants to codirect our film. Would another director cramp your style?"

"Jaeger wouldn't—I would be honored. I could learn a great deal, and I could use the help. He'd bring endless talent to the project. I must confess, I knew I was out of my league with this undertaking. Having Jaeger on board—

we could deliver a masterpiece to the public. Wow, I can't wait!"

"It'll expedite the progress of the film."

"I'm overwhelmed by your faith in me. So much is happening at once—the film, meeting my father—there must be serious activity in the cosmos on my behalf."

"Probably. You have a fan club in God's kingdom."

"Well, maybe, because I need all kinds of backup."

"Did I hear you right? You're meeting your biological father?"

"A long story but will catch you up later. The timing is criminal, and if I start lamenting over it, my blood will boil."

"To be continued, no doubt. Listen, hope you don't mind, I gave Jaeger your number."

"Not at all."

"He knows about the interview and your accident. He'll call you next week. Keep a low profile, and if you need to go out, hit my cell. I'll take you. If I can't, one of my specialists will. Understood?"

Roare grinned from ear to ear, excited to work with Jaeger. "Sloane, not to be rude, but I'm fading fast. Do you mind?"

"No problem. Go to sleep. Christmas is around the corner—consider Jaeger an early Christmas gift."

"Merry Christmas to you too. Tell me, what does one give a man who has everything?"

"An amazing film. I'll talk to you soon."

Sloane gave Odin access to review all the profiles of the journalists employed at TGIET, as well as anyone who knew about the film. In the privacy of his home, Sloane scoured surveillance tapes and obtained cell phone records. Reliable contacts in the CIA assisted with the search. Sloane even had them review bank transactions made by the suspect in mind.

Bingo.

Sloane's intuition had not failed him. Lujza, a journalist, and some guy named Grayson. He found half a million dollars had been wired into Lujza's account from an offshore account. She would be terminated immediately, along with disciplinary actions. As for Grayson, he would conveniently disappear. *Match will soon know we're on to him.*

Sloane called Odin and Roare and updated them on the snitch. He strongly advised, moving forward, anything regarding whistleblowers, TGIET's movement for appointments, and the progression of their film should be kept between them and the trusted few whose loyalties were unwavering.

Alone at home, Sloane gazed at the Brooklyn Bridge lit up against the dark sky, knowing the time would soon come when he'd meet Match again. *Not soon enough.*

chapter twenty-one—convergence

Not everything that is faced can be changed, but nothing can be changed until it is faced.—James Baldwin

Hunter readied himself for a late flight to New York. He leaned up against open sliding glass doors which separated the bedroom from the deck. The day was grim, despite the grandeur of the mid-December sunset. The waves across the seascape sparkled like fireflies. He wasn't in the frame of mind to appreciate the sea, though. His stomach twisted like a tangled rope. *How will Roare receive a man in such a ghastly state of mind?*

He closed the doors and ventured into the bathroom. With a glare, he faced the vacant gray-haired man in the mirror. *Look at yourself, mate. Your bravado has fizzled to embers, and your healthy complexion wasn't spared.* The ten kilograms he'd lost due to cancer didn't help his physique, either.

Layer by layer, God was peeling away the masks Hunter wore, and he was left like an artichoke with its heart exposed. He felt like an old man who'd lost his senses. "God," he whispered, "I can accept my failings. I blame myself for my flaws. Can't say I fancy myself much." He turned from the mirror. He'd have several hours on the plane to contemplate his fate and take jabs at his character.

He shaved and dressed in comfortable clothes to endure the long haul to JFK. Evie had packed his weekend bag—a welcome gesture. Either she pitied him or was looking after him because she loved him. He'd take crumbs if he had to.

He parked himself on one of the stools in the kitchen. He hoped to arrive at the airport early. As soon as the idea came and went, Reynalds walked through the front door and into the kitchen. He eyed the clock on the wall. "Twenty minutes to spare, chill out. The other two will be joining us shortly. We all want to see you off."

Hunter asked, "Are you well enough to be here? My immunity is weak these days."

"Papa, I'm not completely brain dead. Other than a sporadic cough, I'm no longer viral. Gee's Linctus helps."

"Relieved to hear. You don't wanna kill off your old papa yet, do you?"

"You can be ridiculous sometimes."

"Go say hello to your mum."

Reynalds walked into the living room, and Evie stood. "Hey, Mum. I'm just going to wave. I'm becoming paranoid now with papa's condition and all."

"That's wise of you. Good to see you," she said.

The front door opened and Aaden sauntered in.

"Hey, Papa. How's everything? Ready to roll?" He shook Hunter's hand firmly and embraced him.

"I'm doing the best I can," Hunter said. "Guess I have a committee escorting me to the airport."

"In a manner of speaking, yes. What's with the sudden trip to New York? Find a new cancer treatment?"

"Not exactly. I'll tell you on the way. Where's Abbi?"

"A text came in," Evie said. "She sends her love and can't see you off. She has to cram for exams." She followed them to the garage.

"Remind her not to stress," Hunter said, "and send my love back."

"Let's take my Harrier," Aaden suggested. "Why all the luggage? I thought this was a short trip."

"The extra carry-on is mine," Reynalds said. "Did you think I'd let our papa take this trip alone?"

"I'm with you, bro. He's a stubborn old boar."

"All right, pipe down," Hunter said. "No need to be dramatic. I'm not helpless. And you, Reynalds. Awfully brazen of you to invite yourself."

"Glad you came to your senses," Evie said. "Now, stop gabbing, or you'll miss your flight."

Aaden assisted Hunter into the front passenger seat, while Reynalds collected the luggage, then climbed into the backseat of the SUV.

Hunter shifted to make himself comfortable and buckled himself securely.

Evie leaned in and kissed him. "Have a great flight. Everything will go well. Call me when you land." Then, she said goodbye to her sons and asked Reynalds to look after his father. "You're doing something mighty significant—"

Aaden beeped the horn. "We're going to be late."

"Okay, off you go." Evie backed away.

As Aaden drove, he gave a command to the in-dash GPS, directing them to Sydney Airport. "Our ETA is forty-four minutes. Give us your story, Papa. Are you taking this trip to stay alive?"

Hunter explained, "This is my cursed year of misfortunes, I reckon. Rest assured I'm not trying to pin a guilt trip on any of you, and please don't whimper around like lost puppies because you couldn't help. Besides, Reynalds is still a possibility. So—why New York?"

"No drumroll, please," Aaden said. "Just tell us."

"We're going to meet your half-sister. Roare Violet Murdock-Galloway. She's twenty-six, tall like you, and a two-time Oscar-winning film director."

"She sounds remarkable," Reynalds said. "The real question is whether she wants to bother with us."

"Why go when your health is on the edge of oblivion?" Aaden asked his father.

Hunter cleared his throat. "My health and future are in God's hands. I've opened my heart to him, to the one who has power over life and death, and a heart to forgive someone like me. To survive, I need to come clean about the damage I left behind. I saw a small window of opportunity. Hoping forgiveness could be a game changer."

"Since when did you become religious?"

"When you're wading through troubled waters and close to drowning, you're forced to call on a higher power to pull yourself out. Me? I called out to Christ."

Aaden took a long glance in the rearview mirror and cleared his throat.

Reynalds said, "I dunno, maybe I would do the same."

"While you're being philosophical," Aaden said, "I suspect another reason you might be going."

"Fine," Hunter said. "Without pride or prejudice, I'm going to eat crow—get on my knees and grovel—and ask Roare whether she'll donate her bone marrow."

"I wish you luck. I wouldn't. You're still hung up on this DNA business. Family doesn't have to be absolute! I wouldn't give a rip who donated bone marrow, as long as I could be healed. Don't lose your head over this."

"I get you. I'm working through things. Good for me if she is the intended donor. If not, I'll need to abandon my comfort zone and explore other avenues. Don't judge others until you've had similar experiences."

Aaden parked the Harrier close to the T1 terminal entrance and accompanied his father and brother to the security point. "What you did or didn't do, doesn't matter," he said to Hunter, "or affect what we think of you. What should matter is who you think you are. I hope everything works out. Sorry I was such a pest all these years."

"Now who's philosophical?" Hunter said.

Hunter reclined in his first-class seat. Reynalds sat behind him, stretched out himself. The long trip gave Hunter a chance to formulate what he'd say to Roare. Prepare for the worst and pray for a reprieve. He hoped he'd speak with his heart instead of pleading desperately for help.

Forty-thousand feet above the Pacific, he finished a healthy dinner, then washed down his nightly collection of meds with warm lemon water. He feebly attempted to unwind by watching a film. The sleeping pills would kick in soon, though. He desired the nice glass of wine he usually had on these flights. Those days were gone—at least until he got past his health crisis. However, his outcome depended on his willingness to trust God. *Christ, where do I begin?*

A simple "sorry" will do, came the reply.

Had God spoken to him, or was he dreaming?

He fought off the gradual heaviness of his eyelids as the medicine sedated his active mind. He rehashed his candid exchange with his children and pursed his lips gently. They were far more mature compared to when he was their age.

A clever bunch—morally grounded, purposeful, and they had gracious, inspiring traits, thanks to Evie. They were outspoken too, not easily intimidated. He prayed he could regain their respect. As for Roare, he could never bring back the time they'd lost, but maybe he could say something meaningful to her. He moaned and finally drifted into a deep sleep.

Roare was certain God had orchestrated her convergence with Hunter Barraclough as carefully as he'd manipulated the alignments of stars and planets. Why now?

She forced herself to eat a light breakfast yet still felt foggy from the concussion. Within a few hours, she'd meet her biological father. A root canal might be a better option.

Cup of jasmine tea in hand, she moved to the dining room table and opened her laptop to work on her interview with the next whistleblower. She rubbed her forehead.

Her cell phone rang. "Mom, hi."

"Hello, baby girl. How're you?"

"Not sure. I have a feeling things are about to get interesting with Hunter arriving soon." She dared not tell her about nearly being killed. *She'd harass me to death about dropping the film.* "When I try to unwind, a tsunami washes the life right out of me. Seems like my light is leaving me. Any insights?"

Lane sighed. "You're overwhelmed. I would have the same mixed bag of emotions. Mental conflicts are okay, though you're forgetting a few facts."

"I'm all ears."

"We should respond with dignity and kindness—even when we want to rip a person's heart out. You're above this. Do you get my meaning?"

"Don't lose my cool and explode on him. Part of me wants to hurt him because he hurt me. Another part wants to look him in the eye and see what kind of man he is—I guess I have a morbid curiosity. Even though holding hatred close to my heart almost destroyed me, forgiveness is a sobering thing. Either way, I'm not in any position to judge him."

"Remember the prodigal son in Luke 15?"

"Sure. He spends his inheritance and comes back in rags. I'm no prodigal."

"You're missing the point."

Roare conceded. "His father welcomes him back and treats him like royalty, and this angered his older brother." God would want her to be like that father when she met Hunter. Besides, her mom had taught her manners.

"Those who love you will say Hunter doesn't deserve grace, and this is exactly why you must grant him grace. It's not a requirement to be best pals, but at least hear him out. Help him with his medical crisis and move on with your life."

"Sounds simple in theory, Mom. This situation isn't a movie. Real life will always present complications. If I could assist him, would I be at fault for doing so?"

"I can't answer your question. You need to make up your own mind. You've been a believer for a while, you know how this goes. God recalls everything you did with your life—the good, the bad, and the ugly. Wouldn't you want the same consideration Hunter wants from you?"

"Well, I know when I was flat on my face, God definitely gave me grace."

"The prodigal's father didn't hold onto his son's offences. They had history and a relationship. You and your father don't. You have a clean slate in front of you.

Only you can determine how you want to write your history with Hunter."

"Hmm. Forgiving him is one thing, but having closure and writing history with him is another."

"You've got this," Lane said. "Wyatt is going with you, right?"

"Seriously? He would never let me meet him on my own."

"I wouldn't have expected less. You'll have God's company too. Where are you meeting?"

"In Central Park at Le Pain Quotidien, 2:30 tomorrow afternoon."

After the call, Roare returned to prepping for her interview with the second whistleblower, a married couple who were both scientists employed at Cosynthesis.

Roare occasionally bit her lower lip in disbelief while she researched the couple's testimony. *These poor people had their newborn twin boys kidnapped and used like lab rats for DNA harvesting. The lab's overreach is diabolical!*

Digging further, Roare discovered the couple had signed many disclosures with Cosynthesis which included allowing *some* experiments to be done to the boys—borderline entrapment. She could see why the lab wanted to suppress public scrutiny to protect its integrity and avoid liabilities. *CoSynthesis couldn't have their shady practices getting out, but they didn't count on the Kovacs resigning and becoming whistleblowers.*

Creak.

Roare jerked her head toward the noise. Her chair scraped backward as she jumped out of her seat.

"Good grief, Pilar. I almost ran for a knife! When did you come in?"

"Sorry I frightened you." Pilar stopped at the kitchen counter. "You were engrossed in taking notes, and talking to yourself, I didn't want to disturb you."

"I don't mean to be nervous. The research on this project is macabre."

"It may be a good time to give it a rest." She frowned at Roare. "I hope you weren't on your laptop too long. Maybe take a break to eat. How're your migraines?"

"They're diminishing slowly. I'm resting a lot."

"I'll be glad when you're done with this film. Have you blessed your project with a title?"

"*Rage Against the Machine.*"

Wyatt and Roare walked through the park, arm in arm, approaching their destination. "How're you holding up, Gobo?"

"My nerves are in turmoil."

"The timing is lousy. But remember who you are in Christ. Be yourself. Keep your queries simple, give short answers, and focus on the purpose of your meeting. Don't let your emotions cloud your decisions."

"Seems like a commercial endeavor." Roare cleared her throat to push aside her emotional strain.

"Sort of, in a way. Be open, but guard your heart. I'm right here with you."

"Don't let go of my hand."

"Brace yourself," Reynalds said. "She's here with her husband, I gather."

Hunter ran his fingers through his hair and allowed Reynalds to help him up.

As Roare approached the door in long, confident strides, her coat flapped in the wind like her long hair. A man opened the door for her, and she stepped inside, pausing momentarily as her eyes swept the room.

Manus had sent Hunter a photo of Roare before their meeting. He waved slightly. She returned the gesture and headed toward the table. Reynalds stood close by while Hunter moved forward to meet her. He nearly tripped over his feet. Reynalds took his elbow to steady him.

His daughter looked like a goddess. And he'd contributed nothing toward raising her. His pulse revved like a high-performance boat. He was the biggest half-wit on Earth to have missed out.

Maybe now is the time to pray for mercy, eh, God? Keep your head up, man. Use what remnant of pride you have left and use this trait for good.

Hunter paused. Took a couple of steps back. "Hello, Roare. You're as beautiful as your mother was when I met her. I feel privileged to meet you."

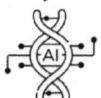

Roare kept a careful distance from the man before her. Unimpressed, she tightened her lips.

Giving compassion is fruitful. And for your sake, necessary. God wasn't cutting her any slack today.

She bit her lower lip to restrain herself. Blast! She had his square face, the same turned-up nose, exactly as her mother had said. However, something else told her his face was familiar.

"How was your flight?" she asked.

"Long. I managed a nap, thankfully," he said.

"I'd like you to meet my husband, Wyatt."

Wyatt stepped forward and shook his hand.

"My eldest son, Reynalds," Hunter said.

The reality of having a half-brother struck her like a tidal wave. Finally, she shook his hand.

"An honor to meet you," he said. "Trippy we're brother and sister, eh?" His face turned red, and he flashed a wide, dimpled grin.

"Totally a surprise," she said.

Thank goodness Reynalds took the seat across from her instead of Hunter.

The waiter arrived to take their orders.

Awkward silence followed.

Wyatt took Roare's hand under the table.

Finally, Hunter said, "Since I asked for this, I'll start. Recent events have convinced me to apologize for my offenses against you. Abandoning you must've caused great turmoil and pain."

If he only knew how much. She fought off a snide comment.

"I did you a horrible disservice in life. My spineless, irresponsible actions were despicable. I was a heavy drinker and doper back then. My father was furious—either I'd come right, or he'd disown me for seeing a Black woman. I had no guts to stand against him." He glanced at the table briefly, then met her gaze again. "I'm sorry I turned my back on you. I can't undo the years we've missed. I wish I'd been the father you deserved. I was never worthy of your mum. She honored me by letting me into her life at all."

Wyatt gently squeezed Roare's hand.

Hunter's spirit was broken. Roare wasn't sure what to make of him. Either he was emotionally transparent or a master of deceit. *God, please let healing words flow from my lips to his ears.*

"You showed a lot of courage traveling so far to come meet me, share your story, and ask me to forgive you." She spoke quietly, and the others leaned closer. "Regardless of everything else, I respect you for being frank. I don't know what to say. Life can change us—sometimes willingly, sometimes by force. Between those two points, a transformation took place in my life, maybe for you too."

"Yes, my life has been altered forever, I feel."

She sighed. "I used to dream of killing you. I wanted to destroy your good name and the perfect, privileged life you had."

"I can't blame you," Hunter said.

"I had to curb my hatred, or I wouldn't have turned my life around from my own poor choices. My godly, praying family never gave up on me when I wanted to cut out any resemblance of you. They got me through a few dark years. Just so you know, Mom never shared details about why you disappeared. She only said you weren't fit to be a father at the time. I don't know what kind of man you are now, so I can't judge you."

"She always was a diplomat. If I were a different man back then, the story would've been more pleasant to tell."

The right corner of Roare's lip curled. *Don't smirk.* "The three of us weren't destined to be. Mom didn't abort me, and she ended up finding Jesus instead. Now I believe in him, and I'm grateful to be her daughter. What an amazing lady who sacrificed everything for me."

"It must've been difficult for her early on, being on her own, but I'm sure she never once regretted her decision."

"We managed okay. I'm not here to make you feel bad, but I'm compelled to lash out at you a little, out of self-preservation. All those years as a young girl, questioning who my father was, where you were, if you gave a second thought about me at least once, if you were dead. For me, I would've coped better if you were—would've been easier to cope."

Another hand squeeze from Wyatt.

"I did think about you, Roare, in the beginning," Hunter replied. "When I left America, I also left behind a life that was bigger than my ego. My wife Evie gave me a different perspective from your mother's. I failed to see it until after I finally told her about you."

"No one can understand what I've gone through emotionally except those closest to me, but I appreciate what you admitted. I depended on those years to face what I could not change, and I became numb to get over you." Roare turned to Reynalds. "I mean no disrespect to Evie."

Reynalds nodded. "None taken. I'd feel the same."

Roare's lips turned downward. She could feel bitterness rising in her spirit like a loaf of bread baking in an oven. *This is not how I wanted the exchange to go. I have to speak my piece and end on a positive note.* "We did okay. We held each other through the rough times and the triumphs. Look, my success is inspired by God and those I surround myself with. In the interest of my soul, I forgive you, Hunter, and I have found my peace."

He tilted his head back and dropped his shoulders. "You have no idea how much this means to me."

"You have no idea how hard it was to say this to you. I'm glad I did. To carry resentment takes tremendous energy. I'm blessed I was able to finally release my burdens." Roare squeezed Wyatt's hand tightly. She prayed a strong gust of wind would find its way into the restaurant and whisk away the years of malice she had for him. She felt exonerated from bearing the strain of holding a grudge like a sentimental companion.

"Isn't she amazing?" Reynalds said to Hunter. He turned to Roare. "We appreciate you for making this meeting happen."

"There was something else you wanted to ask me, from what I understand?" she asked Hunter.

"Well, ah, yes," he said. "I believe Manus Cross filled you in on my health dilemma."

"He did."

"Over the past few months, I've had reoccurring nightmares. I believe they're from God, and he wants me to deal with my past. Now I've got this wretched bone cancer. Matching genetics for bone marrow replacement isn't easy. Evie wasn't the best candidate, and neither are our children. I need your help. My bones are deteriorating rapidly. I'll accept whatever answer you give me. I'd be the last person on Earth to hold anything against you."

Was he here making amends or wanting his needs met? She took a deep breath. "What'll happen to you without a match?"

"The longer the treatment is prolonged, the more the cancer will spread. I don't have much time."

"How bad is the pain?"

"Pretty vicious when I don't keep up with the meds."

"I'm already involved with a new project that demands my full attention."

"Say no more. I wouldn't forgive myself for interfering. If by chance this doesn't work, I'll have to pursue other donors."

"I'll call you this evening with my answer. Our get-together was overdue and necessary."

Reynalds said, "The day has been full-on, and Papa gets tired easily. I'd better take him back to the penthouse, so he can rest and take his meds."

How many times had he visited the city and stayed at his penthouse? We've been near each other before. Did we pass each other on the street and not know it?

198

"Yes, I'm exhausted," Hunter said. "If you agree, we'll exchange information and work out the details for the tests. I'll look after all your expenses."

Roare said, "You won't have to concern yourself with my finances. I'm doing well enough." She didn't need handouts.

"Duly noted. The offer still stands."

"I'll consider it. Reynalds, I enjoyed meeting you as well. Perhaps one day ..."

"You're awfully generous." Reynalds handed her a business card he pulled from his wallet. "Here's my phone number and email. I'm going to hail a taxi."

"Take care of yourselves and have a safe flight home," Roare said as she left the table.

Hunter stood and nearly lost his balance. He latched onto the back of his chair. "I have to say, you turned out pretty well. You inherited my tenacity and drive, and your mum gave you the rest. Tell her she's done an outstanding job raising you. Had I been a part of her life, I would've only interfered with your mum's wise decisions. Meeting you has been one of the best days of my life. Maybe you and Wyatt will visit Australia, yes? And meet a few relatives. She is a treasure, Wyatt. Look after her."

"We look after each other," Wyatt said.

Before she exited the café with Wyatt, Hunter gently grasped her left forearm, and she, his. She and Hunter gazed at each other one last time.

"Well?" Roare asked as she and Wyatt retraced their steps through the park, hand in hand.

"Well, what? Let's stop and take a breather." He stepped in front of her and reached for her other hand.

Roare cocked her head. "What's the matter?"

"Gobo, when these ordeals with your dad and your film project are over, why don't we find a place together, someplace else, make a new home, and start a family? I want our lives to be wholesome, healthy, and at a slower pace."

"What a genius idea."

"I'm relieved to hear. Otherwise, I'd have to kidnap you, drag you by your hair caveman-style, and torture you with horrible poetry day and night until you gave in."

"Well, since you leave me with no choice." She giggled.

"I knew I was missing something, your laugh. We've had a monumental day, haven't we?"

"Unforgettable and draining. I must admit, the meeting wasn't as bad as I believed. I grieve for him, Wy."

"You handled yourself like a heavenly angel. Don't feel bad for him. God's going to do something extraordinary with his life. My spirit senses this."

"I'd love to witness the transformation."

chapter twenty-two—the bittersweet

One of the hardest things in life is having words in your heart that you can't utter. —James Earl Jones

With her knees drawn to her chest and arms wrapped around her legs, Roare perched on the window seat in her bedroom, where she had spent many nights reviewing scripts, decompressing, or contemplating.

What had her mother ever seen in Hunter? He had probably been handsome and charming until she saw through the façade. Nonetheless, when Roare had decided to forgive him, this freed her to progress spiritually for the sake of her soul. *Helping Hunter will be cathartic, release me from the bondage of abandonment, and grant me closure.*

She leaned her head against the window frame and replayed the many times she'd tried to destroy her life because of him. "I can't allow my past to dictate my future." Roare gave a short bob of her head, accepting the words.

There was something to be said for solace—a fresh perspective crept in. Roare's muscles relaxed, and her shoulders dropped as her confidence grew with her decision.

Meeting her biological father and half-brother created an opportunity. Maybe the connection she'd experienced with Reynalds during those few brief minutes had opened a door to building a friendship and getting to know her other siblings. Did she want further communication with Hunter? *No doubt a question I have no capacity to answer at the moment. But, God of heaven, can you walk alongside me? I need your strength.*

She retrieved her cell phone and called Reynalds.

Roare sat next to Sloane at the Qantas gate for their flight from JFK to Melbourne. "I'm glad you're going with me," she said. "These days, I've become suspicious of anyone I don't know."

"Just natural instincts. Wy was very generous to let me come with you."

"He was comfortable, after some persuading. He's wrapping up a critical work project, and I couldn't bring myself to ask him to leave. Mom didn't want to join me."

"And why should she? Why aggravate an old injury," Sloane said.

Roare took out her first-class boarding pass, granted as a medical emergency. "You're looking around a lot. What are you up to?"

"Scanning." Next, he stared hard past the wall of windows. "The plane checks out, although ..." He turned to his right, where a young couple across the way whispered to each other, and he cleared his throat. Their eyes darted away.

Wyatt would've liked how protective Sloane was.

"How credible is this cancer center we're going to?" he asked.

"Supposedly, one of the top twelve in the world—the Olivia Newton-John Cancer Center in Heidelberg. Hunter's in capable hands. My bone marrow extraction will be at Austin Hospital, two minutes away. I prayed over this."

"Good move. And I'm happy to be your advocate. It'll show your father you have a support force."

"You're right. I do hope the transplant cures his cancer. Here I am, but doing this for him is mystifying to me. You know what, though? There will be some positive outcomes," Roare said.

"I couldn't agree more. Your courage is commendable," Sloane said.

"You can believe that if you want, but truthfully, I'm not the one driving my heroic efforts—not under my own power anyway. God provided me with supernatural strength to meet my father and help him, and the guts to do this film."

They both chuckled. Without God's authority, neither of them could accomplish anything.

"Right now, I'm looking forward to kicking back, eating a decent meal, and having a rest on the flight," Sloane said.

Roare lowered her voice. "Or you could transport yourself to Melbourne without the use of a jetliner and meet me there."

"Shh. I prefer blending in. Pretend I'm normal."

After the procedure, a five-day rest in her hotel room revived Roare. With an explosion of vitality running through her veins, she could run a marathon. However, her lower back still hurt. Enough of the dramatics. She'd done her good deed. She'd carry on with the farewell lunch today and move on with her life.

At midday, Sloane and Roare left their luggage with the concierge and flagged a taxi to Cutler & Co., one of the finest restaurants in Melbourne. The plain, beige, two-story building with large windows revealed the bustle inside.

When they entered, a slender young woman with waist-length, wavy blonde hair walked toward them—must be Abigale. She returned Roare's wave.

Sloane's head swept slowly from left to right, his lower jaw slightly open—his scanning look. His subtle sapphire hue in his eyes meant he was processing information. Everything must've been clear, or he would've had her out of there immediately.

"Hello, I'm Abigale, Hunter's daughter. I love your films."

Roare paused, bewildered. "Pleasure to meet you. This is Sloane, a family friend."

Abigale gestured toward Hunter's table. "We're over this way."

They followed her to the middle of the room, where Hunter sat beside a lovely blonde woman in a half-circle booth. Beside them were Reynalds and a slightly younger man, which left two chairs open on the side of the table closest to Roare.

Being unfamiliar with Hunter's family made her uncomfortable, yet she'd deal with it. She'd soon be on a plane back to her life in New York and her future. Besides, she was ravenous.

When the three of them arrived at the table, Hunter and Reynalds stood.

"Glad to see you again," Hunter said to Roare.

"How're you holding up?" she asked.

"As of now, I'm doing okay."

"I knew you would."

Hunter glanced at Sloane. "I see you brought someone along."

"Oh, sorry. This is Sloane, a dear friend of the family."

"Welcome. I appreciate you traveling with her."

Sloane shook his hand. "A pleasure."

Reynalds gave her a huge smile. "So glad you're here."

She beamed back at him.

The younger man got out of his seat and shook her hand. "I'm Aaden. Doing this for a person you barely know gives you angel status and scores massive points with me."

Aaden and Sloane exchanged pleasantries.

He sure wasted no time. Roare winked. "I like you. You're a straight New Yorker in your heart."

"I guess you've figured out I'm Evie." Hunter's wife seemed friendly enough.

"Save the best for last, I always say." Roare accepted the chair Reynalds held out for her, and the others sat—the Barracloughs in the booth, she and Sloane in the chairs.

"Brilliant answer," Evie said. "I hope one day we'll have a real visit."

"You're way too kind." Evie was probably one of the primary reasons Hunter had come to see Roare. Mom would like her.

Hunter asked Roare, "How're you doing after your hospital visit?"

"Not too bad. I've gotten a lot of rest. I was finally well enough to venture out around Melbourne. Artsy with an edgy vibe."

Aaden concurred. "Spot-on. I'm a resident of Sydney but prefer Melbourne—suits my personality better."

"Apparently, the two of you are the only people in the family who have a fondness for Melbourne," Hunter said. "Aaden, you now have an ally."

I believe I have," Aaden said, then slipped Roare his business card. "Call me if you need anything."

Roare smiled. "Will do. Thanks."

"You seem like a creative," Roare said to Aaden, "direct, observant, and confident. And Melbourne is a city bursting at the seams with fertile imaginations. Just sayin'." He was so much like she used to be—rebellious and bold.

"I'm a techie and have carte blanche on my creative output. I hear you have an artistic flair. I must admit, I haven't seen any of your films, though."

Abigale seized the moment. "I have, and they're both different and fantastic."

"I'm grateful for your positive feedback," Roare said.

Sloane shook his head. "She's an accomplished director."

Heat rushed to Roare's face.

Hunter jumped in. "I'd love to see your work. You must be sought after and have a stockpile of new projects."

Roare glanced at Sloane.

"I saw that," Abigale said. "You are working on something new, aren't you?"

Roare should've known these questions would come up. "Well, I am but can't reveal anything yet. The subject matter is sensitive, and I'm in the middle of research and interviews."

Hunter said, "I can't blame you for protecting your information. I had no right to probe."

"Nice to know you're interested."

Evie picked up her menu. "We'd better order. You're probably anxious to return home."

"I'm enjoying myself, though. Lots of work ahead of me, and I do want to get home to my husband."

"Wyatt, yes?" Hunter asked.

"That's right."

"Reynalds and I were impressed by him. He's strong, classy, and protective of you. You deserve the best."

Roare's face heated again. "He's a special guy."

Evie reached over and squeezed her hand. "I'm pleased you have an abundance of love."

"This is the consequence of a praying mom," Roare said.

The group ordered a medley of dishes that left a table of empty plates and satisfied palates.

"I don't want to see any food for three days," Abigale said.

Aaden raised his eyebrows. "Don't be dramatic."

She pinched his arm.

"Ow! Mum, did you see what she did?"

"You brought this upon yourself." Evie set her napkin aside and addressed Roare. "Since we're in a food coma now, you two should head back to the hotel, so you won't miss your plane."

"Thanks kindly," Roare said. "The food was delicious."

Aaden excused himself from the table and headed out. While Hunter settled the bill, Evie, Reynalds, and Sloane headed toward the door. Abigale and Roare lingered.

"What are you studying at the university?" Roare asked.

"Can you believe archaeology? I took an elective class in documentaries, though." Abigale spoke animatedly. "When I make a discovery, I'm going to make a documentary." She seemed like a tender-hearted girl. And smart.

"Definitely a clever idea. Any plans for a specialty?"

"I'd love to lead digs to find ancient civilizations and biblical discoveries."

"Could be a phenomenal adventure. I can see how passionate you are."

"I suppose you feel the same when you make a film?"

Roare beamed. "Absolutely I do."

"You're really cool. Wish we had more time to talk. Maybe we'll meet again?" Abigale was unpretentious.

"We'll see."

Sloane held the door for Roare and Abigale as they joined the others outside.

"You two need a ride?" Hunter asked Roare and Sloane.

"I ordered a taxi," Sloane answered.

"Well then, we'll say goodbye here. Roare, we deeply appreciate you flying out to do this procedure and for your time," Hunter said.

Evie stepped up beside him. "I hope meeting us under these strange conditions wasn't an unpleasant experience. We were as surprised as you were by Hunter's ... situation. Things happen for a reason, don't they? We're indebted to you for your time. We wish you continued success and joy in your life. We'd like to stay in touch to update you on his progress if you wouldn't mind."

Roare blinked to ward off tears. "Please do. I'm thankful you all welcomed us. Yes, updates would be good." The taxi pulled up. "We'd better go."

"Have a safe flight," Hunter said. "Please let us know when you land in New York."

"Will do. I have Reynalds's number. Keep well." Roare didn't want to get too comfortable with them yet, especially not Hunter. Her history with him—or lack thereof—wouldn't allow her to trust him.

She walked away with no malice in her heart toward him. *Lord, I did what you called me to do. Now, return us home safely. We want to complete the course you've set us on.*

chapter twenty-three—divine intervention

Have I not commanded you? Be strong and of good
courage; do not be afraid, nor be dismayed, for the Lord
your God is with you wherever you go.
                                        —Joshua 1:9 (NKJV)

"Your meeting with Chips tomorrow will go well,"
Sloane told Roare over the phone.

"I hope you're right, but I'm nervous."

"Don't be. He's pretty laid back, not as temperamental
as he lets on. I've arranged a bodyguard to accompany you
the entire time and see you home."

"Can he be trusted?"

"He's capable. There's a board meeting I must attend,
otherwise I'd go myself. You should be fine. Stay alert."

At nine the next morning, Roare bundled up, shoved
her hands into her gloves, and grabbed her tote.

Her angst over meeting a film giant was enough, and
now she had to look after her safety with a stranger. *God,
send your guardian angels to protect me, and let there be no
incidents.*

A hairless, bulky man stood in the lobby, garbed in black. The tall, serious type. Maybe a good thing ... or not.

She strode up to him. "Hi, I'm Roare."

"Vance. I gather Sloane filled you in on the details?"

"Enough. Are you ready? Don't know how long my meeting will be."

"Not a problem."

"All right then, lead the way."

Vance glanced around frequently as they walked toward the subway station at Eighty-Sixth and Central Park West. At least he was observant.

The F train to Park Slope was due any minute.

"Rush hour," Vance said. "Lots of commuters on the platform. I'm right beside you."

"Okay."

Vance pushed his broad shoulders through the sea of people waiting for the train, and she followed him to the front of the crowd.

Roare eyed their surroundings, even though Vance stood close to her.

A few minutes later, the rumble of a train approached, the station filled with the sound of screeching wheels as the subway rolled in.

"Do you have the time?" a woman asked Vance. "I don't have my phone on me."

He glanced at his watch.

A hard shove hit Roare's back. Someone pulled her tote backward ... Vance? Too late. Her arm slipped past the strap as the shove propelled her into the air.

People yelled.

Roare thudded onto the steel tracks.

The lifeless face of the train bore down on her.

"No! Stop!" She covered her face. *Oh, God, I don't want to die.*

A man jumped off the platform as she squeezed her eyes shut. He rolled her underneath the platform.

People above gasped, while others screamed, "Somebody call 911!"

She cringed as the train screeched to a halt. *Still alive.* Her head throbbed. Everything was blurry.

"Roare? Roare!" Vance jumped down to the tracks. "Can you hear me?" He was beside her now.

She nodded weakly.

"Good." He turned to a tall young man next to him. "Let's lift her onto the platform." He touched Roare's elbow. "Squeeze my forearm if the pain is unbearable, and we'll wait until EMS arrives with a stretcher. Understand?"

She groaned.

"All right, on my count, you lift her legs. I've got the rest of her."

The man took hold under her calves. "Ready."

"One, two, three."

They gently moved her onto the platform. By then, the police had taken over, and EMS was on-site.

Roare shook profusely as she lay on her back. Tears ran down the sides of her face. "I saw them. One angel pushed me under the platform. The other halted the train. They were huge. Sparks flew off the brakes. Thank God he wasn't going any faster. They saved me." She cried harder, breathing heavily.

One of the paramedics flashed a penlight in her eyes. "Her pupils are dilated. She's in shock, signs of a recent concussion. Let's get her over to Presbyterian Hospital."

While she was strapped onto the stretcher, a policewoman interviewed Vance.

"I was with her," he said. "A woman distracted me, asked me for the time."

The officer pointed at the bright digital display that hung from the ceiling. "The time is right above you." She called to a couple of police officers. "Lewis, Ryan. Head over to the transit authority and have a look at the video of this."

Sloane glanced over his shoulder when the boardroom door inched open. As he conducted a meeting with TGIET financial backers, an administrative assistant came up behind him and whispered in his ear.

He rose from the table. "Excuse me, everyone. I have an emergency. Please continue without me." He went into his office and called Vance. "What happened?" he demanded.

"Roare's on the way to the hospital. Someone pushed her off the subway platform." He briefed Sloane on the details.

"Where are you now?"

"With her in the ambulance, on our way to Presbyterian Hospital on Seventieth. She has cuts and bruises, and she's pretty disturbed by the drama."

Sloane's eyes cast a bright blue haze on the desktop. He gritted his teeth as he attempted to stay calm. His voice dropped an octave. "As soon as you arrive at the hospital, and she's in the doctor's care, I want you to leave. You know my policy: Failure to protect the client is a failure to recognize the danger. No exceptions. Your contract is terminated immediately. I'm coming to the hospital. By the time I arrive, I don't want to see your face."

"I'm sorry, Mr. McInerny. I screwed up."

"If Roare had been killed, the outcome for you would've been a crime scene." Sloane hung up on him. The poor girl. He predicted Wyatt would grow volatile at the news.

rage against the machine

Sloane dialed a reliable contact who lived near the hospital. "Hey, Scout, have a minute?"

"For you, definitely," she replied. "What do you need?"

"Can you spot me for an hour and watch a client until I arrive? Her name is Roare Murdock-Galloway, and she's at Presbyterian Hospital."

"Gotcha. I'm leaving now."

Wyatt reached the hospital in forty minutes. Outside the curtain at the foot of Roare's bed in the ER stood a tall, muscular redhead dressed in navy blue.

"Hi," she said. "You are?"

"I should ask who *you* are," Wyatt said. "I'm her husband. Are you security?"

"Yes. Can I see your identification?"

Wyatt huffed, then pulled out his wallet.

The woman returned his driver's license after having a good look. "I'm Scout. I'll be here until Sloane arrives."

"I need to visit with my wife."

"Go right ahead."

Wyatt pulled back the curtain and entered Roare's ER bay.

Barely coherent, she squeezed his forearm. He held her hand while she lay in bed, attached to an IV and heart monitor. The blankets were pulled back a little, which exposed black-and-blue discoloration on her right thigh. He ran his fingers across the bandages over her right shoulder and hand.

"I'm torn up, Gobo, seeing you injured," he said. "How could this happen *again*? Sloane's supposed to be your bodyguard, not anyone else. Ro, this project isn't worth losing your life for. You need to give this a pass, and I'm going to push hard on this. What you've taken on is madness."

She shook her head. "I can't. There's a great deal at risk."

"Since when have you stopped valuing your life? And what about us?"

"I'm going to be okay."

"I'm not sure. Look at you, Gobo!"

"I look jacked up, I know."

"You've been knocked around enough. Your face not being shattered is a miracle."

"I need to share something with you later. Right now, I want to rest. I'm scared, Wy. Please don't leave me."

"We'll talk more tomorrow, babe."

Later, heavy footsteps approached. Wyatt glanced toward the curtain. When Sloane appeared at the foot of Roare's bed, he glared. "Where in blazes were you?"

Sloane ignored his question. "How is she? Is she asleep?"

"How do you expect her to be? The doctors assured me she has no broken bones, fortunately. She's on sedatives and pain meds. They're going to keep her for a couple of nights. I've been with her the entire time." Wyatt's face turned red. He tightened and opened his fists repeatedly to release his tension.

Roare held his hand. "I'll be okay." She sounded dazed. "Chips. He doesn't know. I was going to meet him."

Sloane said, "Don't concern yourself with that. I'll call him."

"Tell him I'm sorry. In a few days, maybe we can do a Zoom."

Wyatt patted her arm. "You have nothing to be sorry for."

"Chips is the last person who should be on your mind," Sloane said. "He's not going anywhere."

Roare's grip loosened on Wyatt's hand. He turned to Sloane. "We need to talk."

"I guess you met Scout."

"Yeah. At least she's here, doing *your* job. She seems competent, but I question whether you are."

"I understand you being upset. Scout will leave after the testing is done. Once Roare gets to her private room, I'm going to be on guard all night."

"Finally."

Wyatt sat on a padded chair in the small empty chapel near the hospital lobby. In the quiet, beneath subdued lighting, he took a few moments to calm himself. To his right, Sloane sat silently with lowered head, his hands folded in his lap.

"Your track record isn't looking great," Wyatt said. "My wife now has had two attempts on her life. We both knew the risks involved in this project. Should've been your cue to take the reins to protect her. You. Not someone she didn't know. I find myself questioning whether you're protecting her or warring against her. You're spearheading this film, and Roare is on the frontline. Step up security with direct involvement, or your movie won't happen." He kept a steady gaze on Sloane.

The bodyguard pursed his lips, stared at Wyatt, and took a deep breath. "What happened was unforgivable. The direction of collateral damage has to change now. I also need to warn you they might come after family members. These people are treacherous. Things can get rough. Therefore, this movie *must* be made. Controversial documentaries have their dangers. Roare knew this."

"We take chances every time we step outside," said Wyatt. "I'm asking you to keep my wife alive."

"I intend to, Wyatt. We take a gamble inside our homes too. But we must rely on our faith to get through these troubling times. I'd like to have her confidence restored, and yours."

"I'm a man of faith, but give me some hard evidence to go on. I'm counting on you to keep our families safe. I'm pleading, for her sake and theirs."

"I won't disappoint you," Sloane said. "I'll beef up security. And, as an apology, I'd like to provide you with a full security system to be installed in your home, on me."

"I appreciate your generosity, but that won't do. The ultimate focus here is to not fail Roare."

"I won't. When Roare heals, I need to run something by both of you. The gloves are off. We have to lure out these maggots and confront them on our terrain."

"I'll have to tell her our families may be in danger. This could influence her decision about continuing the movie."

"I'll take the risk."

Alone in the chapel later, Sloane rang Chips's cell phone.

"Hey, man," his friend said. "The prodigy was a no-show."

"Sorry, bro, not her fault. She was pushed in front of a train. I should've been there."

"Good grief! Is she okay? I know you assigned her a bodyguard, what's the story?"

"He dropped the ball, a complete dereliction of duty."

"Some of these projects can be volatile. Safety affords no errors."

"Roare has a few cuts, bruises, and a concussion. Her nerves are on edge. She was thinking of *you*, wanted to set up an online meeting with you in a few days."

"Bless her soul. What do you want to do?"

"Give her a few days to recoup. Whenever you do work together, I want you to stay close to her. And she's gonna need additional protection."

"Protecting your assets?"

"Exceedingly more than you know."

From the chair beside Roare's hospital bed, Wyatt cupped her hand in his and bowed his head. *Lord, heal each wound, all her bruises, and more importantly, her heart so fear can no longer reside in her.*

A few moments later, she covered her mouth and yawned.

He smiled at her. "Hi, Gobo."

"Hi, yourself. Was I sleeping long?"

"No, not long. You're in and out."

"Oh, honey. I'm sorry I'm putting you through this. I know I took a bad fall, but how come I don't feel anything?" Her voice rose in pitch. "I'm not paralyzed, am I?"

"No, you're not. Don't even utter those words," Wyatt stroked her right thigh.

She smiled faintly.

"I'm grateful you're not in pain. The morphine won't last forever."

"Morphine?"

"Go easy on yourself, babe. Those subway tracks weren't made of rubber."

"I suppose not." She lightly fingered the bruises on her thighs and arms and winced. "Wy, I don't want to do this film anymore. I'm not sure if I'll live through the project."

"You're emotionally wrung out right now. Wait a couple of days until you've healed a bit. You were knocked around, and had the wits scared out of you. The fact you're still with us says a lot."

Roare looked tenderly into Wyatt's eyes. "I wasn't alone. They saved me. One slowed the train. The other pushed me under the platform."

"Who did?"

"I wouldn't be here without them." Her voice was barely audible. "The angels were huge."

He couldn't believe what he was hearing. "What? You mean you saw them? You sure the meds they gave you aren't making you imagine things?"

"They were as real as you are. God sent them to me. They saved my life. They exist, Wy. They're with us, even now."

"How do you know?"

"I sense them nearby. I can't see them but somehow, I know."

Wyatt stroked her hair out of her face. "Gobo, I believe you. Seeing those angelic beings must've been an indescribable experience. All those testimonies we've heard—they're all true. God spared you and the project." He took her hand again. "I have to warn you, Sloane says our loved ones might be vulnerable too. Do you think you're prepared to continue despite the threats?"

"I can't give you an answer right now. I'd choose to die instead of having any of our family harmed, but what is the point of living if we accept a dictatorial depopulation plot?"

"You've decided, then?"

"Not yet. I need to think this through—he's the one who put me up to this."

"And he'll get you through this. Put your trust in him, not people. The Lord has his reasons for putting you on this path."

rage against the machine

"He's right," Sloane said, entering the room. "Don't give fear energy. This is precisely what these terrorists want."

"Plus reducing me to seven cat lives. I may not be fortunate the next time. Vance was useless."

"You won't be seeing him ever again. Chips will schedule another meeting with you after you've recovered. Get your rest. Everything else can wait. We'll handle the interviews meanwhile. When you're better, I need to run something by both of you."

"Okay." Roare's eyes were barely open now. "I need to sleep."

"By all means rest," Sloane said.

"Wait. Is anyone staying with me?"

Wyatt said, "I'll be here overnight."

Sloane butted in. "A heroic idea, however, not necessary. You don't want to burn out. Why don't you stay here until visiting hours are over. I'll take the night shift. I'll be able to sense danger, and I'm in a foul mood. Anyone flinches wrong, I'll be on 'em like a Doberman."

"No use having both of us here," said Wyatt.

"The transit authority caught the man who pushed her. And he's been arrested—a petty drug hustler paid well by someone who made sure he couldn't be traced."

"These hitmen seem to have the upper hand," Wyatt said.

"I'll be outside her door while she sleeps and inside when they're giving her meds."

Wyatt remained silent for a minute, then asked Roare, "Are you okay with this?"

"As long as one of you is here," she said.

Wyatt looked at Sloane. "Thanks."

Sloane reaffirmed. "She'll be safe. I'll tell Scout she can go now."

219

As Roare drifted off to sleep, the remaining tension left Wyatt's body. He turned on the television—local news. The second story was a one-minute blip of a woman who was pushed onto the subway tracks at Eighty-Sixth Street. He snatched the remote off the table and turned off the TV.

Healing had its moments. Roare's wounds itched, and the bruises had faded through a vivid range of colors. A couple of weeks planted at home were nice—soon, she'd want to bust out of there.

Sloane had greatly fortified security. He'd worked around his schedule and Wyatt's to install a security system—must've cost him a small fortune. The coverage ranged from intruder sensors and hidden cameras to internet security.

Roare leaned her head back against her office chair and propped her feet on the ottoman. Her friend Drue phoned. Wyatt had notified her about the attack.

"But I'm miffed," Drue said, "because you never called me yourself. Why?"

"You're obviously pregnant. I didn't want you worrying about me. I'm still alive, and I'm grateful."

"Ha! Barely! I could've gone with you to your appointments. Who's going to mess with a pregnant woman?"

"You don't know how corrupt people are these days, do you?"

"Judging by what's happened to you, I can only imagine. I'm sorry I've been neglecting you. I've been too focused on the baby, and he or she isn't even here yet."

"Drue, don't apologize. You're bringing a new life into this world. I'll be all right. I've got Wyatt and my bodyguard looking after me."

"Your bodyguard is questionable."

"He can't be with me all the time. Besides, Mom recommended him. And he's intricately involved in my life right now. Wyatt has sorted him out. No matter what, keep me in your thoughts."

"Not necessary to mention. Next time Wyatt calls me, he better not tell me you're dead."

"Despite how grim things look, I'll be fine. It's all part of the role I'm playing."

"Which is?" Drue asked.

"Film director and superhero?"

"Look, I'll settle for my friend remaining above ground, not six feet below."

"I love you too," Roare said. They agreed to have another call soon, and Roare thought lovingly about her friend.

Right away, Roare switched hats and logged in to the Zoom session Chips Jaeger had set up. She tweaked her camera to make certain her image was clear and brushed the hair from her face.

The soft, dark-brown eyes beneath Chips's arched eyebrows were as stunning as in his numerous TV interviews. His mostly silver hair was short on the sides, long on top, and paired well with the salt-and-pepper beard shaped by his distinctive square jaw.

"Mr. Jaeger, such a pleasure to finally meet you," she said.

"No, I'm honored. Please, call me Chips. No formalities here."

"Great. I see you're wearing your trademark blue specs."

The man was a lot older than her and barely had any wrinkles. He had a genuine, friendly smile too. "I'll take all the compliments I can get. Hey, you're one tough lady. Most people would give up. Are you up to this meeting?"

She rubbed her leg. "I'm still sore, but I'll manage. At one point, I did want to give up, but God persuaded me otherwise."

"Excellent. Listen, Sloane's got security covered. I'll look after you too. I can be a bad papa bear."

"What a relief to hear."

"We have lots to talk over." He held up a flash drive. "Sloane scored an interview with another whistleblower. But the footage isn't the greatest."

"Yeah, I noticed. We still have enough to salvage though."

"I concur."

They were like-minded thus far—a positive sign.

Roare checked her watch—1:15. Sloane had better pick her up soon before she changed her mind about meeting Chips at his studio. Besides the two visits to hers and Wyatt's parents, she hadn't left the house in the month since her accident.

She paced between the kitchen and living room, her mind and heart racing. Flashbacks of being pushed off the platform still haunted her. *Lord, I'm trying to move past this, but on my own, I can't. Can you lend me a hand? Should I be doing this at all with my life on the line? Why don't you answer me?*

Be still. The reply was nearly audible.

She stopped midstride.

You don't have to pretend with me. You love getting to the truth despite the risks involved. You tell the stories of those who are forced into silence. I am he who gives you the courage to pursue this.

"You?"

rage against the machine

From the moment you were born, I have shaped you for such an occasion. I cherish you. I'll shield you from those who stalk you. Do you trust me?

Roare muttered, "Yes."

A powerful fragrance of frankincense and myrrh filled the room as if someone had walked by with incense. Abundant peace saturated her spirit like a security blanket wrapped around a newborn. She felt safe. Completely safe. *How could I have doubted him?*

"Forgive me, God. My unbelief caused doubt. You always show up when I need you most."

She took a deep breath of the woodsy, spicy scent and rested in the hands of her Father.

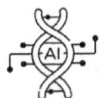

A muscular man of medium height opened the steel door to the film studio—a spacious, multilevel brick warehouse in Brooklyn, where Chips and his staff worked.

"Happy to see you again," the man said to Sloane. "He's in the usual spot." He led them to a corner sectioned off by white brick columns—kitchenette, seating, and adjoining office. There sat Chips Jaeger.

He came around the desk. Roare didn't expect him to be as tall as he was. And he looked sturdy.

She stepped forward. "To meet you in person is a treat to me. Seems like I've known you a long time."

"You have since our video meetings, and you're more stunning in person."

Roare felt her face warm up. "I'm blushing."

"No need, I'm telling the truth."

Chips gripped Sloane's shoulder. "This guy loves to make himself at home here. This is a second home for my buddy, and this is yours too. Guess what? We're going to make an incredible film together. Let's get to work."

Sloane entered the office area, clutching a coffee mug. These creatives were amazing. By 9:20 p.m., Roare and Chips had made tremendous progress.

Chips rubbed his eyes. "Great idea to shoot the opening in Canada."

"I like authenticity—the environment and the cold?" Roare said.

"I'll text my contact in Alberta tomorrow who's scouting a location," Chips said. "Once we've secured a spot, I'll handle the travel arrangements. You've done a good job today. How're you feeling?"

"Excited and exhausted."

Sloane eyed two copies of the documentary script on the table. Notepads had blue scribbles and whole lines crossed out. "I can see you're in your element here," he said to Roare.

"I believe I am, for now," she said.

"Well, we'd better move out. I want you home before midnight."

"Or I'll turn into a pumpkin?"

"There's always a possibility."

When Sloane brought Roare home, he asked for a few minutes with her and Wyatt. They sat in the living room.

Sloane propped his forearms on his thighs and clasped his hands together. "I ask you to trust me once more—I must tell you there will be an increased level of risk ahead."

Roare closed her eyes for a second, as if praying. "What's on your mind?"

"To be blunt, we need to bring this fight with our enemy to *our* territory. Match has been taking jabs at us. High time we make an advance on him," Sloane said.

Wyatt stood and scratched at his beard. "I think you're expecting too much from us. We have no experience in combat."

Roare waved her hand. "Wait, Wy. Hear him out first."

"Thanks. I see an opportunity here," Sloane said. "I did some research on Match. One thing he loves is attending charitable events. He uses philanthropy as a front, so the public will view him as a humanitarian. His constituents praise him for his 'good deeds.' If we send him a personal invitation to an event—say an elegant auction that you'll organize, Roare—I'm certain he'll make a special appearance."

"Then what, we tell him we're on to him about his depopulation plans, and how he'll use borgs to finish off the human race? Our guests won't buy it," Roare said.

"Nearly. Roare you'll threaten to expose him to the public to tarnish his image as a hero. If he pushes back, and I'm banking on him to resist, then you'll tell him you'll broadcast the whistleblower interview of Dr. Ponte and what really happened to him, and how he's tried to have you killed."

"And what if this all backfires?" Wyatt demanded. "You know he's not going to come alone. He'll have his killer borgs with him to take out everyone at the event. What then?"

"Nah, won't happen. Someone could easily livestream him going on a killing spree, and any insane action on his part will leave CoSynthesis vulnerable. His benefactors wouldn't go near him with a hot poker. It'll destroy him."

"But, Sloane," Roare started cautiously, "if he has nothing to lose, what would stop him from activating Armageddon on us?"

Wyatt snapped at Sloane, "She makes a valid point."

"I know this man. He'll bail out of an embarrassing situation to avoid any blemish on his character. He'll retreat, then prep for a more severe attack against us. From a distance, he has the upper hand. When we have him close to us, we have the advantage."

"I see why he doesn't want this film made," Wyatt said.

"Precisely."

"Do you think we can pull this off without getting murdered?" Roare asked. "Apparently, I'm the bait."

"I don't want to guarantee anything, but I'm pretty sure he won't be able to do much. I'll have my special security team there."

"You mean Scout?" Wyatt asked.

"Yes, and a few others like her, whom I trust implicitly with my own life. I've also shared my plan with Chips, and he offered to bring his security team as well. They're loyal to him. I only need to give the word, and he's on board. You see, he has a protected interest too."

"Sloane, would you be able to organize the gala event? My assistant can help you. I can send an invite to Match," Roare said.

Wyatt clenched his jaw. "So, you're going along with this plot? Shouldn't we be making this decision together?"

"This man is after me and TGIET."

"Yeah, and what affects you, impacts me as well. You're not the only one involved in this."

"You're right, Wy, but this is about every human being on this planet, not just us. Ask yourself, given the prospect of a fatal outcome for humanity, knowing what we know, do you want to sit on the sidelines and watch the dismantling of civilization?"

"Ro, you know better. I'm a man of action, but I'm not ready to die."

"None of us are," Sloane said. "But if we don't respond to this madman's attacks, we give him power over our lives."

Wyatt tilted his head back. Defeated. He looked at them. "I better fish my tux out of storage."

chapter twenty-four—the invitation

Will this journey of mine ultimately take me to a pinnacle or a pit?—Craig D. Lounsbrough

Match began his December Monday morning staring down at a four-by-six box, wrapped in black paper and pink ribbon. Was this a joke? CoSynthesis didn't recognize holidays. *Unlikely a bomb, my security team would've never placed this on my desk, otherwise. A gift from her.*

Without further contemplation, he opened the box. An invitation to attend a fundraising gala to support children rescued from human trafficking. His AI sight allowed him to see her fingerprints. *How did she find me? Who told her about me? Something for security to handle. But how can I refuse? I'll RSVP right away.* Then, Match noticed the other items in the box. *Hmm, Teuscher dark champagne chocolate bonbons from Switzerland. Is this her way of waving the white flag? One way to find out.*

Roare fidgeted in her form-fitting, strapless, black gown. The split on one side would allow her to run or kick someone. She worked the crowd with her head held high.

Attendees marveled over the grandeur of the Rainbow Room at Rockefeller Plaza. Roare could feel the buzz of excitement and chatter of patrons mingling with one another. Through her muso contacts, jazz musicians had volunteered to play.

From across the room, Roare caught sight of Sloane near the door. He was turning his head from left to right as guests came through the door—security scans. She and Sloane had agreed on 140 guests, excluding caterers, servers, and the auctioneer. He had even organized forty security personnel to blend in as guests in the required black-tie attire. A clever strategy on his part, but she couldn't help but hold her breath each time someone walked through the door, anticipating the archenemy's arrival.

She focused on remembering Match's features, knowing she'd spot him easily. She had peace about her safety as Wyatt and Chips stayed close to her, and Sloane lagged only a few feet behind for vantage positioning. The four of them communicated through wireless earpieces.

After patrons settled into their seats, Roare stood on a platform in a corner of the spacious ballroom. The lights dimmed, and the spotlight shone on her. Wyatt, Chips, and Sloane stood three feet behind in the shadows, but close enough. Four other defense personnel stood at both sides of the platform. She introduced two CEOs of children's rescue organizations, along with some retired military veterans who volunteered their time in recovery operations. Each special guest gave overviews of their humanitarian efforts and the reasons behind their passions. Everyone stood and applauded, some cheering and even whistling.

When Roare presented the auctioneer, the lights turned on. Auction items ranged from a staycation package, to valuable artwork, to an all-expenses-paid cruise to

Antarctica. She didn't have to guess who'd submitted that one.

And there was Match, in the middle of the room, two other guests flanking him.

He's here. Don't panic. She peered at Wyatt, then Sloane. *Do something! Just don't stand there flustered, he'll sense it.* She took a quick breath and exhaled. She looked directly at him and nodded.

He returned the gesture.

Roare, Chips, and Wyatt stepped down from the platform and took their seats with the honored guests. She watched Sloane step away to speak to his security team, alerting them of Match's arrival. While wait staff distributed trays of desserts to each table, the auctioneer initiated the bidding.

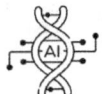

When the auction ended, the jazz band played subdued melodies. Roare took the stage and thanked everyone for their generous contributions and invited patrons to enjoy the music and the rest of the evening.

Be done with this already. This is no time to be a coward. Roare whispered to the others, "I'm going to start the dance. Cover me."

Sloane said, "Copy that."

As she made her way toward Match, she prayed others would dance too. She didn't want to be the only one on the floor, especially with him.

She had been waiting all evening for this moment. As she drifted toward him, Roare could feel Match's piercing glare on her. *Stay calm.*

Roare sensed all eyes were on her. She stopped in front of him and held out her hand. "I'd like to have the first dance with you."

Match stood and buttoned his dinner jacket, then nodded and smiled. "I'd be more than honored." He took her hand and led her to the dance floor.

He was warm and pleasant to look at, but she could feel her anger slowly rising. *Keep your head cool.* "Mr. Matchithew Tekeda, meeting you is unprecedented. Thank you for accepting my invitation."

"Please call me Match. I was pleasantly surprised but would've traveled around the world to meet you. You have a brilliant way of commanding my attention."

Roare was relieved to see the dance floor fill up. She searched for Wyatt, Sloane, and Chips. *Ah, I see them, they're all nearby, chill out.* "In what way?"

"You caught me off guard. Your invite found its way to Antarctica—and those delicious chocolates. How did you know?"

Roare smirked. "I have my ways. Nothing about the chocolates is a secret. You were gifted those often through your philanthropic work. You didn't come all this way to talk about chocolates, did you?"

Match pulled her closer to him. "You know I didn't. Tell me, was your invitation a form of surrender, signaling the end of your film project?" He spun her as the music intensified.

When he pulled her closer, her concern grew. She peered over his shoulder.

Then, she heard Wyatt's voice in her earpiece, "Ro, we got you. Keep him engaged. We're recording him."

"If I had any good sense, I would," she said to Match. "After all, you made two attempts on my life. You must be protecting something vital to your life's work."

Match glared, his tone sharp. "My existence. You have no idea what you're stepping into or who's involved to improve the continuation of humanity."

rage against the machine

"Don't you mean to diminish the advancements of humankind?"

"You sound like a conspiracy theorist. Don't you have a reputation to protect?"

"We all do, for different reasons. The thing is, Match, I can expose your laboratories and shut you down." Roare's anger rose. Her mouth twisted on one side. "You despise humans, don't you? Why else would you build an army of AI borgs to wipe us out?"

Sloane and Wyatt drew closer.

"You don't understand, Ms. Murdock. What I'm doing goes way beyond what mankind has achieved. I don't despise humans—I pity them. We had our time here on Earth, accomplishing very little. We never seem to learn from our past, we keep repeating our bad history. Humanity hasn't evolved. We still kill each other over drugs, land, things, infidelity, war, and blackmail, to name a few. We're antiquated creatures—"

"You're no better. You've tried to kill me, and you've already taken out one whistleblower. How many more need to die?"

"I won't tolerate you standing in my way. Nothing personal—this is about the future. My partners won't appreciate any interference. Your film won't happen."

"Are you threatening me?" Roare raised her voice.

A few onlookers stared at them.

Match tightened his grip around her wrist, pulled her in closer. "Yes, I am. I can finish you instantly, and everyone in this room." He clenched his teeth.

"Go ahead. But, if you don't let go of me, I'll broadcast the dead whistleblower's interview across all social media platforms. The entire world will know within minutes."

"We'll finish each other together, then."

Roare drove her stiletto heel into his right leather shoe. She kept the pressure on, driving the point of her heel further into his foot. He flinched. But when Roare yanked her wrist from his grip, he managed to transfer something slightly wet onto her wrist. Roare rubbed her wrist and felt a burning sensation.

From the corner of her eye, she saw Wyatt rush over. He pushed her away from Match and whisked her to a table in a corner of the ballroom. Her husband's face was red with rage. He snapped his head around to eyeball Match. Gratefully, Chips stayed with her while Wyatt confronted Match.

But before Wyatt could reach him, Match smirked and stalked her way.

Sloane jumped in front of Match.

"You," Match snarled.

Sloane's laser blue eyes glowed. He didn't want to cause a scene.

Match met his gaze with his own blue eyes.

"I never suspected you'd forget me," Sloane said.

Match's two borgs sidled up beside him, while Scout and other members of Sloane's security personnel stood behind Match's borgs.

"Is everything okay?" Scout asked.

Two more of Sloane's bodyguards rushed over and stood behind him.

A few patrons whispered among themselves.

Wyatt rushed to Match and grabbed him by his collar. He growled, "What have you done to my wife? Her wrist is inflamed!"

"You'll soon find out." Match grunted.

Wyatt balled up his left fist, but Sloane shook his head.

Sloane told Wyatt, "Go look after your wife. She needs you."

Match and Sloane faced each other toe-to-toe. Sloane believed Match was reading his mind. Then Sloane said, "Whatever you did to her will be done to you. If she dies, you die."

"You're driving this film project, aren't you?" Match asked.

"You can say I have a personal interest in the film and in you," Sloane said.

"I left a lasting impression on you. How unfortunate you didn't use your energy and capabilities wisely." Match folded his hands in front of him and widened his stance.

"Neither have you." Sloane sneered. "Judging by your grim achievements."

Match looked around the room.

"This isn't the kind of publicity you need at this moment," Sloane said.

"I'll fix this and deal with you later." Match gave an icy smile, and patted Sloane's shoulder.

Sloane didn't react.

Match stepped past Sloane and onto the platform where Roare had stood earlier. He projected a professional speaking voice to the audience. "Ladies and gentlemen, if you'll allow me to have a few moments of your time, I have an important announcement."

Everyone fell silent, even the musicians.

Sloane gritted his teeth. *I know what he's about to pull— to dig himself out of the embarrassing scene.*

Match continued, "I apologize for the disruption of this evening's festivities. None of us meant to cause a scene and draw attention to ourselves, so please forgive us, we aren't normally this rude. As a form of vindicating ourselves, I will donate one hundred thousand dollars to each of the child rescue organizations. I hope this gift will assist you in furthering these important causes that we're all passionate about. Thank you for your time, and I wish you a goodnight."

As he walked off the platform, the two CEOs shook his hand, and thanked him while others clapped.

Sloane kept his eyes on Match's every movement from a short distance. *His arrogance is nauseating.* His gaze shifted to Roare as she winced in pain. *God, what did this madman do to Roare? You can't let her die. I could strangle him right where he stands.*

Sloane eyeballed Match in disgust, then saw Roare's frantic expression toward him, Wyatt, and Chips, terror gripping her face as if she'd had seen a monster. She had.

Match headed out the door, his minions following.

Sloane decided to catch up to Match and walked in front of him, security officers flanking him and two more behind Match's companions. He faced his adversary. "You put on a great show. When we meet again, neutral territory would be better, so we won't tear up our towns."

"Acknowledged. Can't wait to see you again."

"Meanwhile, you should take care of your foot."

When Match returned to his hotel room, he removed the shoe damaged by Roare's heel like a dagger. She had punctured the top of his foot. Swollen, bloody, and red. *Nothing I can't repair. However, I'm certain I injured her more.* His eyes gleamed wildly with satisfaction.

He retrieved a smooth, silver, oval-shaped disk from his overnight bag and waved the gadget across his foot.

A yellow light illuminated underneath it. Within a few seconds, the wound healed, and the redness disappeared completely. The blood evaporated.

Wyatt wasted no time taking Roare to the toxicology wing at NYU hospital. His experience in pathology told him the redness spreading across her hand and up her arm was poison. Then, when her symptoms intensified and the doctors suggested merely food poisoning, Wyatt fumed.

After a swift reprimand and acknowledgement of his credentials, the doctors finally ran more extensive tests. They administered medicine to calm Roare's stomach and hooked her up to an IV drip with electrolytes.

She gazed at Wyatt while he held her hand. "Did Sloane take him out?"

"No, not yet. Sloane didn't want to cause a scene but did escort him out of the building. I don't know what happened after. Try to remember what you did tonight. You faced the enemy and showed him you're not a pushover. He tried to intimidate you, but he didn't kill you."

"I can't wait until this is all over."

He squeezed her hand. "Don't fret, Gobo. God won't let you down."

She took a few deep breaths.

Wyatt remained by Roare's side until all the testing was done.

Four hours later, two doctors had the results. The drug was a high dosage of Amatoxin, and the hydrogel was used as a weapon to release the poison into her bloodstream quickly.

Wyatt asked, "What stage did the poison reach?"

One doctor said, "Stage two. You were smart to bring her in immediately. We have her on a high dose of penicillin, and a gram of activated charcoal every two hours. To help the meds work faster, we gave her something for sleep."

"Dr. Galloway," began the second doctor, "we're going to have to inform the police. We believe this was attempted murder. She's going to be okay, though."

Wyatt was taken aback. "Thank you, doctors. I'll provide you with any information the police will need." He rubbed his forehead. "How long before all of the poison is removed?"

"A few more hours. The good thing is that you got her to us early. We found no liver, kidney, or heart damage."

Praise God. Wyatt felt the stress release from his body. He looked at Roare—she was fast asleep. He found a quiet spot in the hallway and called Sloane.

"You've been in there a long time. What's happening?" he asked.

Wyatt briefed him on her progress and what the doctors had found.

"Thank goodness, Wyatt. But let me tell you, your wife was a champion tonight. She didn't back down from his threats. Therefore, more importantly, she remains strong— we all must—to get through this."

"Yeah, but at what cost?"

"We're doing our best to minimize the cost. We had a small victory tonight, despite our *challenges*," Sloane said. "That stunt Match pulled raised a few eyebrows, despite his efforts to smooth things over with his donations. The thick layer of armor he hides behind is starting to crack. One, we have his conversation with Roare recorded, and two, what he did to her is attempted murder."

"Sure, if he doesn't find a loophole to get himself off the hook. He's a nasty piece of work, and this situation has come down to us versus him. Even if Roare stops filming, she knows too much and can still harm his agenda." Wyatt scratched at his light beard.

"We all know too much. We're all targets. He'll become desperate and careless. The moment is not far off before he'll take this fight too far and will regret it."

"I hope time will work in our favor. Sloane, I wish to God you had never approached my wife. If not for your film, and your desire for retribution, we wouldn't be in this dilemma."

"Wyatt, this isn't about me, this concerns the extinction of our species. God won't allow this horrific event to take place. I'm doing this because I am a foot soldier of the Lord. So is Roare. We were chosen for this."

Wyatt sighed. "Then I need to take up my grievances with God."

"Or join the fight."

"I'm up to my neck in this, not by choice. I better get back to her."

"I'm not going anywhere. Not until Roare is released. I need to do a security sweep of the area, in case Match's assassins are still around, and prepare for his next move."

Wyatt shook his head. This was really happening.

chapter twenty-five—rage against the machine

Never give up, and be confident in what you do. There may be tough times, but the difficulties which you face will make you more determined to achieve your objectives and to win against all the odds.
—Marta Vieira da Silva, Brazilian athlete

Roare refused to allow her disgust for Match to deter her efforts, and instead focused her awareness on who she was in Christ. She would push forward with the film.

She insisted on using as many unknown actors as possible to create authenticity. By mid-February, Jules Proust Casting had carefully selected actors, stunt personnel, and extras to support the film.

They prepped for filming at Athabasca Falls in Canada's Jasper National Park. The falls powered down a gorge, both sides made of quartzite and limestone layers like pancaked rock formations. The dark edges contrasted sharply with the frothy, aqua-and-green glacial water. Tons of water converged from banks and cliffs that cascaded with dramatic cinematography effects. Mountain peaks towered above pristine blue lakes.

Finally touring the falls in person, Roare took her umpteenth picture. She placed a hand on Wyatt's arm. "Wy, we have to come back."

"I know. The power of water is terrifying and captivating at the same time."

The cliffs and ledges were too slippery for humans to trek. During the first portion of the film, drone specialists would capture the footage of the stunning scenery, as well as the interior of an underground cavern.

"Wish I could stay to explore instead of heading back tomorrow," Wyatt said. "You'll concentrate better without me anyway."

"Given the insane schedule, I don't even know when I'll sleep."

Chips approached. "All right, you two can sightsee later. Roare, take hold of this location with all your senses. Then we'll head to the house for the first scene." He glanced at Wyatt. "Sloane will stay with her, and his guys will be with the rest of us. Safety first."

She kissed Wyatt. "We'll connect with you later."

"Stay close to Sloane," he said.

She loved this man.

Filming began at midnight at a residential hillside home—on loan for the film—in Calgary, Alberta. For the opening scene, two actors would portray the highly acclaimed scientists-turned-whistleblowers. The husband-and-wife team would sleep upstairs in the master bedroom. On the nightstand, a baby video monitor would display their twin boys, asleep in their cribs.

The owner of CoSynthesis had found their children to have brilliant genetics, beauty, and intuitive characteristics, and desired to use their DNA as a blueprint to further AI science. The parents refused. CoSynthesis took the children anyway. Thus, the scientists became whistleblowers.

The scene began. Roare hid herself in a corner of the kids' room to film the kidnapping.

Chips managed the camera drone outside. He and one of his experts watched from a van at a distance, and Chips navigated the drone slowly over the grounds of the estate, then to the front door. Once past the front door, a smaller drone floated and panned through the foyer, then up the curved staircase. The drone floated down the corridor and reached the master bedroom, where the parents slept. Chips zoomed in to observe the couple sleeping soundly, then panned out of the bedroom. The drone entered the children's bedroom and approached the cribs.

Roare began filming:

Moonlight beamed through the children's window, and light streaked across the torsos of humanlike trespassers. Otherworldly cuneiform symbols produced a faint, orange glow under their translucent, graphite-gray bodysuits.

The cyborgs were seven feet tall, muscular, and hairless. Their almond-shaped eyes cast a faint fluorescent orange gaze at the children. Each passed a hand over a twin's face. The beings locked eyes with one another, then snatched the babies like vultures. The captors held the sleeping children to their chests and hurried toward the exterior wall without a sound.

The parents remained asleep down the hall.

"Cut!" Roare said from her corner. She set aside her camera. With small cameras and biometric screens strategically placed throughout the home, the opening scene needed only one take. The CGI team would add the details of the intruders passing through the wall with the children and teleporting to an underground facility behind Athabasca Falls.

Roare rubbed her arms, glad she'd cranked up the heat. She leaned back against the wall. The kidnapping details she'd learned during the interview with Fleming and Astrid Kovac played vividly in her mind:

The intruders had disabled the home's alarms and motion sensors, and then telepathically wiped out the data on the baby monitor. Through quantum photonics—aiming a massive amount of charged electrons on their outer "skin" at a solid mass, such as a wall—the cyborgs resumed their forms outside the house. The babies had passed through with them, each encased in a translucent pod on the cyborgs' chests.

The film would use CGI to capture such activity.

"Hit the lights." Roare packed her equipment and stepped outside as the pale pink of dawn kissed the horizon. She yawned relentlessly on her way to the food trailer, her breath smoking in the frigid air. Crew members stomped and stretched beside the refreshment table, as others consumed coffee and donuts under heat lamps.

Chips stepped forward. "Listen up, everyone. Be on-site and on time to shoot the next scene at noon, at the cavern opening to the right of the falls. Grab sleep while you can."

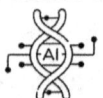

Water thundered down the turbulent river. Park rangers and emergency medical teams stood by as a precaution. People huddled together like smokestacks, exhaling warm breath into the frigid air. A welcome distraction from being terrified. Roare shuddered. With one wrong move, any of them could be swept away by the current. *Heavenly Father, please keep us safe.*

She and Chips carefully stepped over moss and flat rock formations to avoid the icy water. Chips's younger brother and cameraman, Gavin, followed.

The three of them stationed their cameras and crouched in separate nooks in the cave. Dressed in wetsuits, stuntmen and divers waded in a large cavity of water, at the ready with underwater drones. Security positioned themselves close to Roare and Chips, and near the opening of the cavern.

Roare removed her thick puffer coat.

Chips laughed. "A minute ago, you looked like an ice cube."

"The cavern is warmer."

Swampy patches and green plants sprawled across parts of jagged edges and smooth rocks, and water fed into a series of small tunnels and nooks. Their prearranged lighting gave the cavern an eerie look.

Roare asked Chips, "Ready?"

He nodded.

"Cyborgs"—her command echoed off the walls—"take your places."

Chips said, "Action."

The two cyborg actors held baby dolls against their chests as they entered the cave through the waterfall, then veered to the right toward the tunnel, into the depths of the cavern.

Chips deemed the fifth take to be perfect. When he stood, he clutched his lower right abdomen and swiped a hand across his pale face. He pulled an Alka-Seltzer packet out of his pocket, plopped the tablet into his water bottle, then drank the mix.

Gavin glanced at him. "Are you all right?"

"Yeah. Probably ate something bad last night. My stomach will calm down soon."

Roare decided she'd check on him later.

As the afternoon soldiered on, the natural light dimmed. Chips and Roare zoomed in at different angles to shoot the cyborgs. Then, stunt doubles stood on a round translucent platform while they slowly submerged. Professional divers beneath the surface filmed the whirlpool created by the disk.

As the divers helped the stuntmen out of the water, Roare and Chips reviewed what they had recorded.

Roare grinned. "Gosh, this is fantastic and eerie."

"Precisely what we want," he said.

"Assuming we're done here, I'd like to pack up. After a long day, I really need my beauty rest."

"Beauty is the least of your worries. Let's wrap this up for today, rest at the lodge, then meet at the restaurant for dinner around seven. I reserved a quiet table for four near the fireplace."

"Great. I'll join you in a few, I need to jump on a Zoom call with CGI before dinner to review the vision we want for this scene."

"You don't miss much, do you?"

Roare shook her head. "Can't afford to. C'mon, let's go."

In the comfort of her cozy cabin at Tekarra Lodge, Roare lit the fireplace. She read her notes and grabbed a pen next to her laptop to jot down additional details for the CGI directors. She clicked on an MP3 file and listened to her interview with the Kovacs:

"Doctors," came Roare's recorded voice, "can you describe the subterranean city?"

"I'll take this one," Astrid said. "When CoSynthesis first took us to the cavern, we didn't know what to expect. This place was over four kilometers underground in an undisclosed location in northern Canada. A vast self-contained futuristic city thrived. The walls were curved and smooth, made of a silvery, translucent material with patches of green, purple, and blue plants. Small sections of grass with soil and roots hovered in midair. In the center of an enormous space, a large flat silver disk hovered a meter off the floor. And floating above were holographic cubes marked with hieroglyphics, ancient cuneiform, and a third script I didn't recognize."

"How did you know what the writings were?"

"I studied ancient languages as a hobby. The centerpiece display was detailed and intentional. An Oort cloud intertwined with the holographs. Names were engraved on the edge at the top of the disk—Jeqon, Azazel, and several others—fallen angels worshipped as heroes. CoSynthesis exalts them as gods."

"Anything else you'd like to share with me?"

"I'm a gardener," Fleming said. "Noticing plants comes natural—large bonsai, and vibrant greenery. Abnormally healthy—I suspected a heightened level of oxygen. Ethereal lily ponds dotted oval areas around the main floor. The walls ascended fifteen stories and housed hive-like spaces as living quarters. Silver hover disks docked at the landing pad at each household, summoned by thought and used to move around the complex.

"The city behaved like a living, breathing organism. Humans and hybrids lived together as emotionless automatons. Each wore full-body, second-skin suits, made from matted milky-blue latex. The hybrids had pale-blue eyes, fair skin, and platinum-blond hair, unlike the humans' various traits."

Roare paused the recording. She rested her forearms on her knees and bowed her head. If only the information had ended there. She continued listening:

"Farther below," Fleming's voice resumed, "the cavern was a stark contrast to the subterranean city. The walls of a narrow, arched passageway resembled the rings of Saturn. The black, iridescent floor moved like mercury to a teleportation pad. Bioidentification authorized us, and the pad enclosed and teleported us to the Genesis lab a few miles away.

"We were greeted by lead scientists and a hybrid CoSynthesis representative. Giant tactical robots stood to one side, their arms and legs the size of cannons. Their heads were helmets, their faces black monitors with two piercing orange eyes. Such vacant eyes … they had no souls. When provoked, they would raise a hand across their chests, and then the orange light under their silicone skin would intensify, and their eyes would emit beams of destruction. The lab workers told us the soldiers even used high frequency waves to implode enemies. In fact, one time—"

Roare skipped the details that followed, and instead closed her eyes and focused on Fleming's description of the lab. In her mind, Roare could see an enormous circular lab with a huge, black lily pad with liquid titanium petals opening to unveil a command center. She pictured control panels and holographic monitors that displayed blue and green graphs, and biostats of the children housed in the lab. She visualized glass capsules suspended in midair in one of the research rooms down a corridor. She recalled Fleming's description of scientists harvesting the DNA and adrenochrome of chosen children to integrate into AI.

rage against the machine

What horrors these children must have endured, so these sadistic freaks could obtain the purest quality of adrenochrome. Wicked monsters! Worse still, their bodies were discarded like garbage. Let these demons rot in Gehenna.

Roare's stomach soured. She skipped ahead in the interview to another clip of Astrid.

"We played along," she said, "so we wouldn't stir suspicion, didn't want to compromise our loyalty. They never intended to advance human beings, only AI. They're trying to create a perfect hybrid god-man to replace us entirely! They'll deceive people while their secret societies openly control the world through the technology we created. We had no desire to participate.

"Their plan goes against life itself and against God. Yes, we're scientists. But while pursuing our life's work, we discovered the Creator of the universe. For the sake of our twins' lives and for humanity, we couldn't walk away. We're not afraid because we have a deadman switch in place if they kill us."

This interview would help CGI specialists recreate what the Kovacs had seen. Roare turned off the recording, stood to stretch her legs, then sat in front of her laptop.

She allowed the first attendee into the Zoom meeting. "Dresdyn, glad you could join us. Let's see, you're the ..." She consulted the staffing list.

"Lead CGI Engineer for Visual Effects. Nice to meet you. Mathieu will log in shortly. I hope you're keeping warm up there. You might need to come to California to thaw out."

Roare welcomed the diversion after reviewing the gruesome testimonial. "Oh, not a bad idea."

"Hopefully you'll have a chance to try the ski slopes while you're there."

Roare shook her head. "Unfortunately, no time to play."

The Zoom app signaled Roare, and she admitted the next person.

"Hi, Mathieu here. Animation Engineer." The olive-skinned man in his late thirties swiped dark hair out of his eyes.

"Nice to meet you both. How's the project going?" she asked.

Dresdyn said, "You and Chips provided a good visual for us—lots of details to go on. Those scientists logged a lot."

"How's the performance-capture transformation coming along?"

"We're still building the framework from the sketches," Mathieu said. "The drone downloads will help. The actors and extras can be worked in with 3D photorealism later."

Roare held up her notepad. "I wrote more today."

"The more info, the better," Dresdyn said. "To create the underground cavern, lab scenes, and hybrids will take a lot of time."

"Do you need more staff to keep to our timeline?"

"Yeah, we could use more hands to support 24/7 shifts—soon preferably."

"We'll do what we can to support you and arrange more techs."

"You're perky this evening," Sloane said as he drove Roare to meet Chips for dinner.

"I'm revved up after the shoot today and a productive meeting with CGI. I still can't digest the things the Kovacs witnessed. I don't want to come across as a whack job, but I read a few articles on demon-possessed borgs. How is this possible?"

"Depending on who makes the robot, a demonically-inspired scientist can implant a virus into AI, which can be triggered by keywords under *special* circumstances. Once the fiends are unleashed into society, they will eventually turn on their creator. When scientists understand the evil they've invoked, it'll be too late."

"I see your point. Was this virus embedded in you?"

"Had that been the case, I would've classified you as a threat and destroyed you already. Anyway, my will was too strong to let my soul be captured. I still have my humanity. I still believe in God, and I've kept my faith, despite what I am now."

"Thanks, Sloane."

"For keeping my faith?"

"For confirming why I'm making this film. I've had my doubts."

"I'm happy you have the vision. This job isn't for the weak and may not reward you with an Academy trophy."

"Don't tell Chips I can live without a trophy. He's overambitious, despite his accolades. Besides, there are other honors."

"Absolutely."

chapter twenty-six—wrath of betrayal

> There is a darkness in you. In all of us, probably. Beasts
> we keep chained. Ordinary men have to keep the chains
> strong, for if we let the beast loose then society will turn
> upon us with fiery vengeance. Kings though ... well, who
> is there to turn upon them? So the chains are made of
> straw.—David Gemmell, *Troy: Shield of Thunder*

Upon his return to Antarctica after attending Roare's
fundraiser, Match pruned his bonsai trees while Phamie
Gow's "War Song" piped softly through the speakers in
the glass atrium. He evaluated the fallout of his meeting
with Roare—and seeing his old nemesis. *I should've known
Sloane was behind the push to expose me. I should've never
let him return to the world. Revenge can be sweet and
diabolical. Roare is a special woman. I admire her tenacity,
but it's wasted on her love for God and mortals.*

Given the data his adversaries had on him, Match
decided to expedite his agenda—severe actions must be
taken to avoid greater risks. *No more liabilities.*

Match held a private meeting with his uncle in the
tearoom to gain insight for his next move. He divulged
the chain of events that transpired between him and the
enemies of CoSynthesis.

They both sat quietly across from each other, sipping tea.

Raidon poked his mouth out like a fish. "Nephew, you've fallen into a snare. As a result, you have drawn attention to CoSynthesis. Our constituents are not happy. You chose ego over discretion. Yes, you revealed this to us, but only after you had already RSVPed."

Without emotion, Match stared at his uncle. "I disagree. If you meet the enemy face-to-face, you may obtain insight on who you're dealing with and discover their weaknesses."

"I'm concerned about your judgments lately, as well as your motives."

Match's eyes flared at the jab. He snapped back, "My actions have always been in the best interest of CoSynthesis."

"Not true. I've been observing you the past few years, after you obtained off-world technology. You have never shared any information with me about your source. You have partnered with unknown entities and excluded us from it. I deduce your actions are for your benefit alone, not CoSynthesis's. You have forgotten I made you who you are, but—"

"I exceeded you in every way," Match snarled. "Uncle, don't think I'm ungrateful for all you did for me, but you still think and behave like a human instead of accepting an advanced frontier beyond this planet. I thought by standing alongside me, we'd share the same vision. This is no longer the case."

The silence in the room was stifling as they glared at each other.

Raidon set down his teacup and peered over his glasses. "I'm proud of you, Match, for achieving what no one else has. Perhaps I should've taken the next step in becoming part cyborg myself. My lack of courage is my inadequacy. However, I never let emotions dictate my decisions. I fear you're on a power trip, therefore your actions can be unpredictable."

"Are you finished?"

Raidon shook his head. "No. One other thing. That film director will not be as easy to kill as you believe. There is a supernatural element to her. She is a young prodigy with the mark of Jesus on her life, and she is a warrior for him. She's protected by angels. Maybe there is something to be said for my brother's faith in God after all."

"Oh yes, *him*." Match turned his intense gaze on Raidon.

"I haven't forgotten what you did to him. You were aware of what you were doing when you killed him with the defibrillator. You didn't want your mother to discover what you'd done, but you chose to tell me. Why?" Raidon stood and placed his hands on his hips.

Match snickered, stood, and faced his uncle with his hands folded in front of him, legs spread apart. "Because you didn't care for your brother and didn't respect him. Back then, I idolized you and wanted to impress you." Match cocked his head to one side.

"And you did. You were the son I never had. But now, the power you wield will drive you into the deepest pits of this world." Raidon snatched off his spectacles.

"Well then, Uncle, there's nothing more to say. I detect rage and distrust in your spirit. Your growing hatred for me will cost you. Your memory is slipping." Match thrust a finger at his face. "Do you recall you were the one who taught me to be unscrupulous and ruthless?"

Raidon walked toward the door, then turned back, and said calmly, "I admit my faults. What little humanity is left in you should've been discarded when you became a cyborg. You're as cold as a reptile."

"And you've gotten soft in your old age."

"And now, you've given me regrets." Raidon placed his specs back on his face and walked out.

Indifference breeds contempt.

After the exchange with his uncle, Match decided in the best interest of CoSynthesis to have Raidon step down from his place on the board. He coerced the other senior members into a unanimous decision to have Raidon release his position.

Due to Raidon's intricate involvement with CoSynthesis, Match would not allow his uncle to take vengeance against him or leak vital information. *Before I eliminate him, I'll have to buy him out to spare us legal repercussions. He will have to be disposed of. Without cyborg logic, he won't have the means of self-preservation, instead he'll be just a messy, human "accident."*

Raidon had learned how to block Match's telepathic abilities. Using visualization exercises, Raidon kept his mind clear of negative thoughts and remained calm.

He suspected Match would soon get rid of him and had to act quickly before he met his death. Raidon hired a private detective to find Sloane, who traced him to his midtown dojo. In the aftermath of Match's recent activities, Raidon decided to assume the role of a whistleblower before he met his end.

He mailed Sloane a small parcel containing documentation of Match's murder of his father, and the thousands of missing children CoSynthesis held captive in their AI lab. Raidon included further corroborating data that verified the testimonies of whistleblowers and investors in CoSynthesis. *This will force him off the planet sooner than later. As for me, I'll have an honorable burial.*

chapter twenty-seven—blindsided

Sometimes, she had discovered, you had to walk around
the holes in your life, instead of falling into them.
　　　　　　　　—Priscilla Cummings, *Blindsided*

To Roare's surprise, filming finished early *and* without
incident. The crew left exhausted, eager for warmer
climates. She had survived the cold. Nonetheless, she
missed the familiarity of home and feeling Wyatt's body
next to hers.

In the stillness of late morning, a vibrating sound roused
Roare from sleep. She rolled onto her back. Her cell phone
buzzed again on the nightstand. She moaned and pulled
the covers over her head. They could leave a message.

Thirty seconds passed, and Wyatt's cell phone rang.
"Hello." He sounded groggy. "Yeah, right here. I'm putting
you on speaker." He nudged her. "Gobo, wake up. It's your
mom."

Roare bolted up and rubbed her hands over her face.
"Mom? What's going on?"

"The boys were kidnapped!" Her mother's voice was
frantic. "The police and FBI are here. I told them about the
film you've been working on. They want you to come as
soon as you can."

"What? Wait. Slow down."

"You heard me. Maddox and Noland are gone. I dropped them off for tennis practice at school this morning, and they never showed up for first period. I got a call from a muffled voice. They're going to kill the boys unless you quit your film. They gave us forty-eight hours. Please come and bring Sloane with you. We need his help. I want my babies back."

Roare covered her mouth. "This all seems surreal. We'll be there as soon as possible." She took deep breaths. *God, don't let me hyperventilate. Please protect my brothers. Lord, what have I done?* "If my brothers are harmed, I'll kill them!" Roare hung up and hurried to get dressed.

Wyatt called, "Sloane's headed over. We'll meet him downstairs."

Her cheeks flamed. "He warned they'd come after our families. I don't want to believe this is happening."

Sloane arrived in his armored Conquest Knight, and the three of them headed to New Jersey. "You need to stow your phones and other electronics in the Faraday box by Wyatt's leg. The whole vehicle is secured from listening ears. Although, I prefer to be extra cautious." As Roare handed Wyatt her phone, Sloane continued, "We're going to get your brothers back. I know the news is disturbing. Only, can you do me a favor?"

She returned his gaze, her eyebrows furrowed together. "Yes, I'm listening."

"Hold firmly to your faith. We all knew there would be retaliation. We have time, and we'll use each second to our advantage. My guys are already collecting intel for me."

"Look, I know you can't be in multiple places at once," Wyatt said, "and you did warn us about thugs who would come after our families. Now, here we are. What's your next plan?"

"Preparations are underway as we speak. I don't want my team to run into law enforcement before we need to. If this becomes a federal situation, I have access to military personnel eager to assist. I cannot tell you anything more right now."

"Fair enough."

Roare stared blankly out the window. This was certainly the "intruder" the Lord had warned her about, and she now had some ideas about his identity. She scoffed at herself. She should've told her mother but hadn't wanted to scare her. She whispered vehemently, "Satan, I rebuke, bind, and break every stronghold with the authority of Christ in Jesus's name. Lord, I need to hear from you. I don't want to cancel this film. Oh please, help my family."

I charged you with this task. Don't you believe I will see you through to the end?

The corners of her lips turned down. Her family was hurt! People had taken risks and *died* doing what they believed was right. She'd nearly lost her own life.

Taken risks? Abraham did with Isaac. If the angel hadn't stopped him, he would've killed his son because he trusted me. Do you trust the I AM? The voice in her mind faded.

They stopped at a red light. A billboard to the right displayed a bright, neon-green sign: "God sacrificed his Son for us. Jesus completed the mission for you. If the mission cost you everything, would you do it? Genesis 22— Want to know more? Visit us Sunday at 11:00 a.m. at Trinity Fellowship Church."

What are you saying, Lord? Roare retrieved a small Bible out of her tote bag and found Genesis 22: Abraham's willingness to sacrifice Isaac to obey God. *Okay, I hear you, but my brothers' lives are in your hands.* Roare cleared her throat. "Listen, Maddox and Noland are going to be safe."

Wyatt said, "I've been praying myself. I'm sure they'll be home soon."

"Then, we're on the same page," Sloane said. "Now to convince your mother."

"Don't push her too much." Roare smiled. "She's a mama bear and would rip your throat out if any harm came to her cubs."

"This I know. But one, I wouldn't expect any less. Two, I would do the same, and three, her faith is like the Rock of Gibraltar. She never could trust people fully."

chapter twenty-eight—unsung heroes don't wear capes

A hero is an ordinary individual who finds the strength to persevere and endure in spite of overwhelming obstacles.
—Christopher Reeve

A cloud of dread hung over Tenafly. Nosy reporters tried to pry information from tight-lipped officers, who asked them to leave the premises. As Roare and Wyatt walked past the police line in front of her parents' home, terror rose in her like a crawling, erosive vine. A familiar policeman tipped his head to Roare and let the couple pass the crime scene tape.

"Sloane McInerny will be coming up the driveway shortly," she said to him. "He's a close friend."

"No problem. We'll let him through."

She and Wyatt rushed inside, where her mother and Ben sat on one of the living room sofas. Two plainclothes detectives occupied the opposite sofa, notepads in hand. Another two men stood behind them with FBI badges on their lapels.

Roare ran into her mother's arms.

Lane pulled away and latched onto Roare's forearms. With a stern glare, she said, "You have to kill this project for the sake of your brothers."

"Mom, please. What kind of person do you think I am?"

"A sister who loves her brothers, who would do anything to save their lives."

"Where's your faith? I know you're upset. I am too. You can't put this burden solely on me."

"If you hadn't taken on the documentary, this would all be a moot point."

One of the men stood and cleared his throat. "Ladies, bickering wastes precious time. Ms. Murdock, is there anything in your film that would implicate anyone? We'd like some insight on why your brothers were targeted."

Roare explained the controversial nature of her film, Dr. Ponte's murder, and the attempts on her life as the detectives took notes. As she spoke, some of her concerns eased as she noticed Sloane enter the living room and stand away from the others.

During the details about Dr. Ponte, Lane chimed in. "Yet another reason to give up this insane project."

The men eyed each other.

The taller detective said, "Your movie sounds interesting. Would be a pity to halt production."

Lane sucked air past her teeth. "What an insensitive remark! My boys may be murdered as a result of her film!"

"Sorry to be callous. First, there's no guarantee they'll return your boys whether your daughter pulls out of the movie or not. Second, they haven't made any financial demands yet and the kidnappers wanted your full attention—"

"I'm captivated."

The detective continued. "This is a typical scare tactic. Let's use the time we have to find bargaining leverage. Ponte's murder and the attempts on Roare's life may be keys to who these kidnappers are. If we can link all these incidents, we'll have a stack of charges in addition to kidnapping. I wouldn't cancel the film yet."

"And what about our boys? Don't they have a say?" Ben asked.

The other detective's brown eyes intensified. "We will be their voices. Nothing would give us more satisfaction than to bring them home safely. All available law enforcement is on this, and there's a team reviewing the school's security footage."

The first detective asked, "Mrs. Anakoni, was there anything unusual you noticed when the kidnappers called? Any sounds, noises, accents? And the boys—did you speak to both of them? How did they seem to you?"

"They were frightened and upset," Lane answered. "I told them to remain calm, as best as they can. My oldest, Maddox, breaks out in hives when he's frightened, and my baby, Noland, laughs when he's nervous. Their voices echoed like they were in a large, empty building, but the kidnappers' voices sounded muffled."

"Could be anywhere. Since this recently happened, they can't be far."

As the detectives circled the officers in the entryway to assign tasks, Sloane walked over to Lane and Ben. "I'm sorry this happened. If there's anything I can do—"

"I want my kids back." She looked up at Sloane with eyes bloodshot from crying and lack of sleep.

"I'll do whatever is necessary to bring them home." Sloane tapped Roare on the shoulder and signaled her to step aside to a quiet corner. "Match's henchmen have gone too far," he said. "I'll pull together a rescue team. First, I need a cybersecurity expert who can make us invisible while we gather intel. A tech who's not connected to any AI corporations, especially on US soil."

"I know someone. He's young, hungry, and based in Australia."

"Ah, yes. Aaden's offshore. He could be a good option."

Roare grabbed her cell phone from her handbag and fired a text to Aaden.

He replied immediately: *Glad to hear from you. Was awake anyway, working.*

Roare texted again: *Can you talk—need to run something by you.*

When his call came, she found privacy in the guest bathroom. "Aaden, I hope I'm not disturbing you."

"Not at all," he said. "We were finishing up a software upgrade. What's up?"

"We need help getting through the back doors of some AI companies to give Sloane eyes to track two boys who were kidnapped. Then his team needs to be untraceable for the rescue. He doesn't want to use contacts from the mainland, and you struck me as someone who'd be eager for exciting work. With your background, I thought I'd reach out."

"Do you know these boys?"

She took a deep breath. "They're my brothers. They were kidnapped because of the film I'm making."

"Crickey! Don't say another word. I'm in."

"Fantastic. I'll text you Sloane's info, and he'll take it from there. I can't thank you enough."

"I owe you one after you saved Papa's life."

"How is he?"

"Coming along, tough old bloke. He said God gave him a second chance with his life. His health's improved nearly a hundred percent. We can never thank *you* enough. Let's chat after your brothers are rescued."

Roare joined the others on the living room sofas.

Sloane scratched the top of his head. "I've got people who can pinpoint the boys' location. We'll bring Maddox and Noland back. Trust me."

"I'm counting on you," Lane said. "My only consolation is that the boys are together." She added under her breath, "Lord Jesus, spare them."

Sloane eyed Roare and tilted his head toward the door.

She followed him out to his vehicle before telling him Aaden was available. "He'll need access to your dedicated network. I told him you'd call. Sloane, I—"

"I know what you're going to ask. Don't. Consider why you're doing this film and for whom. Now you have two more reasons: Noland and Maddox."

Sloane slid open the hidden panel behind the clothes in his bedroom closet and entered his high-tech control room. As the door clicked shut, he sat at the desk and switched on the dedicated server. He logged on to the computer, picked up his private landline, and dialed Aaden's number.

"Your help is critical, Aaden. Roare said you're one of the best. Listen, this is top secret information and remains between us. Can I count on your discretion?"

"I'm capable!" Aaden's voice was high-spirited. "I was born to do this sort of work. I can sign privacy documents whenever you want."

"I'll fax you a nondisclosure. Meanwhile, I'll need remote cyber support for a recon-and-rescue mission. Six of us have to slip in and out undetected at the recovery points. I have an implanted tracking device from my days at a private tech company. I disabled it myself." The fewer people who knew his cyborg nature, the better. "All I can say is I want certainty the satellite is blocked to prevent any trace of my whereabouts. Can you handle the break-in codes if I give them to you?"

"Give me four hours to get familiar with the network and the security traps. I can hack in."

"Great. My black-ops undercover source was able to acquire the boys' exact location. Criminals love shooting off their mouths to their inner circles."

"Brilliant."

"Not if we're discovered."

"Cloaking you will take another hour."

"The sooner, the better."

"Once you get me what I need, I'll have satellite and drone interference for you within five hours."

Sloane boarded a dark-gray Boeing CH-47 Chinook at 0115. He inspected his team, outfitted in black combat gear, and took stock of the weapons and equipment in the belly of the rotorcraft. At the rear, two F470 Combat Rubber Raiding Craft were anchored securely.

Sloane yelled into his headset to address the three men and two women through their helmets. "Attention team. Our ETA is 0145. Infrared data shows two gunmen inside, two snipers on the roof. The kids are together, executing the snatch will be easy."

Carson, a wide-bodied man of color, said in his deep voice, "We're good with those numbers right?"

"The source is legit. They're holding them in the vacant building next to Blazing Star Cemetery. The boat graveyard along Arthur Kill is a direct pathway and would rip our crafts to shreds. The Isle of Meadows will be available for docking. And we'll be far enough out of their sight. Then we make our way through the marsh. Once our infrared has them in view, we're a go."

Scout brushed her fiery red hair away from her face. "Carson and I got the two on the roof."

"Check. Keep 'em engaged while the rest of us slip in the back. We need to drop them fast and move out."

Vlad, a tall, muscular Nordic man, checked his weapon. "We'll be ready."

Six-foot-two Atticus tightened the black bandana around his dark hair, scratched his beard, and slipped on his leather gloves. "Yeah, you got that right."

Sloane frowned. "This could get ugly. The less the boys see, the better."

"No worries, chief." Serenity placed a sturdy, fair-skinned hand on Sloane's left shoulder. "Carson and Scout can meet me at the rear after they're done outside, and we'll extract the kids before things pop off."

"Copy that." The secure phone in Sloane's pocket vibrated. He raised his hand and gave a thumbs up to the team as he answered the call. "Tell me something good, cyber guru."

"You're fully cloaked," Aaden said, "and satellites show you in Coeur d'Alene, Idaho. If anyone attempts a reverse trace, they'll be redirected to Liechtenstein."

"You're a talented man. I'll be in touch when the op is over."

When the team landed, they synchronized their watches and double-checked their gear. With everything prepped, Sloane cleared his throat. They paused and bowed their heads.

Serenity tucked her short blonde hair behind her ears and said, "God, keep the kids safe and us too. Cancel whatever these goons have planned. Intervene on the boys' behalf, and may the battle be yours."

"May the battle be yours!" the others shouted.

Atticus added, "Yeah, let's get kinetic!"

The team disembarked the helo and launched the F470s. Like ninjas, they cut silently through the marsh and closed in on their target. Within twelve minutes, they reached the shoreline and took their positions.

Carson and Scout turned on their infrared goggles. The others dropped their heads low, and Sloane motioned them forward.

Two watchmen paced back and forth across the rooftop. A large bald man caught sight of movement from a nearby tree. "Did you see something?"

The average-sized man scanned the area through his infrared binoculars. "Yeah, a hawk just flew off a branch."

The bald man shrugged, then continued pacing.

The other watchman paused, reached for his CB radio attached to his shoulder, then suddenly fell to the floor of the rooftop.

The bald man heard the thud, pivoted, and saw his partner's dead form. He crouched low, readied his M16, and peered through the scope.

Movement in the distance. Two people.

He had them in his sights, and he itched to pull the trigger.

Thwip!

The bald man joined his partner, dead on the roof.

Sloane and the others ran toward the farthest door on the left side of the building, and Serenity took her position around the back. They surveyed the area. Clear.

Sloane stood near a steel door. He held up his left palm and directed a light-blue energy beam at the door. Within seconds, a smoldering heap of ash lay on the floor. He crept inside with Vlad and Atticus.

Something was being dragged across the concrete floor somewhere above them, the sound echoing throughout the stairwell. Sloane used the heat sensors in his eyes and located the assailants two flights up, down a short corridor, in a spacious room on the left, one hundred feet from the stairs. Two smaller figures huddled together in the middle of the room.

By now, the metallic odor of the vaporized door had likely reached the upper levels. As one of the kidnappers pounded down the upper hallway, Sloane's heat sensor pulsated on his wrist. The gunman was running hot, coming downstairs now.

Sloane motioned to Atticus and Vlad, then pointed to the stairwell. He held up three fingers, identifying the assailant's weapons: a firearm in each hand and a knife strapped to his lower right leg. The three of them advanced toward the stairs.

Carson and Scout entered the building behind them and immediately fanned out to sweep the ground floor, while Serenity followed the others.

An explosion of rapid gunfire echoed like a symphony of cannons within the stairwell as the assailant emptied his magnums. Atticus and Vlad blasted him with their .380s. Despite blows to the leg, arm, and ribs, the six-foot-six brute still lunged at them. He hunched over Atticus, who bent low, grabbed the knife out of the man's leg holster, and thrust the weapon into his abdomen. The enemy landed motionless in a twisted heap on the concrete at the bottom of the stairs.

Serenity caught up as Sloane moved to the bottom of the stairs and scanned the man's body. A broken neck and internal bleeding confirmed the end of life.

Sloane grimaced. What a waste. He never got any pleasure when things had to end this way.

Serenity closed the man's eyes.

Atticus and Vlad continued to the next floor. They'd search up there while Sloane took care of the burn bag. He piled the man's ID, dog tags, jewelry, and cell phone on the floor, then emitted a piercing blue stream from his eyes to incinerate them.

"Give us a few, then make your advance as backup," he said to Serenity, then he ran upstairs.

Atticus and Vlad had completed their search of the unfinished second floor. On the next floor, a scuffle broke out. The boys were screaming now, their voices muffled. Sloane and his men took the stairs two at a time.

On the third floor, the last gunman stood behind Maddox and Noland with a gun to each boy's head. They were on their knees in the center of the cavernous space, their mouths taped, hands behind their backs, and feet bound with ropes. Beneath panic-stricken eyes, tears coursed down their faces.

Sloane caught a glimpse of the gunman's laser blue eyes. *Borg. Tread carefully. He can either take them out instantly or go into stealth mode to escape.* Sloane returned the man's glare and scanned him. *A lesser intelligent model. The boys don't need to experience this kind of technology.*

The borg clicked his head to the left.

rage against the machine

The team fanned out, their gazes on the assailant.

Sloane wanted to pounce immediately, but timing was everything. The moment would come. He took a deep breath.

"Welcome, gentlemen." The gunman eyed Sloane. "You woke the kids with all the commotion downstairs. You should've been quieter on your way in."

"Couldn't be helped." Sloane lowered his voice. "You boys will be okay. Try to stay cool. Will you trust us?"

They nodded.

"Since you came at us hard, their lives are forfeit." The man pulled Noland closer by his collar, then engaged the magnum's firing pin. "You decide on how far I take this. Not only will the innocent die—the filmmakers will be next until all are dead. I'm politely asking you once, to drop your weapons. And don't test my patience."

"Trouble is we're not you," Sloane said, "and we're not polite or patient."

Carson crept behind the gunman from the opposite side of the room.

Eyes front, Sloane told himself, *don't want to blow his cover. My man, you're going to be dropped.*

Carson stole forward in complete silence. Three inches from the man, he threaded a piano cord through one of the openings between two steel columns, wrapped it around his fists, then slipped the wire around the man's neck and pulled.

The gunman dropped the magnums and grabbed his throat. He broke the wire. His blue lasers ignited.

Noland launched himself away from the gunman as best as he could with his bonds.

Atticus and Vlad whipped out their knives and threw them at the kidnapper's eyes.

273

The man screeched and clawed at his eyes, reeling backward.

Carson grabbed his jacket and dragged him away from the children, pinning him against a steel support beam.

Vlad smirked.

The gunman didn't make a sound, and Carson didn't release his grip. Serenity and Scout arrived behind Carson, swooped down to retrieve the kids, and carried them downstairs.

Sloane strutted to the kidnapper. "Never announce your plans. Execute them." He placed his right hand over the man's chest and closed his eyes. As his palm emitted a subtle glow, the assailant stopped struggling, and his body plunged to the floor.

Carson asked, "Is he—"

"He's a borg. I scrambled his AI software with directed energy frequency," Sloane said. "The feds will be interested in his origin and who created him." He knelt next to the kidnapper and made sure he was inoperable.

"Let's hope our actions send a clear message to CoSynthesis that we're not backing down from this fight. There will be consequences, especially when they drag innocent children into their sick agenda." Sloane stood and dusted himself off.

"They'll have regrets," Carson said. "If you're done with this junkpile, move him to the bird."

Atticus and Vlad retrieved their knives and returned them to their holsters.

Sloane collected the kidnapper's guns.

Carson helped Vlad pick up the borg and throw the limp body over his shoulder. "I gotta tell you, your timing was perfect."

Atticus clapped Carson on the back. "The invisible bomber strikes again. He didn't even hear you coming."

Carson smirked. "He was too busy talking."

"Good thing. A bloodbath would've traumatized those kids," Atticus said.

"Cut the chatter," Sloane said. "We have work to do before we roll out."

Vlad headed to one of the watercrafts with Sloane, while Atticus and Carson stayed behind to process the scene. Vlad readied one of the crafts and handcuffed the criminal, still disabled, to one of the seats.

Sloane stood next to the other craft, where Maddox and Noland sat alongside Scout and Serenity. "I see my friends have got warm blankets around you. We're gonna bring you back home to your mom, where you belong. You were incredibly brave. Your parents will be proud of you."

"We were a *little* scared." Maddox's eyes glimmered in the darkness.

"There's nothing wrong with being afraid." Serenity hugged him. "I am too sometimes."

"Really?"

She grinned. "Yes."

Noland peered up at Sloane. "You're Mommy's friend, aren't you?"

Sloane rubbed the back of his ear. "Yes, I am. Listen, I need you to do me a favor. We have to get to our chopper in these boats. Would you be able to do this?"

Noland and Maddox glanced at each other. "Sure we can."

"Are you guys superheroes or something?" Maddox asked.

The women laughed. "Kind of," Scout said. "We like to pretend we are. Sometimes, we help superheroes."

Noland gaped. "Wow ... oh, I get it. They can't be everywhere all at once, so you're like extra hands helping them out."

"Perfect! You're so clever." Serenity held out two life jackets. "Now, put these on to be extra safe, okay? We'll be there in no time."

Sloane held the craft steady while Serenity and Scout helped the boys into their life jackets. Doe-eyed, cold, and yawning, Noland and Maddox leaned against each another in the center seat.

Scout said, "See you in a few, right?"

"Definitely." Sloane helped their craft shove off.

"Hurry back, chief. We're waiting," Atticus yelled as he approached.

Sloane headed to the side of the warehouse as Atticus and Carson joined Vlad at the other boat.

Sloane kicked in the basement window. Whew, the guys hadn't skimped on the propane! Time to light this place up. He backed away several feet and engaged his eye laser. The beam targeted the tank his team had placed in the basement. A moment passed while the liquid started to boil inside the tank. He sprinted toward the water and jumped into the craft. They barely cleared the shore before an explosion lit the sky.

Cinder blocks crackled and steel groaned as orange and white flames shot high into the night air. When the team reached the chopper, the men lifted the disabled kidnapper in with them. Atticus and Scout hoisted up the craft and secured the door.

Sloane circled his right arm in the air, and the pilot took off.

Noland peered out the window. "Wow! Did you"—he nudged his brother—"just like the movies!"

"If we were still there, we would've burned up." Maddox turned to Sloane. "Can we go home now?"

Sloane rubbed his scalp. "As quickly as possible." He let out a pent-up breath and called Lane. "We got them, and they're safe."

Lane wept on the other end. "Oh, praise God!"

"Your sons will be in your arms soon."

"God bless you, Sloane, and everyone who helped!"

A faint ribbon of midnight-blue edged the onyx sky, followed by variations of blue, orange, pink, and yellow. Roare lay quietly next to Wyatt as the morning debuted through the window on her side of the bed. She turned toward him. At least one of them had slept.

She reached for her phone as soon as she heard the phone vibrate on her nightstand. Sloane. She scrambled out of bed and raced into her office as she answered. "Hi. Any news?" she whispered.

"I have an update."

"Yes?"

"Your brothers are safe and home with your parents. They're frightened yet animated by the excitement. I bet they'll want to tell you everything."

"Knowing them." Roare looked toward the ceiling. *Thank you, Lord! You didn't fail me or my family. Everything you told me was true. You do care.* She broke down and cried.

Sloane stayed quiet while she composed herself.

"You saved their lives! And those monsters who kidnapped them?"

"I rather not say."

"I guess I can breathe again, thank God. How can we repay you for all you've done?"

"You owe me nothing. With Aaden's help, we were successful. After the film's done—provided we're still on—

I'd like to show him my appreciation monetarily, maybe employment."

"I'm sure something could be arranged. And yes, still on."

"Can't ask for anything more."

chapter twenty-nine—dogpiling

Surely he will save you
from the fowler's snare
and from the deadly pestilence.—Psalm 91:3

A few days after the boys were rescued, every ounce of stress Roare had carried in her heart flew away like a butterfly breaking free of its cocoon. However, her comfort was short lived.

"Ro, before you go tipping out the door to meet Sloane, I need to say a few things." Wyatt stood in the doorway of the walk-in closet while she dressed.

"Sounds serious."

"I think so, but I'm concerned you don't fully realize the gravity of what's going on here. Over the past few months, our lives have been turned upside down. Since this film started, death has been stalking us like a demented panther. I wonder how many more chances we need to take before one or both of us are dead. Have you considered how this is affecting me and our relationship? I can barely concentrate at my job, and every time my cell rings lately, I'm not sure if I want to answer the call."

"Wy! How could you? Who am I supposed to call if I'm in trouble or half dead?"

"You're not seeing my point—so many ugly things have occurred, I can't keep up! This film is making our lives frantic and too dangerous to even breathe. I don't want to continue living this way. Not only is this unhealthy, it's tiresome."

Roare sat on the ottoman. "Why haven't you said something before?"

"I thought all these skirmishes would've resolved, and these psychopaths would have been dealt with by now. I want my old life back."

"And you think I don't?

"You don't behave like you do. You're so eager to run off to the studio—as if you already forgot you nearly lost both of your brothers. I assumed you'd take some time out and reflect."

She retrieved a sweatshirt and slammed the drawer shut. "And what in blazes do you expect me to do—brood over the carnage, give up and allow sociopaths to intimidate me into an early grave? Why can't I make you understand I'm beside myself with this film and what I've taken on? Do you think I enjoy seeing those I love harassed?"

"Am I included on your list of those you love?"

She pushed past him with her handbag, then spun around. "You've got some nerve. Are you insinuating I don't love you or care about our welfare, our marriage, our future? I want my life back too! I'm doing my darndest to cope. I didn't expect to be forced off the road, thrown on subway tracks, or poisoned. Yes, I took on this project, and I'm committed through to the end. Our species is at stake. This isn't about just us anymore, Wy."

He sighed. "I'm certain you love me. I'm frustrated and have a difficult time coming to terms with what's at stake. I love you, Gobo, and I don't want to lose you."

"I don't want to lose you either, but the only way we're going to get through this is by taking leaps of faith. Otherwise, we're as good as dead." Roare checked the time. Sloane had texted her.

"You're right, and I'll stand by you. Go and do what you have to do, but I'm holding Sloane accountable if this project takes your life." Wyatt walked over. They embraced.

"So will I." Roare hurried to meet Sloane in the lobby.

He escorted her to the black Conquest Knight, double-parked in front of her building.

"You seem tense," he said.

"I had a fight with Wy, and I can't blame him for how he's feeling." She explained their exchange.

"Hmm. Given his position, I'd voice the same concerns. I'm not taking sides, but what I'm praying for is an end to this—soon. The more pressure we put on Match to come after us, the better off we are."

"Makes no sense to me."

"Why not? He's already exposing himself and getting sloppy. If his *partners* value anonymity, they'll be anxious to cut him loose—something I'm banking on as well as on God."

"I'm trusting my instincts we're doing what's right," she said.

"So am I. Shifting the subject—your mom. Give her time. She'll come around soon."

"I hope so. I miss talking to her, but I know the film is something I've got to do. People have to know before the situation becomes hopeless."

"I'm pleased you're standing your ground with the film."

"I'd disappoint myself and God if I walked away now."

Roare and Sloane arrived at Chips's studio. She prepped her equipment in a roomy corner for an OR scene with the cyborgs. Green lighting provided a placeholder for the CGI team to program the scenery and lab action. The cast and crew moved to the filming area. Sloane took a seat with a cup of tea to watch.

Roare and Chips hovered near the three actors, gave final instructions, and began rolling:

The female cyborg stood over the human on the operating table and used a microscopic syringe to inject a sensory entity into the patient's heart. "Report on the SE's activity."

The assistant to her right hovered his hand over the patient's heart. "Data should appear on the monitor in a second."

All four cyborgs raised their heads toward the large screen at the end of the table as pale rings of white light passed across the human, scanning vitals.

Two of the cyborgs monitored biometrics while the others reviewed the 3D monitor.

As the scan continued, the lead cyborg looked at the patient. "SE invasion complete." She hovered her hand over the human's heart, and a faint ribbon of white smoke rose from the body into her palm. She trapped the smoke in both hands.

The assistant opposite her held a translucent, egg-shaped pod over her hands, and the light mist transferred to the pod.

The lead took the pod. "I'll place this soul with the others in the alchemist's chamber. We begin soul infusions next week for the new hybrids. Right on schedule." She left the OR.

Chips recorded her departure from the front while Roare captured footage behind her.

"Cut!" Chips called. "That was perfect."

Roare peered over her camera and gave him a thumbs up.

As the crew clapped, the actors appeared to breathe a collective sigh of relief. The scene was over.

Smack! The sound echoed throughout the warehouse.

Roare jumped and spun toward the noise.

"Ugh!" Chips lay crumpled in a ball on his left side.

Gavin nearly tripped over Chips's camera as he rushed to his side.

Sloane carried Chips to the sofa. "He's sweating and shaking."

"Try to relax." Gavin patted his brother's shoulder. "This will pass."

The assistant director, Phoebe, spoke into her cell phone. "Okay, we will. Please hurry!"

Roare got a cold washcloth from the bathroom and placed it across his forehead.

Chips moaned and his eyes rolled upward.

Phoebe walked closer. "A medevac'll be on the roof in five minutes."

"I can carry him," Sloane said. "Someone, open the emergency exit door."

"You bet," Gavin said, "and I've got the key for the roof."

Gavin took the stairs two at a time, setting off the automatic lighting, and Roare brought up the rear.

When the medevac landed on the helipad, EMTs hopped out, strapped Chips onto a stretcher, and moved him into the helo.

Over the whomping of the helicopter blades, the doctor yelled, "Looks like his appendix ruptured. We'll reach NYU emergency in a few minutes."

"Right, we're leaving now," Gavin shouted as one of the EMT assistants shut the door.

Roare sat with Gavin and Sloane in the ER waiting room. She turned her head and closed her eyes. *Not now, Lord. Chips still has more to do. Please remove this affliction from his body.*

A few minutes later, a senior staff surgeon approached, grave concern in his features. "Gavin Jaeger?"

Gavin stood. "Yes?"

The doctor came closer. "I'm Dr. Ghaderi. Can I talk to you privately?"

"These are close friends. You can speak freely in front of them."

"As you wish. Your brother's pain is stabilized. An ultrasound confirmed acute appendicitis, and we're prepping him for immediate surgery. Laparoscopic surgery involves a single incision, the removal of the appendix and any infection. I suggest you come see him before we start."

"Hey, buddy, how're you doing?" Gavin asked.

Chips's pale skin stood out against his blue gown as he lay in the bed of a private ER bay. "Hey. Going under the knife soon. I'll see you on the other side."

"C'mon, you've got this."

"Maybe. But, in the end, God makes the final decision. Listen, can you do something for me?"

"Anything."

Chips gazed at him intensely. "You and Roare will keep filming, won't you?"

"Absolutely, goes without saying."

"One more thing. Can you look after her? She's amazing— truly talented and not tainted by the industry."

"I know, and I will. Love you, big brother. I gotta leave now. The doctor is waiting." Gavin kissed his brother on the forehead and returned to the waiting room, where Phoebe and a few crew members had joined Roare and Sloane.

The anesthesiologist administered sedatives through Chips Jaeger's IV. Within a few minutes, he went into a deep sleep.

Dr. Ghaderi turned to the surgical technician, then glanced at a headless, tentacled, white AI robot. The foreboding claws and scorpion needles hung over the operating table. "You have Apollyon ready?"

The tech gave a grudging nod, disapproving of the doctor's nickname for the machine.

Ghaderi observed the video feed on a 3D monitor, while the tech activated the robot.

Apollyon opened the abdominal wall, entered the peritoneum, and isolated the appendix.

The doctor gingerly grasped the finger-shaped tube and removed the organ with a scalpel. "Please close the abdominal layers."

Apollyon responded to the tech's joystick controls, threading a collagen suture through the delicate claw. The arms extended and began stitching the deepest tissue. Two more layers to go.

Within seconds, a gash to the main artery caused massive bleeding.

"Good grief!" The doctor shoved the robot away from the patient after he activated the override switch. "Clamp!"

The nurse pressed a vascular clamp into his outstretched hand.

Dr. Ghaderi deftly secured the artery. "Electrocautery." He cauterized the artery, suctioned out the reservoir of blood, then stitched the abdomen layers.

"Heart rate is dropping." The anesthesiologist tapped the patient monitor. "His blood pressure is falling rapidly. We're losing him!"

A long tone exuded from the monitor.

Ghaderi grabbed the defibrillator paddles and applied gel to the pads. Charge already!

The nurse began chest compressions.

The doctor pressed the paddles on the patient's chest. "Clear!"

The others backed away while he administered an electrical current.

Jaeger's chest jerked upward.

No heartbeat.

Again, they tried chest compressions followed by the defibrillator. Again and again, they tried for more than an hour.

Roare checked her watch. More than two and a half hours. Gavin had passed her fifty times as he paced the waiting room.

"This shouldn't take this long," he said. "I thought this was a straightforward procedure."

"Yeah," Sloane said. "I have to tell you, my spirit is disturbed. I have no idea how to stop a plague descending upon us."

A few minutes later, Dr. Ghaderi entered.

"How's Chips?" Gavin asked.

The doctor glanced at the group. "Let's talk somewhere private."

"That alone tells me the news is bad. You can speak freely with everyone here." Gavin shoved his hands into his pockets.

"We were too late. We removed the appendix, then a blood vessel burst. While we stopped the bleeding, he went into cardiac arrest. We worked on him for more than an hour and couldn't bring him back. I'm deeply sorry."

A bead of sweat trickled down the side of Sloane's face, and his fists tightened. Roare could almost feel heat radiating from his body. She saw a hint of his blue laser eyes peek out from under his eyelids.

"You're lying. You know full well what went wrong in there." Sloane gritted his teeth.

Roare gently placed her hand on his back. "There are other ways to unveil the truth ... legally."

Sloane regained his composure. His sapphire eyes returned to brown.

"How could a routine operation go wrong?" Gavin asked. "Was his heart weak?"

"You'll need to ask his general practitioner," Ghaderi said.

"Can I see him?"

"Yes, follow me."

Gavin left with the doctor.

Roare dropped onto a chair in the corner of the room, placed her hands over her face, and wept. How could Chips be gone? Were criminals trying to stop the film again? Vengeance came to mind. Maybe Sloane was right. She'd better not let unhealthy thoughts contaminate her spirit. She closed her eyes and shivered. The film was leaving a trail of human carnage.

A small, still voice whispered, *This was no coincidence.*

Sloane seated himself next to her. "Sorry I lost my cool. Chips is ... was a dear friend. Sabotage is written all over this. I'll investigate further. Guarantee."

Phoebe approached. "Life doesn't make sense. Chips—always euphoric when he'd make a film." She removed her glasses and wiped her eyes. "Everyone here worked with him for several years. We lost a family member. Such a shock to ..."

Roare placed an arm around her, and the assistant director buried her face into Roare's chest.

Sloane stared out the window, a clenched fist against the sill.

Around the room, crew members grieved together.

Gavin returned with red-rimmed eyes. "Today's been horrific. Why don't you guys go home? I'll reach out to you before the funeral. I'm too numb to say anything else."

Roare and Sloane refused to leave. She touched Gavin's forearm. "Now isn't the time to be alone."

"I suppose not," he said. "One thing is certain. There will be an investigation and an autopsy. He was the epitome of health. I need to know what went wrong."

"We're with you, one hundred percent." Roare patted his arm. "C'mon, let's take you home."

Chips's family had digested the news like a poisoned pill. Gavin chose to celebrate his life and legacy in an intimate setting. Family, close friends, crew, and plainclothes security—thirty-seven altogether—gathered on a crisp Thursday evening in late March, two weeks after Chips had passed.

"How're you doing?" Roare asked Sloane as she sat beside him. "Why didn't you speak at the service?"

He puffed and gazed downward. "I birthed this project to expose the people who turned me into a freak and what they intend to do to all humanity. One of my best friends is dead, your brothers were nearly killed, three attempts on your life, and look what happened to Dr. Ponte." He pounded his fist on his leg. "Maybe your mom was right."

"Are you telling me to shelve the film?"

"Yeah."

"You overestimate your responsibility for this."

"I do blame myself for Chips's death, but I won't, however, allow them to get away with this." He looked her in the eye. "Dr. Ghaderi's father is a high-ranking member of the Illuminati. The AI surgery robot severed a major artery—intentionally."

"You and I both know these *incidents* are all Match's directive. We need to take down this monster." Roare rubbed her left temple.

"I agree," he said. "Stopping the film no longer matters. We know too much. Match retaliated. Our turn now. What I blurted earlier about quitting was my guilt talking. Finish the film. The decision is yours. Anyhow, Chips's crewmembers make a great team. They're committed as long as you are."

"As the bodies stack up, I'm not so sure anymore."

On the way home, the weight of Chips's demise pressed against Roare's soul. When they entered the apartment, Wyatt pulled her into a strong embrace. As she leaned her head on his shoulder, she teared up.

"What else, Wy? I've returned from the front line of a battlefield, and death is lingering like a vapor. I can't take much more of this." She wiped her eyes with the back of her hand, and they walked to the living room sofa. "I'm numb and beside myself with anger," she continued. "I want to leave everything behind, hide somewhere, never to be seen again."

"No more negative talk, Gobo. Satan knows your intentions, knows why you were chosen. Therefore, his puppets are coming at you hard. He doesn't want any good to come of your efforts. On behalf of the lives already lost and the countless billions who are clueless, on behalf of our future children and life on earth, you *must* finish. Chips's passing was cruel. I know you'll honor the work he's done, but his is completed. Yours must go on."

Roare closed her eyes and rested her head against the sofa. Though she couldn't linger on remorse, she didn't want to hear those words. "I know, babe. At times, I want to take the easy way out."

Wyatt cradled her hand in his palm. "Doing something significant will never be simple, and ultimately worth the cost."

She pursed her lips. "I hope so."

As Wyatt left for work, Roare ran to the kitchen to answer her cell phone. "Morning, Gavin."

"Why aren't you here at the think tank?"

"You don't know why?"

"Let me rephrase my question. Chips never liked unfinished projects. You are a director on this project, right?"

"I suppose I am, but am I to be excluded from mourning a friend in peace?"

"My brother would reject your answer. You've been around him enough to know he'd say"—he imitated Chips's voice—"'You've mourned me enough. We've got work to do until God says otherwise. Wasted time is lost opportunity.'"

"You either have nerves of steel, or you're cold-blooded. You only buried your brother yesterday. Chips inflated me to be a superstar, and there's no way I can deliver the film without his signature. Anyway, I'm not certain of anything now."

"Horsefeathers. If you weren't capable, he wouldn't have put his reputation on the line. Before he went under the knife, he told me to finish the film. Unless you're on our team, our efforts will be pointless."

Roare paced. "Is everyone else on the same page?"

"The crew wants you back. CGI, even the actors are on board."

"And when was this decided?"

"After you left yesterday. Are you in?"

She stopped short. She'd put her family, the whistleblowers, *herself*, and Chips through hellfire. Why should these people trust in her?

Wait a minute. The entire project never had anything to do with her—this was God's decree.

"I'm highly regarded by you all?"

"Chips too. Let's shake the boots off humanity, to give people a preview of things coming to their doorsteps. Besides, we could use the money."

The corners of Roare's lips turned up. "Do I hear the cry of poor starving wolves?"

"No, but I had to hook you to make you laugh."

"You did. Between God, my hubby, and all of you ..." she took a deep breath, "I'm in."

chapter thirty—adrenaline rush

Courage is not the absence of fear. Courage is action in spite of fear. Courageous people never really overcome their fears. They just become determined to push through them and to use that adrenaline to their advantage.
—Jeff Myers

Sloane still fumed over the loss of Chips and the trail of decimated lives in the wake of the film. But as he gazed at the skyline from his apartment, he considered his next move against Match.

He sat behind his desk and began opening mail. Noticed a yellow envelope. He gave a cautious squeeze. Documents, something squarish and hard. *Who is this from?* No return address, but the postage showed Zürich, Switzerland. His AI eyes scanned the contents—safe to open. The envelope contained a bubble-wrapped external hard drive in a mini hardcase, along with a flash drive and a three-page letter from Raidon Tekeda.

Match's uncle. He could've found me years ago. Why now? He read the letter.

I can't believe what I'm reading. Match is not only a megalomaniac, he's also demon-possessed—the true agenda of CoSynthesis. Sloane leaned back in his chair and pinched his earlobe as he continued reading.

From the details Raidon provided, Sloane surmised Match was no longer human. *He's gone off the rails!* "Once Match becomes a complete cyborg," he read aloud, "he believes he'll be able to live in another planetary system. Meanwhile, he'll betray humanity and his military constituents."

Sloane shook his head in dismay. How could the employees at CoSynthesis live with themselves for using children in their experiments? *I shouldn't expect anything less from the monster who murdered his father as a boy.* He continued reading, "Match's goal is to provide the Drexans full access to all the resources of Earth. When all humans are eliminated, the planet will be pillaged, then destroyed by the Drexans and the god-like CoSynthesis cyborgs." *We don't have much time.*

After this confession, challenging Match's authority, and possessing intricate details of CoSynthesis, Sloane realized Raidon's death had been sealed. Raidon had nothing to lose. By now, Raidon *was* dead. *This parcel was a missile, not intended for me but for Match. His own nephew, whom he'd groomed. All I need to do is detonate it. What am I but half a mortal with a soul, unafraid to die. But not just yet. Outstanding matters warrant a conclusion.*

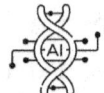

Sloane had a tight window in which to organize his global mercenary group, Loyalists for Peace—former military personnel, black-ops members, and rogue CIA assets from all over the world, committed to protecting the planet and its species from domestic, foreign, and intra-terrestrial invasions. Sloane and his team hashed out a plan to infiltrate Match's Canadian underground site, where the mercenaries would demand his presence and take over the site.

As the last meeting was concluding, Sloane emphasized, "Raidon gave us leverage. We have access to schematics, security codes, the best undetectable entry points, plans to destroy the lab and AI borgs. But," he paused, "there will be casualties."

A military officer asked, "Will our arsenal be enough to stop them?"

"I haven't room for doubt. Raidon's notes indicate implanting a nano-virus into an orifice of these borgs will render them useless. Schaefer's idea to infuse the utility fog with the nano-virus is not only brilliant but will have massive impact in a short amount of time."

Scout said, "Well then."

"Ladies and gentlemen, the goal is to eliminate the army of borgs, take out Match, and destroy the facility. At 2200 hours three days from today, we'll gather at Raven Rock at Blue Ridge Summit in Canada."

Scout asked, "What about the girl?"

"Roare? I don't want her involved in this operation, but she will be a catalyst. I'm going to have her disseminate a film teaser on all social media platforms, showing an interview with a CoSynthesis whistleblower."

"Yeah, he'll be pushed over the edge," Atticus said. "Coinciding the two offensives will bring him out of his hole."

"With anticipation," Sloane said. "This is not only a tech battle, but it's of supernatural and other-worldly origin. Don't be surprised if you see unnatural activity."

When Sloane picked up Roare to drive her to Gavin's studio, he brought her up to speed.

"I can't believe what I'm hearing," she said. "Match has gone off the rails. Infighting among blood relatives? Are you going to take down his labs? When do we go?"

"Ah, no. There is no *we*. I promised Wyatt I'd keep you alive. You'll have to sit this one out. I'd like you to create a film teaser with a clip of Dr. Ponte's testimony. Gavin and the crew can help you distribute it."

"All right then. I like to pretend I'm a fighter, but I'm just a pacifist artist."

"No one should like violence. Unfortunately, there are some who do. Roare, everything we're doing is critical to the future of our planet."

chapter thirty-one—insurgence

We both have war inside us. Sometimes it keeps us alive.
Sometimes it threatens to destroy us.
—Veronica Roth, *Insurgent*

Forty members of Loyalists for Peace boarded the MC-130P Combat Shadow with high tech equipment, body armor, drones, lead shields, robotics for bomb detonation, scuba and tactical gear, armaments, and medics. Sloane was pleased the Canadian Special Operations Forces Command agreed to cooperate and assist. They too had a special interest in shutting down a shadow-government operation.

At 2330 hours, the aircraft landed at Jasper-Hinton Airport. Sloane and his team arrived at 0030 hours and divided into three groups: Red Dawn, Door of Destiny, and Gideon. Park rangers had provided detailed electronic terrain maps of hidden tunnels and caverns, while Sloane and two geoengineers cross-referenced them with the info from Raidon.

The Red Dawn team carried tech equipment down a private path to a shaft that descended to the outer wall of the underground AI facility—the wall they'd breach.

The Door of Destiny team hiked through the forest two and a half miles to an underground geothermal energy station which powers the AI base and quantum computers. Their objective was to implant a nano-virus into the computer, kill the energy source, and contaminate the targeted satellite.

The Gideon team would dive underwater to vacuum tubes, taking them farther below to electromagnetic trains that would arrive at the AI center. The Canadian military would capture the rogue scientists, while Sloane's three teams surrounded the cyborg factory and destroyed the small army of borgs.

Sloane would wait for Match. Realizing his own shortcomings—his own humanness—brought concern over the icy conditions and the inability to control the impending chaos. *I'm not pleased with the odds. In theory, this should all work out. Which side will have the bigger body count? God be with us.*

Sloane and Co-commander Gage relied on satellite ground terminals and Personal Role Radio—small transmitter-receiver headsets—to communicate tactical orders to the other teams. The two commanders eyed each other, signaling readiness. Sloane gave the word. The Door of Destiny team broke the locks on the geothermal station. Sloane and Gage exchanged smirks—couldn't believe the station didn't have any alarms.

The Door of Destiny team, led by Canadian squadron leader Paxton, got the green light from Gage to proceed into the two-story building. They peered above the rails. Four men in white lab coats sat in front of transparent display screens in a glass computer room housing several quantum processors. The team moved below the grated floors in a labyrinth of cables and wiring. They relied on the memorized blueprints to disable biometric sensors and cameras. Disabling the geothermal system alerted the CoSynthesis IT techs. Now, the Loyalists' tech engineers could implant the viral software.

Just as one of the Loyalist techs reached the nearest computer, a call went out, "Breach! Breach! Inform security!"

A CoSynthesis tech pressed the alarm key, but a red error message popped up. He screamed, "There's a malfunction!"

Other Loyalists swarmed on the IT techs, who lunged at the intruders. But they dropped dead—plasma phasers, which destroyed their internal organs.

Two more IT techs responded to the alarm and immediately rushed the Loyalists. A team member drop kicked the IT tech. The man flew back and slid across the floor.

He got back up. "Ugh!" He charged again but met his demise with a plasma phaser. With a loud thud, he dropped to the floor.

Meanwhile, another Loyalist wrestled with the last IT tech. They exchanged blows to the face and stomach. The Loyalist grabbed the tech's hair and drove his head into his knee. Bloodied and dazed, the man lost his footing and reeled back. The Door of Destiny team member finished him off with a snap of his neck.

He ran to the console and entered the override password provided by Raidon. He inserted the viral software that would also infect the satellite.

Paxton informed Sloane and Gage the geothermal station was disabled, the virus was installed, and would take nine minutes for the virus to run through the quantum software.

The Door of Destiny team had needed only twelve minutes to succeed. By now, the Red Dawn team would have their laser ready to break into the lab. As soon as an opening was created, the two teams would meet. Meanwhile, the Gideon team had donned their neoprene scuba suits with armaments around their waists, back, legs and forearms.

Phase Two began.

At 0115, the Red Dawn team breached the AI lab where the borgs resided. The team dispersed in threes and moved silently, surrounding the borgs in the dark, spacious factory. The Door of Destiny team joined them with net launchers loaded. Other Loyalists hid behind pillars with drones and utility fog in position.

Red Dawn's leader said to the drone operator, "On my mark, as soon as you see their blue laser eyes, fire up. Turn them and this place inside out."

The drone operator saluted. "We'll let 'em have it. You think they know we're here?"

"They do if they're sentients, but only one way to be sure," the lead said.

The room was dead silent for twenty seconds. No one breathed.

In the corner, a borg's eyes pulsed. The head pivoted to the left, as if communicating with the borg nearby. The second borg acknowledged and came to life. Its eyes glowed blue. Within seconds, all the cyborgs activated. Like a Roman testudo, they formed a layered circle in the center of the spacious cyborg plant and faced out in all directions. Their eyes opened and brightened.

Paxton signaled with a closed fist, then a thrust of his arm. Hasty ambush.

A swarm of drones hovered over the circle of borgs.

The borgs fired their lasers.

Most of the drones dodged and fired back. Twelve were taken down.

With the borgs distracted, the Red Dawn team moved in slowly with lead shields, net guns, and utility fog. They waited for the command.

Boom!

White fish nets flew in the air. The borgs looked up. Some borgs fired their lasers, while others triggered high frequency waves to blast the ears of the Loyalists. Team members backed away and covered their ears. A couple of men screamed.

Then, the nets engulfed the borgs, and the utility fogs took shape. Their arms protruded and mirrored the borgs. The CoSynthesis borgs stood confused. The UFs attacked with lasers and plasma phasers. The borgs on both sides moved with lightning speed, creating a blinding, moving funnel, like a tornado.

The Red Dawn team took cover and watched until nothing remained but a pile of mangled silicone, metal, and computer parts in ashes.

The medics tended to the Loyalists. Those injured by the sound waves did not survive the damage to their brains. Other team members had suffered laser blast burns. When most of the men were patched up, Paxton signaled to return to the command center. He radioed Sloane the update.

"Excellent news considering the odds against us. How many casualties?" Sloane asked.

Paxton said, "Two down for good. A few of us are injured, but we'll recover. We'll meet you at the command center. Call us for backup if you're having trouble getting past those security borgs."

"Oh, we'll get past them all right. Stay sharp. We're heading down," Sloane said.

The virus was snaking its way to the satellite. Match would've been notified. He would appear soon.

Sloane and Gage signaled the Gideon team.

They pulled on goggles and engaged breathing apparatuses before diving in. Twelve members found six liquid chambers. Upon entering, the cylindrical space drained, became airtight, and vacuumed them farther down.

When they reached the bottom, the chambers opened to a dry cavern floor. Electromagnetic trains awaited them. Sloane warned, "Expect a fight at the end of this ride."

"We're ready. Are you?" Atticus asked.

Lord, shield us. "I was ready ten years ago." Sloane waved them on.

The team boarded the train. The speed was something to behold—warp speed as smooth as silk.

One team member observed, "I guess they don't make local stops."

A couple of others snickered.

Gage snapped his head. "Spare the jokes."

"Apologies, sir. Wanted to take the edge off," the Gideon team member said.

Sloane warned, "Weapons out, we're about to go live."

The doors opened. The team spilled out and checked the area. Sloane sensed they weren't alone.

Six large borg guardsmen appeared like apparitions. They touched their chests in unison, creating a shock wave that knocked back the entire team. Two men yelled out in pain when their backs hit the doors of the train. One of them crumbled to the floor, dead.

"Plasma phasers!" Sloane shouted. His blue laser eyes sent a series of beams at the borgs, but they didn't flinch. *The virus had better take effect soon, or we're all dead.*

Eight Gideon team members fired their plasma phasers. Four of the guards blocked the energy with their palms, but two succumbed to incineration. The remaining four advanced, but stopped midstride, like sculptures.

Gage nodded at Sloane. "The virus is working."

Sloane ordered everyone to proceed and radioed the other teams. "We're on our way."

Paxton said, "Good to know. We have visitors. Hurry."

Match. No better time.

Match appeared in all-black ninja gear. Two cyborgs flanked him. Sloane recalled them from the gala event. The Loyalists surrounded the pad, but they had been immobilized.

Sloane glared at Match. He was the only one able to move. Even Match's guardians were suspended in time. *How is this happening?*

"I froze time so we can have a private chat," Match said coolly.

"Your talents are endless. What have you done to my team?"

"I had to even the body counts. You took out half of my borgs, so a proper response was for me to do the same."

"Not exactly the same, Match. Your army consists of cyborgs with the souls of children you destroyed. These people are human beings—"

"Whom I care nothing for."

"What can you possibly gain by wiping us all out of existence?"

"Full access to all of Earth's resources." He scoffed having to state the obvious. "The Drexans hate the way useless humans waste resources. Once your species is eliminated, this planet will be pillaged, then destroyed."

"And what's your next step afterwards?"

"Once I become a complete cyborg, I won't need to live here anymore. I'll be able to embrace my eternal life on a star of my own in their solar system."

"Sounds perfect for you. You'll never grow weary of yourself."

"Hardly likely," Match took a step closer. "Now you've placed a wrench in my plans. I should've completed you as a cyborg. You and your sidekick have become quite the nuisance. My constituents dropped me because of you and her."

"Not my problem." Sloane crossed his arms. "You must've inherited some demonic souls—how else could you've murdered your father at such a young age? If only your mother knew what you'd done."

"Leave her be. How did you know? No one knew except ..."

"Yes, you've been betrayed by your own. Even if you become a full cyborg, your soul will still be tied to your mother, father, uncle—all your ancestors."

Match's blue eyes lit up as he went for Sloane's throat.

Sloane forced his arms under Match's to break his grip. Freed, he staggered back and coughed. But Match kicked him in the stomach. Sloane doubled over and clutched his middle.

Sloane harnessed his rage and blasted a blue laser beam through Match's forearm. Match groaned but remained unfazed.

The fiend climbed to the top of the command center and jumped, then used his legs to wrap around Sloane's head.

rage against the machine

They landed on the floor with a thud. Sloane maneuvered out of the headlock, jumped into a jujitsu stance.

Fists, kicks, headbutts followed.

Match threw three ninja stars.

Sloane dodged, but one grazed his left cheek. Blood drawn.

Need to end this now. Sloane retrieved a plasma phaser from his utility belt and fired.

The blast stunned Match. He recoiled into a ball. He dropped. But in the next second, he sent a laser toward Sloane.

Sloane's arm sliced open. He phased again. *His intuitive abilities are gone*, Sloane realized. *The level of sensitivity to his surroundings has diminished.*

Match stood, glared at Sloane, then soared to the ceiling. And disappeared.

Wounded but not destroyed, yet. Sloane sighed, fighting discouragement. *He'll return to base, transition to a full cyborg, and leave the planet. He's made a pact with demons and doesn't even know it.*

With Match gone, the Loyalists reanimated. They had no memory of what transpired.

Match's two cyborgs remained incapacitated from the virus.

Sloane ordered two team members to finish them off.

The borgs dropped to the ground.

"Chief, what happened?" Atticus asked. "You look like you've been at war."

"We'll debrief later. We need to take our fallen back home. By the way, I planted a utility fog on the back of Match's neck while we were engaged in fighting. He might be attacked in his sleep."

Everyone grinned.

Scout said, "Nobody more deserving."

"I concur," another team member chimed.

A medic attended to Sloane's wounds, while Gage and some soldiers rounded up rogue scientists to be turned over to federal agents.

Match made his choice a long time ago, and Satan stole his soul. And all the souls of those children, God will hold them dearly.

chapter thirty-two—the flight of the godwit

Endurance is not just the ability to bear a hard thing,
but to turn it into glory.—William Barclay

Roare was overjoyed. If all went well, the film would wrap mid-March and move on to editing. "What a wonderful surprise we have use of the federal courthouse Saturday *and* Sunday," Roare said to Sloane and Wyatt as they drove to Springfield. "We have to finish the scene this weekend."

Sloane glanced at her in the rearview mirror. "There will be extra security on-site."

"Great. Sunrise will be stunning." Roare took a sip of tea.

Wyatt glanced back from the front seat. "You couldn't have chosen a more beautiful setting."

Roare radiated. "Well, of course we did—your brilliant suggestion."

As sunlight inched through the courthouse at dawn the next morning, Gavin maneuvered a camera drone above the building's spine, supportive ribcage, and circular three-story form. The glass gave the appearance of weightlessness.

The drone entered the building for a timelapse of the light edging up the white-marble-and-glass staircase, through the corridors, and into the courtroom.

Meanwhile, Sloane reviewed safety integrity over the entire site.

When Roare and Wyatt entered the room with her gear, her mouth fell open. The Scandinavian theme presented straight, contemporary lines in honey-colored wood—a clean, minimalist design. "I thought a courtroom would be dark and menacing, but I was wrong. Here, I thought I was walking into a room to accept the Nobel Peace Prize."

"I know, right?" Wyatt's eyes glistened in appreciation.

"I'm gonna perch behind the judge's bench and get my camera ready. Can you ask Gavin to send in the actors when he finishes his shot?"

"Sure."

As the actors took their places, Sloane stood to Roare's left. With a glazed, serious stare, he studied each person who came through the door. Other security personnel posed as part of the audience. When everyone had taken their positions, filming began:

Before an eleven-judge panel of humans and cyborgs stood attorneys representing the international case The People v. CoSynthesis Dynamic Ventures Inc. On the left side of the gallery sat the multinational physicists and transhumanists. Many of them glared at their opposition.

A middle-aged, bearded physicist said to the young woman beside him, "These people are mentally deranged. They're too closed-minded to look far into the future."

She nodded. "You're so right."

Pro-humanists filled the right side of the gallery. Men and women, young and old, shot contemptuous looks at the transhumanists and scientists. Two women stood holding signs. "Refuse to alter your human genetics!" read one sign. "We oppose the new humans. Robots will turn against you!" was on the other in bold red letters.

A woman wearing a blue wool coat shouted, "You sit there looking smug. You mark my words—you are nothing but monsters creating demons!"

A forty-something man from the left rose and shoved his fist in the air. "Ignorant fools! Scientific advances will improve humankind. Homo sapiens would never evolve to perfection without science. You people are clueless!"

Six UN military personnel stationed around the room shifted on their feet, semiautomatic weapons at their sides.

A group of attorneys pleaded their case on behalf of defendant CoSynthesis, which had brought in a team of doctors, two scientists, and several global futurists. Across from them, a legal team spoke on behalf of the plaintiffs: three creationists, two psychologists, and a few bio-conservatives.

Despite the efforts of the People's team, a motion passed in favor of AI cyborgs being accepted as citizens of all nations and incorporated into every society. Their ruling warned humans who did not assimilate into a new society with cyborgs would risk being repurposed.

Two men on the right side stood on their chairs and threw eggs at the judge. Another threw a shoe.

Security tased the perpetrators. As they dragged them out of the courtroom, one of the pro-humanists turned to his associate and said, "A dystopian society is being formed before our eyes. We're finished as a species."

The courtroom erupted—as rehearsed, Roare and Gavin captured their reactions.

"Cut!" Roare smiled widely. "Powerful."

She was surely on the right path, and the triumph was sublime. With her purpose fulfilled, her confidence increased sevenfold. *Thank you, my Lord.* Tears threatened, as the pressure of the film released from her body like steam spewing from a radiator valve. She stood and clapped.

One by one, the others joined, and a couple of people whistled.

"Amazing job, everyone!" Roare said. "That's a wrap."

Filming was finally complete, and Roare couldn't wait to plunge into editing. She gathered with Gavin, Phoebe, two senior editors, a visual-effects director, and the two CGI leads. A sea of computers, large monitors, and specialized software ran in the background of the large, gray, and highly advanced technical room.

Dresdyn and Mathieu had already created a mock background. Now, using wire-framed models for robots, they merged each movement into scenes, frame by frame. Their high-power graphics computers allowed them to seamlessly blend photorealistic objects as if they were camera shots.

Mathieu glanced at his screen. "Merging CGI into your film is an art. You can't imagine the enormity of particulars."

"Well, yes, we can imagine," Roare said. "All of us have tremendous respect for the creativity and patience you put into your movie magic." She whispered to Gavin, "I'm out of my league with this technology. I can visualize what I want, but I haven't used CGI until now."

"Yeah, pretty mind-blowing. I'm still playing catch-up myself," he said. "Chips was the expert. I'll stick to my camera."

rage against the machine

"And those composers next door live on another planet with their headsets on. The score is as important as the editing."

"Both take massive focus and manpower," Dresdyn said over his shoulder. "The extra techs have been a big help."

"Do you need any more hands on deck?" Roare asked.

The visual-effects director conferred with the CGI team. "We could deliver the project by late summer if we had three more engineers, provided there aren't many changes after the cut variations."

Roare smiled at Gavin. "Granted." Relief washed over her like a gentle wave.

"Presume we have a hit film," he said.

She smiled.

Dresdyn stopped what he was doing. "When we're done, and you two sign off on the final cut, I know our film will be spectacular."

Roare settled into domestic bliss. She hibernated from the world and gave Pilar a month's paid vacation. Roare and Wyatt spent time with their families and a few weekends at their friends' vacation homes in Nantucket.

Every now and then, she thought about Match, wondered if he was still on the planet. Prayed she'd never see him again. *Things have gone quiet. What has become of the Antarctica lab? Hmph. I'm not going to let peace spook me—or go to waste.* CGI was nearly finished, and the sample clip they sent would've brought joyous tears to Chips's eyes. Gavin had reported CGI would be done by early September, and Roare told him about the wrap party she and Pilar were planning.

At Pilar's suggestion, Roare decided on 74Wythe, a charming urban space in Brooklyn. Jbird Cocktails Lounge was lavishly retro Hollywood—green velvet, clamshell barstools, parquet floors, black-and-white marble bar, and icicle-shaped chandelier. Super glam.

The first week of November brought a sharply frigid Thursday evening. In Sloane's SUV, Wyatt, Pilar, and Roare headed to the celebration.

"Now confess, who's on the A-list for tonight's soiree?" Wyatt asked.

"The usual suspects," Roare said. "The film crew, the CGI team, Arlo, and a couple of TGIET journalists. Phoebe and Gavin invited some of Chips's close friends, and I invited Drue and Ram."

Sloane cleared his throat. "And I invited extra security."

Roare placed her hand gently on his shoulder. "I value your efforts."

When they arrived, most of the guests were already mingling to a mixture of alternative music and jazz. At Roare's request, the movie trailer of *Rage Against the Machine* looped on large screens.

At a high point in the evening, Gavin raised his voice above the gaiety. "Excuse me, everyone. I want to make a toast."

The talking and music stopped.

"Everyone, raise your glasses to toast Roare and my brother, Chips. This film was a massive effort, and none of us could've gotten this completed without them. Most of you worked with Chips for many years. He thought of you as family, and I know the feelings were mutual." He looked at Roare. "Though we've known Roare for only a short time, she's part of our family too."

"Here, here," a crew member shouted. Others whistled and cheered.

Roare raised her hand. "Working with extremely talented people was a pleasure and privilege. Let's take a moment of silence for Chips, who dedicated his life to film, and to those who lost their lives during the making of this film."

The somber remembrance gave way to more celebration, and the evening carried on until midnight.

chapter thirty-three—vantage point

Live your life each day as you would climb a mountain.
An occasional glance toward the summit keeps the goal
in mind, but many beautiful scenes are to be observed
from each new vantage point.—Harold B. Melchart

Wyatt entered Barachou, took a seat across from Sloane, and ordered a flat white.

"You caught me at a convenient time." Sloane sipped coffee. "What can I do you for?"

"You know this *Rage* project consumed Roare and nearly beat her into the ground. She puts up a good front, but her mind is someplace else. Now would be a good time to retreat. We'll give Roare a chance to rejuvenate her spirit—and mine."

"While the film is being promoted, she could still be in danger. What's your idea of a relaxed environment?"

"You have contacts around the world. Where can I take Roare far from here yet close enough to still see her family?"

Sloane nodded slowly. "I have connections in Iceland. I'll give them a heads up you'll be contacting them."

"I don't know if she'll agree, Iceland's super cold."

"Not as cold as you'd suspect and not year-round. Iceland's rated as one of the best places to live—strong economy, diverse culture. And communities of believers. The best way to hook her is to take her there." Sloane checked his watch. "Sorry, I have a meeting. I'll drop off detailed info at your office. Probably better if we communicate off-grid."

On his way out, Wyatt purchased mini cream puffs. He knew the way to his wife's heart. Roare loved their home, but she wasn't made to live in the city. They needed to leave while they still had a grip on their identities.

"Oh, you've been to Barachou's," Roare greeted.

He held the bag above his head, out of her reach. "You can have a treat after you fix lunch for us. I'll set the table."

"Total bribery!" She poked his side. "Whatever you have smells delicious."

While Wyatt prepared the dining area, Roare made omelets with salmon, salad, and kombucha. She carried everything to the table.

"Candles and flowers too?" She eyed him as they sat down. "Ah-ha, you're up to something."

He took a deep breath. "How would you like to take a trip?"

"Pardon me?"

"We both need a break. You're still recovering from the past year and a half, and I've been working long hours. A change of scenery would do us both good."

"What do you have in mind?" Roare leaned forward.

"How does Iceland grab you?"

She raised her eyebrows and touched a hand to his forehead. "You running a fever?"

He snickered. "No, I'm dead serious. I've had this on the forefront of my mind for a while."

"A move, then, not a trip?"

"Gobo, I want us to have a normal life, even if it's a brief moment."

She let the idea sink in. "Suppose Iceland isn't good for us?""

"We'll find another location. However, I'm going with my heart."

"All right, I'm game. Where'd this plan come from, you or the Holy Spirit?" Roare asked, then tilted her head to one side.

Wyatt laughed. "Pretty sure the Holy Spirit prompted me ... and me wanting to protect you from any more disasters. This film has caused abominable things to happen to us, family members, and friends

"What do you see?"

"We're overdue in writing another chapter of our lives while we still can. We can't become victims of someone else's agenda. With the world changing so drastically, life is fragile. Uncertain. We've worked hard, sacrificed much of ourselves, and I'd like the chance to create a new reality—made sense to approach Sloane for suggestions." Wyatt leaned back in his seat and folded his hands behind his head.

"You mean unplug from this reality?" Roare stretched out her hand across the table.

Wyatt grabbed her hand. "Sounds about right."

"We both may have some degree of PTSD. Reason enough to move. Arlo will submit the film to the Cannes next year. I have plenty of time until then."

"Me too."

"A change of scenery could be great. Can I have a cream puff now?" Roare grinned.

Nine days later, they flew to Keflavik and checked in to the Reykjavik Konsulat Hotel.

"This city is nothing like Manhattan," Wyatt said as they planned a day of museum visits. "Seems easygoing."

"Trendy, with culture," Roare agreed. "I read you need only one day to see everything here."

"Let's take our time and see as much as we want. If we end up moving, we'll have time to see the entire country."

"Wy, I've been saturated in peace over the past two days. Must be the air."

The next day, Roare and Wyatt visited the black sandy beach of Reynisfjara, then bathed in the pale waters of the Blue Lagoon. Roare took a few photos, then they cruised north to meet Sloane's friends.

They parked near the fishing docks along the shoreline of the Eyjafjörður fjords in Akureyri. They were early for their appointment with Freyja and Havarr Jóhannsson. With the extra time, Roare and Wyatt strolled along the harbor.

Roare drank in the beauty. God had removed a veil to give a preview of what heaven would be like, and the view was jaw-dropping. The simplicity of the fjords—the serene water gently rocked the boats. Colorful grass-roofed homes dotted rolling hills.

Wyatt took photos of the ships. "Detaching from the rest of the world is nice for a change."

"I think so, but we'd better get to the restaurant."

They walked to Rub23. Freyja boasted about the excellent Japanese cuisine. Roare was salivating already.

Inside, Roare took a step back to keep a safe distance from the Jóhannssons. They were older by at least thirty years. She politely shook the woman's hand and greeted her with a smile.

Freyja was the same height as Roare, with fair skin, wavy, shoulder-length blonde hair, and pale blue eyes. Her casual knitwear was simple and classy. She was incredibly fit for her age. "I'm pleased to meet you," she said. Her face lit up when she grinned.

"I hope I'm not being rude, but are you an athlete?" Roare asked.

Freyja clasped her hands in front of her waist. "I am reasonably active. We both are."

Havarr towered over Wyatt by a foot, wore dark denim jeans and wool attire. *He seems to take himself quite seriously.* His brown-and-gray hair swept behind his ears, while his thick, dark mustache couldn't be ignored. He held a briefcase in his left hand. "Hello to you. Forgive my manners." He and Wyatt shook hands.

The four of them sat in a corner of the restaurant next to a window overlooking the harbor.

"How do you like our country so far?" Freyja asked.

Wyatt took Roare's hand. "We're charmed," he said, "and surprised by the mild temperatures."

"During the winter, they can dip to minus twenty-three Celsius in the north," Havarr said. "Here is quite similar to what you're used to. I must admit, we still boast about the beautiful northern lights."

"I can imagine," Roare said. "I love the creative atmosphere I get about the city."

The getting-to-know-you exchange flowed effortlessly while they ate.

As the lunch came to an end, Wyatt said, "Sloane thought you could help us settle here if we decide to."

Freyja grinned. "If you hadn't decided already, you wouldn't have come."

Roare said, "You're probably right. Wy has more intuition than I do. We want to slow down enough to grab hold of our sanity. And maybe raise a family."

"To live peacefully in a safe and healthy environment and not have to look over your shoulder every minute. A good thing. This is place where your children can play and explore what God created." Freyja had practically read Roare's mind.

"Our architectural firm is developing a private community of custom homes here on the fjord. There will be only six houses, not far from the town center, churches, schools, and shops. Seen yet unseen," Havarr said.

"What do you mean?" Wyatt asked.

"These are standalone structures with the privacy you need," Havarr said. "Yet, they're still connected by courtyards and glass passageways. The concept is to build small communities where people look after one another, to build a sustainable support system to benefit everyone."

"Innovative," Roare said.

"Brilliant, actually, given the direction the world is going. This is far better to start relying more on like-minded people and less on government."

Wyatt stroked his chin. "You mean, self-governance? We should be moving toward *this* instead of fighting a failing system."

"Agreed," Havarr said. "Sloane helped us ensure strong safety measures."

Roare smirked. "Why am I not surprised? Technology has its advantages."

"One such benefit is camouflage. In case of an emergency, a hydraulic system will lower the houses underground and surround them with bombproof coverings and a layer of grass and rock to blend in. As Freyja described—seen yet unseen."

"Incredible," Roare said. "Let's say we wanted to contact family in other parts of the world, or order medical supplies and food?"

"While you're underground, GPS is blocked. If you need to communicate, there are a broadband radio and landlines," Havarr said. "We advise storing at least a year's worth of food and a medical supply kit. We encourage residents to take CPR and first aid courses."

"Who exactly would be our neighbors?"

"Don't worry. All buyers must have family values, be morally grounded, and advocate a peaceful existence. We also look for a balance of skill sets."

"Like farming, nursing, electrical …" Wyatt offered.

"Exactly," Freyja said. "A nice blend of talents to support your environment."

Havarr leaned in. "We'll help you with the immigration application. The government will consider Wyatt's pathology background a necessity and give your application priority. Iceland allows us to do extensive background checks on potential residents." He placed his napkin on the table and raised his hand toward the waiter. "We have our issues, much like other countries. However, most Icelanders are proud of what we have and value community. Freyja and I have a long-standing friendship with Sloane, and we extend our hospitality to you."

Roare recalled her brothers' rescue. "We've been through a lot with him."

Freyja's eyes softened. "A decision to relocate to an unfamiliar country is a lot to process. Iceland's a lovely place to live as you want. Take time to consider the idea." She handed Roare and Wyatt brochures of the housing project. "We can tell you live with purpose and want peace. We'd love to have you here, and we'd look after you. Check over the material, ask us anything at all, and let's talk soon, yes?"

Havarr took care of the lunch expenses, and the group left.

Roare and Wyatt held hands on their walk through Akureyri, getting to know the city. Back in their hotel room, they were greeted by a huge bouquet and dark chocolates, compliments of the Jóhannssons.

For Roare and Wyatt, prayer was a must with any decision, especially life-altering ones. Home from their trip, they pressed in toward the Creator. They fasted during the day, sojourned quietly during the evening, then waited to hear God's voice.

Three weeks passed, and they sat on the floor cushions in their living room one evening after dinner to read the Bible and pray.

"I had a vision a couple of days ago," Wyatt said. "I saw us surrounded by water and rolling green hills. We'd catch lots of fish, which didn't exactly mean 'fish.'"

Roare braided a few strands of her hair. "Wow, goosebumps. Last night, I dreamed of waterfalls cascading over a mountain high in the sky. Then something came to me during tea this afternoon. 'The sound of water will be part of a different path for you as a couple. I will teach you a new thing.' Does this mean I won't be filming anymore?"

"Maybe God'll use your talents differently."

"Maybe so. My dream reminded me of Canada. But my heart is pulling toward Iceland. Reminds me of when I shop online. I put items in my cart—four or five similar items because I can't decide. At checkout, I eliminate what I don't want and go back to the first item."

"Why?"

"Hear me out. The first item resonates with me, I want to be sure it's what I want. At the end of the day, I decide without regret."

"God's nudging us. Let's decide, Gobo. Let's build a home in Iceland and give ourselves five years. We can always keep our apartment here. How does it sound?"

Roare considered everything one last time. "Yes, I believe I can do this without regret, but there will be times when I'll grieve being away from my family and friends."

"Oh babe, I know how close you are to your family. It would be unnatural if you didn't miss them, but we can have them visit as often as you'd like."

Roare had been saying goodbye to her family for the past six months. She wouldn't be able to just pop over to see Lane, Ben, and her brothers when she wanted, or go for a run in Central Park, or play a jazz gig in the city. *I'm going to miss them. Special places Wy and I shared can never be forgotten or replaced. But there are some memories I'd rather leave behind and can't. What about my career? Am I going to Iceland just to loaf around? Is it normal to have doubts when moving to a new country.*

In early June, Roare looked forward to getting on a plane to Iceland in a few days. As her nerves settled slightly over the past year, she felt secure with Sloane's associate Frost in her home while Wyatt was at work.

While Roare sat at her laptop in the dining room, she felt the hair on the back of her neck stand up. Someone was behind her.

She snapped her head around to find Match.

Startled, she snatched her cell phone and backed away from him. Her mind raced and she eyed the cast iron poker beside the fireplace.

"What in blazes are you doing in my home?" She went for the poker.

Match grabbed her wrist and pulled her close to him.

Her cell phone crashed to the floor.

"We're good to go," came Frost's voice as he descended the stairs to the living room. "The upstairs perimeter is secure."

Roare couldn't speak.

"Roare? Did you hear me? Where are you?"

"Kitchen. I'm not alone." She tried to remain calm. Moving just her eyes, she spotted Frost, gun in hand, inching toward the kitchen door.

"Who's our guest?" He used his serious bodyguard voice now.

"Come and join us," Match taunted. He twisted Roare's arm behind her back.

Roare squirmed and tried to pull away, winced at the pain up her arm.

Frost charged into the kitchen, then aimed at Match. "Get away from her. Get out of here right now!"

Roare shouted, "Frost, stop! Don't come any closer. He'll kill you."

"No, you need to go!" Frost said.

Match shoved Roare to the floor.

She scrambled for cover behind the kitchen island and searched the drawers for something to use as a weapon. The cast-iron skillet. *God, send your angels. Help us!*

Frost pulled the trigger.

A laser beam burst from Match's eyes.

The bullet liquified, spilling to the floor.

Frost looked stunned but recovered quickly and lunged for Match.

Though Frost towered over him, Match charged and rammed his head into Frost's belly, knocking him back.

No! Now Match has room to torch Frost's insides. Roare's adrenaline overtook her fear. Holding the skillet like a bat, she darted out from her hiding place and came up behind Match. She pulled back and whacked Match hard across the back of his head.

He grabbed his skull and wobbled. Went down on a knee, then stood.

Frost scrambled for the fire extinguisher. He sprayed the chemical foam over Match's face and torso.

Match jerked back, screaming. Fumbling blindly, he shook violently and flailed at the foam. But his face was already burnt and blistering.

Roare wanted to run, but she couldn't leave Frost. *If a cracked skull didn't take him out, what will?* She recalled what Sloane had told her about cyborgs retaining their vital organs.

In seconds, the blisters across Match's face were gone. His skin was healing itself.

Frost hoisted the fire extinguisher and bashed Match's head again.

The maniac was down on both knees and disoriented. He wrapped both arms around Frost's legs and squeezed.

Frost's wail was heart-shattering.

Roare grabbed her longest knife and charged at Match, plunging it into his right kidney. Blood trickled from his side.

In those few seconds, Match wondered if he were hallucinating. A plethora of thoughts flooded his sense of reason. *Need to get back. Repair.*

Just then, Match caught a whiff of a familiar scent. Like when his father used to burn incense of peonies, plum blossom, agarwood, and other herbs to heighten clarity, eliminate depression, and increase intelligence.

He inhaled. Instant nauseating pain. He grimaced, struggled to breathe.

"Are you some kind of witch?" he wheezed.

Match disappeared.

Roare fell to her knees and sobbed. Frost lay on his side, trying to control his breathing. She didn't want to imagine the damage to his legs. The scent of peonies, plum blossom, agarwood, and herbs filled the room. *Peace from the Holy Spirit.*

Frost was struggling to reach his cell. "I'll get 911."

Roare shook her head. "They'll never believe us. Lie still, and I'll reach out to Sloane."

Now she found a greater reason to leave New York.

chapter thirty-four—concealed in plain view

Where does a wise man hide a leaf? In the forest.
—Father Brown, *The Broken Sword*

Over the next six months, Roare and Wyatt flew back and forth to approve housing materials, interior design, and security equipment for the house in Iceland. They took courses in CPR and first aid, then started the new year by settling into their new life.

They took in the view through the bulletproof glass at the front of their house. The landscape of rolling hills, fjords, and volcanic peaks along vast coastal cliffs brought peace. Each day, they'd watch the boats move in and out of the Akureyri harbor.

"They remind me of swans," Roare said, "gliding through water."

"I find the salty old fishermen more interesting. They're methodical yet lively. Maybe we need to chill out a bit too." Wyatt peered at her over his coffee mug.

"Could be. Life's different here. Strangely, I don't miss the stress."

"Your giftings are endless—go entirely independent, create feature films, change genres."

Roare laughed. "All good suggestions. Safer for sure."

"Definitely, but you're not done making movies. Once your mind's refreshed, no telling what ideas will develop. Don't force imagination. After all, we've only been here a few days."

"I do want to see what happens to *Rage*. Sloane left me a voicemail. Cannes rejected us. I should be torn up, but I'm not. There are other options. I keep hearing 'wait and see.'"

"While we're waiting and seeing, let's go for a hike and fill our lungs with Icelandic air."

Roare began a routine of early morning sessions in their community greenhouse. Gardening nourished her soul. She'd been given permission to start growing a field of purple coneflower and milkweed wildflowers with assistance from two other residents.

One day, she returned home with a bowl of berries. "Mom would be beside herself over my new hobby. I wouldn't have imagined in a billion years I would help grow food to support our community. The whole process is surreal, rewarding, and spiritual."

Wyatt laughed. "You say the same thing every time you go. I know this *is* spiritually healing. Jesus talked often of the harvest. I'm pleased you're getting into something you enjoy."

Roare beamed. Her cell phone rang. Sloane. "Hello?"

"You're in! *Rage* was accepted to DocFest in June. My instincts tell me you won't be attending?"

"Right. I'd rather maintain my low profile."

"Working through the PTSD will take time, but you will."

"Hmm, speaking of PTSD, any updates on CoSynthesis and Match?

"Canada's special forces rounded up the scientists who were *persuaded* to become whistleblowers to save their skins. TGIET has been inundated with testimonies."

"Wow. What about the Antarctica site and Match?"

Sloane groaned. "Logistically challenging. Only scientists and military personnel are allowed on the continent. Given the spotlight on CoSynthesis now, the military must do their own cleanup because they're indirectly involved. Whistleblowers said after the Canada incident, Match ordered half of his borgs to assimilate into society. This has become a matter of international security. Military agencies globally are working together on technology to detect them and flush them out."

"They'd be hard to recognize. My God, they could be anywhere, even here."

"Unlikely. Larger cities are the targets because they can go undetected. Meanwhile, a portion of his AI team fled. Those who remained assisted him in becoming a complete cyborg." Sloane explained Match's hallucinogenic tea, enabling him to see portals to other dimensions. He told her about the Drexans and the deal Match had made. "Match can now physically travel through portals to a solar system called Xa."

"You mean he's there now? What about the other borgs?"

"The virus we used is still infecting them. Though, not all the borgs—the more advanced ones were able to self-repair. Roare, they're sentients and decided for *themselves* to blend in with the human race. A remnant and two board members left with Match and escaped through the portal to Drexa."

"They did this on their own? My gosh, what a terrifying reality. So, this isn't over. Can these portals be closed?"

Roare's heart started racing. *Lord, not again. I don't want to even try to understand this.*

"Regrettably, no, to both. Scientists found a way to open portals but can't close them. All we've done was delay them a few years. Our species will have time to develop advanced technology to travel to other dimensions."

"This could take decades. Meanwhile, the whole world must come together to prepare for an invasion. I hope I'm dead by then."

"Don't say such things. Your purpose is just beginning. God is still on the throne. We don't have all the answers, but he does. For now, my advice is not to worry about any of this. You've gone through a meat grinder."

Roare huffed. "And, I still have the scars."

Sloane said. "Take heart, God and time will heal your soul. Go live your life."

"Sounds good to me."

"Great. Now, getting back to *Rage*, you'll create intrigue with your fans by not attending DocFest."

"Okay, makes sense." She nodded.

"Listen, I extended an invitation to Hunter and his family to DocFest."

"Great suggestion. I assume you, Gavin, and a few others will attend too?"

"Goes without saying," Sloane said.

"I'd be jealous, if I didn't have to deal with crowds.""

"You won't be left out. We've got a few ... creative things brewing."

"Sounds mysterious."

"I know." *Beep.*

"That little rat hung up on me again."

chapter thirty-five—metamorphosis

And do not be conformed to this world, but be transformed
by the renewing of your mind, that you may prove what
is that good and acceptable and perfect will of God.
—Romans 12:2 (NKJV)

June on the Gold Coast was brilliant. Hunter sat across
the desk from his barrister. "I'm in a good place, Manus.
Since releasing my pride, life has been easier to take. God
gave me a new perspective, and I'm grateful to be alive."

"You still have your family, you found your daughter,
and you kept your wits. I'd say you're on the pig's back,"
Manus replied.

"No kidding. God healed my body and revived my soul.
And Roare gave me a second chance. People touched me
with kindness I didn't deserve. I hope my visit explains
why I'm here to make changes."

"How can I help?"

"I'm going to sell my portion of the firm. My partners
would've liked me to stay on. Nonetheless, they understand
and want what's best for me. I also want to put together a
trust for Roare and Wyatt to pour into their future. My spirit
was nudged to do something for others. Investing in your

organization will rescue and protect children from human trafficking."

Manus nodded, and the men worked on the details.

"I'm overdue on making a difference in people's lives," Hunter said.

"I've never seen you so vulnerable. Shameful a grave illness brought you to your knees. I must admit, you are more human than ever before. Welcome to the real world, and I'll be honored to handle these things."

"I've got a lot of living to catch up on. I'm glad for your friendship. I hope we can bury the past."

"Already forgotten. Better not dwell on events we cannot alter."

"You're a gracious man." Hunter stood and shook Manus's hand. "You'll call me soon then?"

"Yes, when the paperwork is drawn up. I look forward to doing meaningful work with you."

"I'm going to enjoy philanthropy."

Hunter left the office, thanking God for showing him there were a few forthright people left in the world. He couldn't wait to see Evie—to take a walk, hold her hand, or gather a bunch of flowers from their garden. *Only don't turn me into a blubbering sap, Lord.*

Steam curled above a tin cup as Sloane poured himself tea outside his tent. Gavin and another close friend slept in two other tents nearby.

Sloane sat in a director's chair and gazed at Morraine Lake. A pristine morning draped the glacial landscape of Jasper National Park. Quiet. The water was still as a dinner plate. What a pity he and his buddies would disturb the peace with their fishing boat.

He could look at the massive elevations and endless tree lines forever. But if he didn't wake these guys soon, they'd be grumpy the rest of the day. As if on cue, they emerged from their tents and started making breakfast.

He glanced at his watch. Should be eleven in the morning there. "Hey, I need to place a call." He held up his satellite phone. "Back in a few." He walked along the edge of the lake and dialed Roare.

He told her about *Rage* at DocFest. "Did you watch the director's version yet?"

"Don't kill me—I haven't," she said. "Plan to this weekend with Wyatt and the Jóhannssons."

"They're like surrogate parents, aren't they?"

"They're sweet. What were Hunter's and Evie's opinions?"

"Mixed. He was happy they were able to watch the film. They raved about how you delivered your message, but the topic frightened them. They were clueless about how far technology has gone."

"Most people are. Did the rest of his family come?" Roare asked.

"You bet. Aaden's charging ahead, digging more into transhumanism. Everyone was appalled about what's been done to children."

"Did we deliver the message and get the reaction you wanted?"

"Let's say there was lots of buzz." Sloane recalled the audience's silence, glazed looks, and tears over the murdered children. "Many were enraged and wanted to protest, raise up petitions, and fight."

"Wait until it's released to the public."

Sloane cleared his throat. "I don't think Hollywood will happen, though."

"Too close to reality?"

"Now guess who wants to premiere our film?"

"Do tell." Roare placed a hand on her hip and held her head down.

"IFC Films, with further distribution to Netflix. You and Chips have a chance at Best Director at the Critics Choice Awards and, who knows, maybe a documentary award from Sundance."

"Ha, if only!" Roare couldn't stop herself from grinning.

"Why not? The film is spectacular. Arlo and Gavin will be calling shortly."

"You want to make me cry, don't you? All the work we put into this, and the amount of danger involved, I wish Chips were here. Our work wasn't in vain after all then?"

"No, and I miss him too."

"I wanted to tell you, I love the website for the film," she said, "especially the interactive hyper-animation activity between the AI cyborgs and the viewer."

"We also staged simultaneous cyborg invasions to infiltrate the lives of city dwellers in New York, London, and Montréal."

"You're insane. I can't believe ... what was your strategy?"

"Well, let me give you a visual. Tall men and women dressed in those blue silicone skins as expressionless, androgenous borgs riding subways and serving patrons in restaurants and hotels. We mixed them in with the regular staff."

"A pity I'll miss all the antics."

"Wait, there's more. There have been robots resembling humans, except for their eyes, on police patrols in black tactical gear."

"And then?"

"We caught people's reactions with hidden cameras. They freaked out, wondering if they were military or aliens."

"Seriously?"

"A few glared at the blue borgs and wanted to know where they'd come from. People left the restaurants in protest or spooked. Others were intrigued. We caught a couple of geeks talking about hacking into the borgs' OS."

"Good grief! Sounds almost comical. Shame on you and Gavin for scaring the wits out of people. How many days were you able to pull this gag?"

"Only one. Costly but effective. Our stunt stopped traffic."

"I don't doubt it. How did you arrange the *Rage* promo?"

"A week of digital billboards. One type ran a loop of two scenes. The kidnapping—until the two hybrids grabbed the twins. Then, the scientists escorting the robot guards to the underground lab. When the lab doors opened, we showed the workers' shocked expressions. The second type showed closeups of three borgs whose appearances changed to those of random people on the street. Then came a statement, 'We live among you and there's nothing you can do.' At the end, each billboard gave the name of the film and its website."

"That was genius! I pray this will give the public a harsh jolt to a future reality they won't accept. You guys have fertile imaginations for marketing. Something I couldn't do."

Sloane snickered. "Being great at everything was never a requirement."

"A tragic fact for an overachiever."

"Rest easy and welcome a new story to your life. The film is going to be a hit. You only need to focus on your well-being. Now, ask me where I am."

"Wait. You're here in Iceland?"

"Not yet. I'll head your way soon enough. Want to see for myself how you're set up, and I could use a bit of downtime."

"Please, do come see us anytime, but where the heck are you?"

"Fishing in Jasper National Park with friends. I liked the lodge and scenery so much I had to come back. Between you and me, I wanted to feel like a human being."

"Oh, Sloane, God bless your soul—you *are* human. Never forget this."

"See you soon, my friend."

Roare's stomach churned. In a few days, Hunter would arrive in Reykjavik. She and Wyatt planned a series of excursions and talks over dinner. She hoped he'd like the time there.

She and Wyatt strolled along the Eyjafjörður fjord in the crisp air—a way of connecting with the Creator before they began their day.

"God's been telling me you should hold this visit with Hunter lightly," Wyatt said. "Besides, all those activities we planned would keep you from getting to know him. Keep things simple."

"Am I making a federal case of this visit?"

"Easing into conversation with him will diffuse any tension and make a world of difference. You might be surprised by what the two of you have in common. My heart tells me he's a converted man."

"You know, he might actually grow on me." *I never would've guessed I'd be saying this.*

When they returned home, they peeled off their coats and sweaters. "I'm glad we lit the fireplace before we left."

Roare rubbed her hands near the hearth. "I'll make us a snack, and we can figure out our next adventure."

She fetched two mugs of hot chocolate from the kitchen, and they sat on peach cashmere pillows against the sofa as they watched the fire.

Wyatt glanced around the room. "Reminds me of our apartment in New York. Some good memories there."

"While we create new ones."

Roare ran to pick up the phone ringing in the kitchen.

"Oh, Roare," came Evie's voice, "I'm afraid Hunter won't be able to visit after all."

"Uh, not a problem, I guess."

"No, dear, it's not what you think. He was looking forward to spending time with you both. Getting to know you was very important to him. Now he can't."

"Is he okay?"

"No, he ... he died."

"What!" Roare placed her hand over her mouth. "Oh no, not possible." She leaned against the island and forced the next words out of her mouth. "We spoke only a couple of days ago to confirm his visit. He sounded fine and upbeat. Did he have complications?"

"I wish he'd never gone out alone in that fog yesterday morning. The deck on the boat was wet from the fog. He lost his footing and his head slammed into a winch. No one saw him in the fog. I was showing a home. When I returned, the fog had lifted, and there he was—sprawled out on the deck. The coroner said the blow to his left temple killed him instantly.

"Oh, Evie. I don't know what to say. I'm deeply sorry for you and your family. I thought God had given us a chance to connect. I wish we'd met sooner. Your family's been gracious to me. Is there anything we can do?"

"My dear, you'll always be part of our family. We'd love to have you and Wyatt attend the memorial service."

Roare eyed Wyatt, who listened nearby. "Of course we'd be there."

"I'm glad. I better go now. I have more calls to make."

Roare returned the phone to its cradle. She turned to Wyatt, buried her face in his chest, and he held her. *Was this truly an accident or is there something else going on?*

Something kept gnawing at Roare about Hunter's death. Even after Wyatt's pleading to let her suspicions go, she couldn't. She reached out to Sloane for insight—filled him in on what happened. He agreed with Roare. There might be something more to this than an accident. He'd investigate.

Two weeks later, Roare and Wyatt had returned from Hunter's memorial service. The summer morning sparkled, and the sun beamed on Roare as she rushed home after a few hours of pruning at the community garden. She headed straight for the refrigerator, pushed her water bottle under the dispenser, then guzzled the refreshment.

Wyatt smirked from the other side of the island.

She eyed him. "What's so funny?"

"I was hoping you wouldn't get waterlogged."

"Not a chance. I'm dehydrated."

"Obviously. Though, you look cute with dirt smeared all over your face."

"Oh, right. I must've wiped my face with my garden gloves."

He laughed. "You're really into this, aren't you?"

"Careful, or I'll recruit you."

rage against the machine

"Not a chance." Wyatt grabbed a tea towel from the kitchen drawer and wet a corner of the cloth from the water tap, then handed it to Roare.

"Thanks." Roare wiped off most of the dirt from her forehead, nose, and cheeks.

"Now, before you rush off," Wyatt continued, "there were some packages delivered for you after you left this morning."

"Who sent them?" Roare set her bottle on the kitchen counter and walked to the dining room table. She found a long white envelope atop a box covered in brown paper. She checked the labels. Australia.

Before she could dig in, the landline rang. Sloane. A part of her didn't want to hear what he had to say, but she had to know.

"If you're standing, Roare, I want you to take a seat," Sloane advised.

She did. "Go on."

"Raidon, whose disclosures enabled our campaign to proceed, also sent damning information to a woman in Norway. Match's mother, Shenandoah."

Roare rubbed her forehead.

"Once Match knew who was behind the film, he burrowed into every detail of your life. Since he failed to kill you before leaving Earth, he wanted to leave you a memento to show you he's in control. So he took out your father. And then his mother reached out to me—like an informal apology for her son. I didn't have the heart to tell her Match had killed his own father."

Practically in tears, Roare cried, "My God, my God, where are you? So many deaths. His own father. My father and his family were never involved in the film. I take the blame—all this hateful carnage."

"This is war and will involve everyone who values human life."

"And what do I tell Hunter's family?"

"The truth."

"If I smoked, I'd have a cigarette right now. When will this war begin?"

"The war has been going on for some time now, we just didn't know."

Roare took a moment to collect herself before she returned to the kitchen. She didn't have the heart to share with Wyatt what Sloane had revealed to her. Not yet. She couldn't let this psychopath invade her life like a relentless plague. She looked for any reason to distract herself from accepting the *truth*.

"Who called?" Wyatt asked.

"Sloane. He wanted to see how we and the Barracloughs are doing after Hunter's passing."

"You seem troubled. What's up?"

"We'll talk about this later. Let's open these parcels."

Wyatt brought over a pair of scissors and sat next to her.

Beneath the brown paper was a box wrapped in shiny pink paper and a thin ivory ribbon. Inside, she found a silver-framed photo of her and Hunter and a handwritten note from Abigale: "Wanted you to have this."

Wyatt said gently, "What a special picture."

"Strange. This is the only one I have of the two of us. Thoughtful of Abigale to send this to me. My entire encounter with Hunter has culminated in one photo."

"Hold onto your special memory."

"I will." She cut open the white envelope next and removed a document. "You won't believe this." She placed a hand over her heart and finished reading.

Wyatt edged closer. "Are you going to share?"

Roare took a deep breath. "Evie and Hunter have organized a trust for us and our future children—twenty-six *million* dollars! Barrister Cross will manage the distribution of funds."

"Can I have a look?" Wyatt read the document. "Between these gifts and staying connected to his family, you'll have your chance to discover the man he became before he left this world."

"Do you suppose he did this out of guilt?"

Wyatt shook his head. "This no longer matters. He was trying to give unconditional love. And atone for the twenty-six years he denied himself the privilege of being your father. To step into his role as your father, even for a little while."

"Astonishing. I'm overwhelmed."

"I still wouldn't compare how beholden they are to you—being the catalyst to his transformation, babe."

"No, no. I won't take any credit—this was God's doing. Hearing about his faith walk would've been the best gift. I'm comforted in knowing he found peace before he passed." She wiped her eyes. "However, my only chance to get to know him was stolen." She gritted her teeth.

"Perhaps not. Call it intuition, but I believe your ties to his family have just started, and the intersecting paths will mean something greater in the future."

"You sound prophetic."

"Do I? Not sure why I blurted those words."

Roare winced. "The thing is, Wy, you're not far off from the truth."

He scratched at his shadowy beard. "Maybe my overactive imagination is talking. Anyway, what do we do with twenty-six million dollars, besides send a huge thank-you note?"

Roare said under her breath. "Help fund a war."

"What did you say, Gobo?"

"Nothing important right now. Only, we could invest in an extensive survivalist course."

Wyatt raised his eyebrows. "Are you expecting some catastrophe soon? I'd like us to catch our breath for a little while first."

Lord, please grant us this privilege. "Comfort is a luxury no one should take for granted."

epilogue—the harvest

And another angel came out of the temple, crying with a loud voice to Him who sat on the cloud, "Thrust in Your sickle and reap, for the time has come for You to reap, for the harvest of the earth is ripe."
—Revelation 14:15 (NKJV)

Two years had not slowed the pace of Roare's and Wyatt's prepping for an impending apocalyptic conflict. After Sloane and a high-ranking general of the Australian Defense Force shared vital information about Hunter's murder and the threat of planetary security, Sloane invited Aaden to join his special forces team.

The desire for retribution flooded Aaden's mind as he eagerly accepted Sloane's invitation. Neither he nor any member of Hunter's family blamed Roare for his death.

Roare reflected on his passing as she walked along the fjords with Wyatt. *The grace given to me can't be measured and offers no comparison to the monetary gift my father left us. God, you're good. Don't let me torture myself with guilt over Hunter's death.*

Roare was pleased to have Sloane nearby. He visited often and included her, Wyatt, and others in combat training with the Icelandic Commissioner's National Security and Special

Forces Units. For just a second, she was disappointed when she had to end her training—a welcomed pregnancy.

Towering birches swayed along the fjords on the hazy, late-summer day. As usual, Roare and Wyatt gathered along the shoreline with a small following of musicians, preppers of varying essential backgrounds. Some were new believers, eager to understand biblical prophecy. Others repented and recommitted their hearts to the Lord. Nonbelievers remained open-minded and focused on readiness. Everyone found a purpose.

Roare and Wyatt were grateful the five other families of their private community shared the same opinion regarding survival. Invigorating chatter rose over the book of Revelation. Skeptics questioned the integrity of God's Word, but a healthy exchange forced some to do their own research. Others shared personal encounters with God.

When Wyatt was questioned about his faith, he said, "Doubts are normal. But we ask questions and seek the truth. Faith, for us, diminishes unbelief. Believers know God has always had a plan for humanity. He made a way to save us from ourselves. Provided we accept what he offers, we can live for him instead of for ourselves."

"Sounds like what he offers makes you a slave and beholden to him," said a newcomer.

"Not in the way you think. God has freed us from bondage through his Son Jesus. You see, he grafted us into his kingdom to become a part of him, so we can be with him—we're his own family, although it's our choice. And he took away our burden of sin."

"Sounds hard to believe." The woman eyed Wyatt skeptically.

"We don't deserve his love or eternal life. He sacrificed himself to cover our sins. Through his resurrection, our souls are redeemed. Jesus came to have relationship with us all, for love."

"Something I'll have to mull over."

At their group meetings, music made everyone appreciate their humanity. Lately, Roare loved when their neighbors, Bill and Lilija Haskins, would play their mandolins. Apparently, the twins she carried were most active then. She'd rub her side, lean close to Wyatt, and whisper, "The babies love the music."

Wyatt would grin and place his hand on her bulging belly to feel their little miracles moving. Still, Roare questioned whether she and Wyatt should be bringing children into such an inhospitable, fallen world.

Undetected by the humans below, a drone recorded and transmitted their activity through a portal to the Xa solar system.

"Too comfortable in their cocoon. Let them assume they're safe." Sigma Hybrid 12 paced before the 3D screen as he observed Roare and Wyatt. "Peace does not exist, not even there."

about the author

H. Meadow Hopewell discovered a love for creative writing in college but placed it on hold to pursue a career in Information Technology. In various ways, she found herself gravitating back to writing throughout her life. After migrating from the United States to New Zealand, her writing passion flamed—as if a spark ignited in her. She began to document book ideas and take notes. Between her love for science, pursuing God, and writing, her first novel *Rage Against the Machine* was born. When not working on the next installment of The Given Path trilogy, her time is spent on Tumblr nurturing her photography blog. She lives on the North Island with her husband, two spoiled cats, and a farm dog. Check out her blog at hmeadowhopewell. com to read more and connect.

www.ingramcontent.com/pod-product-compliance
Lightning Source LLC
Chambersburg PA
CBHW071158020726
47502CB00002B/458